MW00778006

HIS LORDSHIP'S SECRET

Book One of

His Lordship's Mysteries

Samantha SoRelle

Balcarres Books LLC

To my family, for always supporting me,
even when they didn't know what they were
supporting.

And to Margot, whose fault this is.

Happy Reading

from

Samantha Sabelle

(aka, Laura!)

CONTENTS

CHAPTER 1

Mayfair, London
April 1818

It was some time before Alfie noticed he'd been shot.

The Right Honorable Alfred Pennington the Earl of Crawford had been wondering whether a man of his station could be known to have purchased *The Swiss Family Robinson* when the shop window in front of him exploded. He ducked instinctively, covering his head. A belated crack reverberated off the high walls of Curzon Street and seemed to come from everywhere at once. He recognized the sound, though not from country hunts like his peers, but from a childhood he had spent years trying to leave behind.

A gunshot.

A trio of ladies walking on the other side of the street screamed and fell to the ground in fear. It wasn't until Alfie had gotten them safely into the tearoom on the corner that the blood soaking through his sleeve caught his eye.

Alfie pressed his cravat more tightly against the wound and swore as the coach bumped furiously over the rough cobblestones, sending fire shooting from shoulder to wrist with every jolt. A wheel hit a particularly large rut and Alfie cried out as he was thrown against the door. Darkness bubbled at the corners of his eyes. He tried to focus on his breathing.

Slow in... Slow out... Slow in... Slow out... There you go, Alfie.

But all that ran through his mind instead were the words, *I've been shot. I've been shot. I've been shot,* repeated endlessly until they lost all meaning.

"I've been shot," he said to the empty carriage.

The words didn't make any more sense aloud than they did in his head. Earls didn't get shot. Especially not while perusing bookstores in Mayfair. If every movement didn't cause a spike of agony, he would have kicked himself. He'd bought that blasted sword cane for self defense after the other incidents, and what had he done? Left it at home at the first opportunity.

Not that a blade would have been much use against a firearm, but still.

As he watched the red stain spread across the expensive silk, Alfie realised it would have perhaps made more sense to have a doctor called to the tearoom than to wait and have Doctor Barlowe called once Alfie was already home. But it was too late to worry about that now.

He let out a sigh of relief as the coach slowed and the familiar sight of Bedford Square came into view. As the driver pulled up in front of the bicoloured arch over the door of the Crawford townhouse, Alfie stumbled out even before the horses had fully stopped, hissing in pain and clenching his hand even tighter over his injured arm.

"Doctor Barlowe, Harley Street. There's triple the wage

in it for you if you fetch him here within thirty minutes."

"Right you are, milord." The coachman touched a grimy finger to his cap, then cracked the reins, startling his horses back into the breakneck pace with which he'd brought Alfie from Mayfair.

Alfie lurched up the few stairs to his front door and leaned his good shoulder against it. Seeing no way to keep the pressure on his wound and knock at the same time, he instead kicked the door repeatedly.

"Oy! Whatever gotch-gutted fool be kickin' that door will be passin' teeth when—Oh, Master Alfred!" Alfie lost his balance as the door was flung open and his support was yanked away.

"That is—I mean, *my lord*, sir. Apologies for my language, sir. I had no inkling it was you, I thought it must have been some rabble rousers and I'm not used to—Cock and pie! What happened to you?"

"Just a small accident at the bookseller's, Mrs. Hirkins. One must always be careful around the satirical works, you know. Very cutting."

As regained his footing on the polished marble, he flashed the housekeeper his most winsome smile. But as it was the same one he'd once used when she'd caught him hiding a stray puppy in his wardrobe over term break, it had probably lost some of its effect on her over the years. Old Daisy now being a beloved member of the Hirkins' household and spending most of her hours napping in front of the hearth with Mr. Hirkins notwithstanding.

That his arm was now in utter agony perhaps also made his smile a trifle less effective than usual. It certainly didn't stop her from fretting as she ushered him upstairs to his study to lie down.

"Just a minute, Mas...my lord," she said, untying her apron and laying it down upon the settee. "Don't need for you to be getting blood everywhere. Right difficult to get blood out of upholstery."

Alfie sat gingerly upon the settee where indicated, making sure to keep his arm above the apron-covered section. She couldn't be too worried about his imminent demise if she was concerned for the furniture.

"I'll go send for the doctor then."

"No need, Mrs. Hirkins. I've already had a coach sent to pick him up. Some tea would be fortifying in the interim though, if you would be so kind."

"Hmm." She gave Alfie a look, resting her fists on her ample waist before stalking from the room. He laid down upon the settee, careful to keep the apron underneath him. His feet hung off the far end by several inches, but he had no wish to draw her ire by avoiding staining the fabric with blood only to cover it with mud instead. Alfie found that at over six feet very little furniture in the world suited his height, especially any belonging to his parents, who themselves had barely made it past the five foot mark.

He knew why Mrs. Hirkins was displeased with him, aside from the obvious.

Providing tea should not technically fall under a housekeeper's duties. Or a cook's for that matter. But his mother had whittled the number of servants every year after her husband had died, no longer bothering to throw the great parties or soirees to try to buy their way back into respectability. Alfie had watched as one by one the servants had been let go until the household was just his mother,

Mrs. Hirkins, and himself.

But now it was just the two of them.

And really, what need was there for an army of servants for a man whose greatest social outings were the occasional trips to the booksellers or the theatre? And even then, never on opening night, so as to avoid the cream of London's aristocracy. The most he ever ventured into society were his frequent visits to Angelo's Fencing Academy, but even there he was more interested in honing his skills than in the hobnobbing that seemed the main reason for his peers' attendance.

No, Mrs. Hirkins there during the day, and the occasional visits by the boy who took away the laundry and delivered groceries enough for simple meals, that was all Alfie needed.

He frowned. That really was an awful lot of blood. Would any of his wardrobe be salvageable? When had the boy last come by for the laundry anyway? Alfie tried to think, but his thoughts were like eels, squirming and sliding out of his grip as soon as he had them. In fact, everything seemed a bit dark and slippery around the edges. He tried to stand and ring for Mrs. Hirkins to come back, but there was a reason he wasn't supposed to move, wasn't there? And that really *was* an awful lot of blood.

Alfie took a deep breath and let it out slowly, then another. Maybe he would just lie very still until the doctor came and try not to think of anything.

*　*　*

"There you are, my lord. Well done. Most of my patients

would not have borne that nearly as well."

Alfie looked down at the neat line of stitches now running across his upper arm. Doctor Barlowe had cleaned and tended the injury with the orderly focus and precision that had so impressed Alfie when his father had first fallen ill three years ago.

He was an older gentleman, apparently a friend of Alfie's mother in her youth, but had spent his years firmly establishing his practice in London while she had been off flitting around the world with her aristocrat husband. A more soothing and steady presence Alfie could not have asked for during his father's decline, nor in the years since, including the sudden shock of losing his mother just a few months ago.

Nearly bald, with just a small band of grey hair stretching across the back of his head, Doctor Barlowe had likely been an athletic man in his youth, and his ongoing strength remained evident in his barrel chest and heavy shoulders. But the muscle he retained was layered with decades of fine meals at the tables of his wealthy clients.

His bulk lent him an air of pleasant wisdom, as if his natural place was to be dressed in tweed in some rural cottage, sitting in an armchair by the fire dispensing homey advice to all who came to *him*, rather than dashing about London making house calls. The impression was only increased by the tiny pair of glasses the doctor wore on the very end of his prodigious nose, and the grandfatherly sparkle in his eyes.

Indeed, if by some strange circumstance Alfie were ever to find himself casting the role of a kindly gentleman physician in a play, Doctor Barlowe was such an epitome of his profession that no mere actor could possibly compete.

The doctor took his pocket watch out of his waistcoat, the fine gold charms on the chain catching the light from a lamp that Mrs. Hirkins had placed beside the settee at his instruction. He took the wrist of Alfie's injured arm in his other hand and waited silently, counting out the heartbeats.

"There now," he said, releasing Alfie's wrist and stowing his watch with a genial pat over the pocket. "Everything else seems to be in working order at least."

He handed Alfie the clean shirt Mrs. Hirkins had brought with the tea before securing himself a cup. "His lordship's business is his own of course, but I could not help but notice how much your 'light scratch, hardly worth the effort' very much resembles a gunshot wound."

He added two lumps of sugar and sat in the armchair across from Alfie. "I ask only as a medical professional, of course, concerned for the care of my patient. And while I must admit that I find the custom somewhat barbaric, I do understand that there are times when a young man's honor requires a certain course of action."

Alfie buttoned his shirt as he attempted to parse the doctor's words. *A young man's honor?* He laughed when he realised what Doctor Barlowe had assumed. Alfie in a duel? He'd never even fired a pistol, never mind at another person. Besides, he was hardly the sort to find himself in any kind of perilous adventure, despite his secret fondness for fanciful novels. And if most duels were like the ones he read about, fought over the love of a lady? Well. Alfie was in no danger of being involved in that.

At the doctor's quizzical look, Alfie finished with his

shirt, and reached—carefully—for his own cup of tea. "Forgive me, I only laugh because I think the only creature I've ever shot at was the occasional grouse, and even then, I was mostly unsuccessful."

A white lie, given that Alfie had never been invited to any hunting parties, but still Alfie smiled, expecting the doctor to share in the joke, and was surprised when the man frowned instead.

"You don't mean then," said the doctor gravely, "that this wound was of a self-inflicted nature? I know you have been in low spirits since your mother's passing, but you must know that such actions are against all laws of God and man."

"What? No, no!" Alfie was shocked at the very idea. Even during his worst moments, after his father died and he realised the lies he would have to continue for his mother's sake, or after her death, when everything had seemed so quiet, he'd never considered taking his own life. Alfie knew better than most how lucky he was to have the life he did and would never throw away such a gift as he had been given.

"You can tell me the truth. I have sensed a greater melancholy in you of late. Such symptoms must be addressed early lest they lead to... *unbecoming* actions."

"No, it's nothing like that," said Alfie, setting aside his untouched tea.

He found himself telling Doctor Barlowe the entire story, from taking his routine Tuesday stroll along Mayfair to the sudden noise, to helping the ladies, to the startling realisation that he had been shot.

"My God," the doctor exclaimed. "Did you see who did

it?"

Alfie shook his head. "I didn't even realise I was injured until afterward. In all the commotion I can't say I was in a state to notice anyone. Napoleon himself could have done it, and I doubt I would have recognized him."

"Shocking. Absolutely shocking. That such a thing could happen in broad daylight and in this day and age."

The doctor stirred his tea contemplatively, as if the answer to all of society's ills could be read in the leaves at the bottom of his cup. "Still I suppose it must have been an accident. Surely no one would have taken a shot at you intentionally?"

And that was what Alfie had been trying to avoid thinking about. A month or two ago, he would have laughed at such a ridiculous notion. But with the other strange incidents he'd experienced added onto today? He could not be so sure.

The need to finally unburden his worries to someone overwhelmed Alfie. He opened his mouth, ready to spill everything—his fears, his worries, and even the great secret at the root of them all—when there was a gentle rap at the door, followed shortly by the entrance of Mrs. Hirkins.

"My sincerest apologies for disturbing you, my lord."

Despite the pain he was in, Alfie found himself biting his lip to keep a straight face at Mrs. Hirkins' suddenly impeccable demeanor, right down to enunciation of her words without a hint of the Yorkshire moors upon which she'd been raised. She never paid more than the barest lip service to the etiquette demanded of her station around Alfie, but in front of guests, she would not be caught dead without the most perfect manners and crispest vowels.

That said, the curtsey was a bit much.

"Your cousin, Mr. St. John, has just arrived, sir. I've put him in the morning salon, as you were indisposed in here. I hope that is acceptable."

Alfie groaned. He'd forgotten all about promising to meet Reginald for dinner. It must be late indeed if he had already come to track Alfie down for missing their appointment.

"That's perfectly fine, Mrs. Hirkins, thank you. Has he been here long? I didn't hear the door."

She hesitated. "I'm afraid I can't rightly say, my lord. I came down to the kitchen to fetch more refreshments and found him helping himself to the almond cake in the pantry. He must have let himself in the servant's door. I escorted him to the salon, then came to inform you immediately.

Chased him out with a broom handle, more likely, Alfie thought. Outwardly though, he retained his composure. "Thank you, Mrs. Hirkins. I will see to him shortly. That will be all."

"Yes, sir."

She bobbed another curtsey that had Alfie fighting back a smile and departed. Alfie rose to show the doctor out, pleased when the room only swam a little before righting itself.

"Thank you for your assistance today, Doctor Barlowe. Believe me, if I had known I was going to need your services so suddenly, I would have warned you in advance and saved you such a harrowing coach ride!"

"Of course, of course." Doctor Barlowe did not rise,

but adjusted his spectacles to lie even more neatly on his nose. "My lord, as sure as I am that today's *accident* will not be repeated, speaking as your doctor I am concerned for your well-being in general. I assume I do not need to mention the distressing circumstances of your father's final months. In addition, your mother's melancholy worsened rapidly before her passing, and such traits might be inherited."

Not bloody likely in this case, thought Alfie, but just nodded sagely as the doctor continued.

"While I am still troubled that I was unable to cure your mother, I promise that I will not let her memory be tainted by allowing her son to fall into any ignominy. If you'll permit me, I'd like to start you on a treatment for low spirits. Nothing too strong mind you, just something to head off any risk of a dangerous morbidity before it has the chance to take hold."

"Whatever you think best, doctor," said Alfie soberly. Although he was unlikely to have inherited anything from either the late Lord or Lady Crawford, he *had* been feeling adrift since his mother's passing, unsure of his place in the world or what he should do with himself now that he no longer had her to care for and keep company. He had assumed these were the sorts of feelings every son was expected to experience, but if the doctor thought they were cause for concern, then Alfie would follow his advice.

"Glad to hear it." Doctor Barlowe smiled and slapped his knee, "I won't keep you. Lord knows you'll need all your strength to deal with that cousin of yours. Try not to let him overtax you, and be mindful of your arm. I'll be back to remove those stitches in… let us say two weeks?"

"That works perfectly, thank you."

As they walked down the grand stairs to the main level, Doctor Barlowe waved Alfie off. "No need to see me to the door, I know my way by now. In fact, I may stop in on Mrs. Hirkins in the kitchen if you think she'd be willing to part with any more of that almond cake."

"I'm sure if there's any left, she'd be happy to indulge you." Alfie watched as the doctor descended a smaller set of stairs to the kitchen, before heading over to the closed door of the salon.

He took a deep breath. He'd faced unknown gunmen, mad coach drivers, and the guilt that came with lying to Doctor Barlowe. If he could face those, he could face whatever entertainments his cousin had in store for the evening.

After all that, nothing the rest of the night might hold could possibly shock him.

CHAPTER 2

"Freddie! There you are! I was afraid old Hirkins had finally done away with you and baked your bones into bread!"

Alfie gritted his teeth at the hated nickname. "Or almond cake?"

"It was a risk I was willing to take." Reginald St. John shrugged from where he was lounging on the couch—*not* taking care to keep his muddy boots off the upholstery— and waved an empty glass toward the sideboard. "Be a dear, would you?"

Every morning since his father died three years ago, Alfie had awoken with a ball of lead in the pit of his stomach. Guilt, he knew, because he wasn't the true Earl of Crawford; Reginald was.

Alfie took in his cousin. At forty, the man was almost a decade and a half Alfie's senior, yet still acted like some wastrel of a youth half his age. From what Alfie could tell, any time that Reginald didn't spend whoring, drinking, or gambling with whatever funds remained from his own late father's turn at the tables, he spent purchasing the latest fashions and accoutrements. The problem was, when the bills came due, he never actually paid for the items he ordered.

While Alfie refused to pay any of Reginald's gambling

debts on principle, he didn't have the heart to turn away the scores of tailors and haberdashers who inevitably ended up on his doorstep, looking only to collect fair payment for their hard work. As a result, Reginald took even more shameless advantage. Alfie wasn't sure he'd ever actually seen the man in the same suit twice.

And this was what Alfie thought of every morning for the past three years to convince himself to keep the secret for another day. If Reginald treated his inheritance with such appalling disregard, then how quickly would he bring the earldom to ruin? How many lives of those who paid Crawford rents and tilled their land would be destroyed as Reginald bled them for every farthing or gambled their livelihoods on a turn of cards? It was the thought of whole families, especially the children, going cold and hungry that held Alfie's tongue.

The heavy drinking and smoking his cousin indulged in showed in his figure and the permanent ruddiness of his face. From the few times Alfie had met Reginald's father, the late earl's younger brother, he had been the same way and according to the ton's gossip had indulged in all of the same vices. The rotten apple had not fallen far from the tree. Reginald was of average height, like all Crawford men with the obvious exception of Alfie, and his fair hair hung sweaty and lank around his face, ruining whatever positive effect his costly tailoring might have had on his appearance.

A hog in silk dressings, Mrs. Hirkins had once called him, which was cruel but horribly apt.

Alfie went to the sideboard. The level of whiskey in the decanter was already noticeably lower than it had been.

He debated abstaining, but in the end the prospect of an evening with Reginald won out over blood loss.

He poured a small amount into a cut tumbler for himself before approaching his cousin with the decanter.

"Oh, do stop making that face at me, Freddie. It's liable to stick that way, and then where would you be? Why you'd have nothing to win you a wife at all, except for your wealth and title, and what woman wants that!"

Reginald laughed uproariously at his own joke, causing Alfie to spill whiskey on the carpet as he tried to pour it into Reginald's moving glass.

It was not the first time Reginald had made such a jest, and each time Alfie grew more nervous. His cousin had a cruel sense of humor, the kind of man who would throw pennies in the street to watch beggars dig them out of the filth while he laughed and called it charity. His comments about wealth and titles, when Alfie had both and he had neither, seemed pointed, and only worsened Alfie's guilt.

But it was the other part that really worried him. Reginald's jokes about Alfie finding a wife might have been just one bachelor jesting with another, but the more frequently he made them, the more Alfie worried Reginald might suspect his true nature.

And for all that Alfie told himself that his reasons for not telling Reginald the truth and handing over the earldom were noble, that he was doing it to protect the people who could not protect themselves, the real reason was that Alfie was terrified. If Reginald knew the truth of Alfie's inclinations, that it was not the soft curves of women he desired, but the hard bodies of men, then the only things saving Alfie from persecution or even the noose were his money and title. Without those, Alfie would be at his cousin's mercy, and Reginald had none.

If Reginald knew.

"Where have you been, anyway?" Reginald asked. He took the decanter from Alfie's hand and poured himself an overfull measure. "I was at the club for hours. Played not a few rounds of billiards waiting for you. When I finally glanced at the clock, I decided it was time to come searching."

He looked Alfie up and down, eyes landing on his lack of a waistcoat and still untucked shirt. Alfie silently cursed himself for coming directly to the salon instead of taking the time to dress himself properly.

"From the state you're in, if it was any other man I'd have guessed I'd interrupted you with your mistress but you... Let me guess, you found a book missing a page and had to hunt through the entire library to find it? Or were you out gazing at clouds in the park and only realised you'd been robbed naked when you got home?"

Alfie grit his teeth, "Neither, thank you. I just had an unexpectedly trying day. My apologies for missing dinner, but perhaps—"

"Well, if it's a trying day you've had, I know just the thing!" Reginald sprang to his feet with startling speed. "You'll be pleased to know that I won a fine bottle of port this afternoon while waiting for you. Clearly you need it more than I. I left it down in the kitchen. If I wasn't afraid of that old bat cracking me with a frying pan..."

"I don't know that I'm really up for—"

"Hmm no, that's fair, that's fair. I'm not up for facing her myself. Well, I suppose we could instead—and mind you this thought has only just occurred to me..."

Alfie's shoulders slumped. He knew where this was going.

"...It's too late for dinner obviously, but we could go grab a quiet drink somewhere. I know one or two fine establishments you might enjoy. There might even be some entertainment to be had as well."

Knowing his cousin, Alfie took "*a* quiet drink" to mean "four to eight", "fine establishments" to mean "gaming hell" and "entertainment" to mean anything from "prostitutes" to "bear baiting". Even worse however, for Reginald to actually make the effort to come to Alfie's townhouse meant he wanted something and wasn't going to be easy to get rid of. If buying him a few drinks and funding whatever *entertainment* his cousin doubtless already had planned for the evening was the price it took to get him off Alfie's back for another few weeks, then so be it.

His ploy with the gift of port was new though. Perhaps he thought it would sweeten Alfie up. Or perhaps he really was just too afraid of Mrs. Hirkins to retrieve it.

"Very well, give me a few moments to freshen up. As you noticed, I'm in no state to go out."

"Of course, of course, take your time." Reginald poured himself another measure. "Oh, and don't forget your pocketbook. I seem to have left mine at the club."

CHAPTER 3

The evening was even worse than Alfie expected.

The first pub his cousin took him to had actually been quite pleasant; clean and warm with a clear mix of both nobility and the upper merchant class among the clientele. It was the sort of place Alfie might enjoy returning to in future. Reginald too was surprisingly jovial company, not drinking to excess but nursing a single mug of the admittedly fine ale Alfie bought him. Alfie began to feel ashamed of his earlier doubts about his cousin. Clearly, the stress of the day had simply been taking its toll on him, making him see threats and insinuations when there were none.

"Reginald, I fear I owe you an apology."

"Indeed? Whatever for—oh, I say! Batty! Stokes! Over here!"

Alfie didn't bother to hide his groan.

"Reggie! I say, whatever are you doing here? We didn't expect to see you tonight!"

"Yes, what a coincidence I'm sure." Alfie muttered under his breath.

The stocky man in a garishly striped waistcoat—Batty to his friends, Lord Bartholomew Boyle to the rest—turned to Alfie. "Freddie, is that you? Well, this is double the surprise then!"

His over-exaggerated look of shock would have gotten him booed out of any theatre in Drury Lane, and most of the music halls too.

"Yes," said the man standing next to him, a Mr. Charles Stockton, another of Reginald's reviled set.

He was pale, thin, and dressed to the very cutting edge of fashion. Nearly literally; Alfie worried that if the points of his collar were starched any sharper, the man might inadvertently slit his own throat with an ill-timed cough.

"What a fortunate coincidence running into you both," Stockton drawled nasally. "Batty and I were just heading out, would you care to join us?"

Which was how Alfie found himself dragged from a reputable pub to a disreputable one and finally to an outright gambling hell. His role seemed to be a little more than a human purse for his cousin, "loaning" him money to cover his drinks and hands of poker. Each time he tried to make his excuses and leave the group to their debauchery, they moved on to a different establishment, promising Alfie he would enjoy their next stop more. He did not.

"One more, one more, Freddie. *Truh-trusht* me."

Alfie tried to shrug out from under the heavy arm slung over his shoulder, causing his injury to flash with pain as Reginald slurred in his ear. "This next place is the whole reason I dragged you out tonight. Move along now, we don't want to miss it."

If his cousin was too drunk to remember that this whole evening was meant to have been unplanned, then perhaps it meant the night was winding down and Alfie would have fulfilled his societal obligations enough to reasonably ignore his cousin for a while without feeling guilty or causing gossip.

"Very well. Lay on."

Alfie adjusted his grip on his cane as they approached their final stop. He was glad to have remembered it. Its solid weight under his hand was comforting, but even the promise the sword hidden within was not enough to make him easy in this part of London. His experience with such weaponry began and ended at Angelo's, and he somehow doubted East End criminals would be gallant enough to adhere to the strict rules of a fencing bout. He had no idea if his skill with a foil would be of any use at all in a real fight, but it was better than nothing.

If the last stop had been a hell, this new place had to be one of the lowest circles thereof. The coachman refused to drive them all the way, "Too far into the rookeries," he claimed, so they had to walk the last several blocks, following Stockton's increasingly wavering lead. Alfie tried not to let his panic show. Surely his cousin and his acquaintances must have some idea of the dangers of walking through the stews at night, especially dressed as they were and intoxicated to boot!

Alfie shivered and pulled his coat tighter around himself as they passed yet another dark alley. Something moved within, but man or woman, human or beast, he didn't dare look and risk drawing its attention. Any kind of criminal, from simple mugger to would-be assassin might be hiding within, and Alfie had had enough of attempted murder for one day.

He ran his thumb over the hidden latch on his cane that released the blade, just to reassure himself. In front of him, Boyle belted out another verse from a bawdy song about Mother Watkin's ale as Reginald boomed with laughter.

A pile of rags on a doorstep resolved itself into an old woman. She reached a withered hand out to Reginald who paid her no notice. Alfie fell a few steps further behind to pass her a penny unnoticed. She gave him a gummy smile in return, the coin disappearing back into the tattered folds of fabric she was wrapped in.

He knew it was foolhardy to be flashing any money in this part of town, but he couldn't help but feel for the beggar woman. He was from these streets. If not for the most extraordinary twist of luck, her fate could have easily been his own. This woman might even be some relation of his, an unknown grandmother or forgotten aunt. Sobered by the thought, he pressed another sixpence into her palm before hurrying to catch up with the others.

Spitalfields. What a ghastly part of town. And yet, somewhere in this filthy stinking mess he had been born, precisely when and to whom he would never know. Even his original name had been lost forever.

Lord Alfred of the Mud.

He couldn't help the wry smile. The workhouse couldn't be too far from here, unless someone had finally torn down the grim, damp, louse-infested blight. He could only hope.

That said, if not for the workhouse—or more specifically, one of the boys there—Alfie would have been dead in a gutter long before his new parents, the Lord and

Lady Crawford, had found him and raised him as their own. Maybe he did owe it some credit. Alfie took a moment to remember a gap toothed smile and glittering blue eyes, before releasing the past with a sigh.

Finally, whether by ability or good fortune, Stockton led them to the establishment he had sought. There were several large, rough-looking characters milling about in front of a stairwell that led to a basement entrance. An even larger, rougher man sat posted on a stool beside the door. Immobile as the gargoyle he resembled, he made no move at Stockton's approach, but a few whispered words and several surreptitious coins led to a grunt and a chin bob.

"What are you waiting for then, a formal invitation?" laughed Stockton as he waved his compatriots and Alfie through the door with exaggerated effect. Alfie took a deep breath of the slightly fresher street air, and ducked inside.

He wasn't sure exactly what he had been expecting; some sort of bacchanal, perhaps? But the underground pub seemed almost civilized. The walls were darkened by smoke and age, but clean enough. There was a bar against the far wall that was doing a brisk trade, and the few serving women rushing between the tables that had been pushed to the edges of the room were all fully clothed.

There was a pronounced lack of seating, so the majority of the patrons stood, a definite thrum of anticipation in the air. While most of the men resembled the ruffians outside, there were a few other top hats and silk cravats to be seen.

Alfie loosened his own cravat as much as his sense of decency would allow. The heat and sounds of too many bodies in one place were oppressive. There must have been at least a hundred men in a space designed to hold a third that number. It did not help that most of the space was taken up by what he assumed they were there to see: A boxing ring made of rough hempen rope had been assembled in the middle of the room.

"Not what you were expecting, eh?" Reginald shouted in Alfie's ear to be heard over the din. "Don't worry, it's more than it looks. I promise you won't see a fight like this at Jackson's!"

Whatever Reginald planned to say next was lost as a man in an apron, the publican, Alfie presumed, stepped into the ring and the crowd roared.

The man raised his hands, "Gentlemen! Tonight I have for you a battle for the ages!"

The crowd roared again.

"Introducing... winner of more fights than an old man like me can count... Bill 'The Body Snatcher' Nunn!"

The man who stepped into the ring drew excited cheers from most members of the crowd, and hisses from a few of the braver ones. Alfie could see why. The man was terrifying. He had to be well over six foot, and twenty-two stone if he was an ounce, all of it muscle. Stripped to nothing but trousers and light shoes, the effect was almost that of a caricature strongman, right down to the oversized mustache and mutton chops leading past two cauliflower ears on his completely bald head. "*Almost*" because, where a caricature suggested humour, there was nothing of the sort in the man's small eyes, squinting coldly as he rubbed some sort of grit over his tightly wrapped hands.

"The Body Snatcher?" Alfie couldn't help but ask.

"Well, these fights don't follow that milksop

Broughton's rules. Here there's no rounds, no limits, just two men facing each other the way God intended until one of them calls it quits or dies." Reginald said.

Alfie noticed vaguely that they'd already lost Stockton and Boyle somewhere in the din.

"They call that one Body Snatcher on account of the number of his opponents who've ended up on dissection tables. Wouldn't be surprised if there was a medical man or two here tonight, hoping for a casualty in the ring."

Alfie was so shocked, he almost missed the aproned man's next announcement.

"...your challenger, Nick 'the Terror' Tripner!"

The noise surrounding Alfie seemed to dim as the second man ducked into the ring. He was tall, but closer to Alfie's own height than the monstrous proportions of his opponent, but that was where the similarities between him and Alfie ended. Where Alfie was narrow and lithe, naturally gifted with a body that was the epitome of the aristocratic breeding he pretended to have, Tripner was thickly muscled from his broad shoulders to his staggeringly well-defined waist.

Alfie tore his eyes from the elegant "V" of muscle that cut over Tripner hips and disappeared into the linen of his trousers. His eyes landed instead on Tripner's veined forearms and massive hands that beat at his bare chest as he warmed himself up for the fight, and oh, that wasn't better at *all*.

With effort, he lifted his gaze from that chest, thick with golden curls where Alfie himself was bare save for a faint line of reddish hair leading down from his navel. Their differences continued the higher he looked however,

Alfie's precise features and smooth cheeks in contrast to the rough stubble and a nose that had clearly been broken more than once.

Even their skin was different, Alfie's delicate and fashionably pale from too many hours indoors with his books, while Tripner shone like a gilded statue in the lamplight, those same hours for him spent working and sweating under the sun. His time outdoors had lightened his hair as well, a messy Bedford crop of blond waves that Alfie ached to sink his hands into, to twist and grasp in the throes of passion.

Such a thing could not be done with his own hair, Alfie mused, sad for the first time that he insisted on keeping his own hair clipped close a la Brutus, having endured too many taunts about his auburn curls while at school, and not trusting any tonic to be powerful enough to contain them. For this man though, it would be worth the taunts. To have him dig his fingers roughly into Alfie's curls, pulling painfully until he had Alfie's head exactly where he wanted it, those strong arms flexing as they forced Alfie to take whatever he gave him, again and again and…

Alfie looked away and tried to marshal his thoughts. Those were not things he should be thinking about any man, but he had accepted his deviancy in that regard long ago. It wouldn't do though to have such thoughts in public however, especially not in a place like this. Once he was sure he had his physical reactions under control, Alfie looked back.

There was one place they were similar, he realised. Tripner's eyes were blue, just like his own, although even there Tripner was the superior. His eyes shone like sapphires, lit with a fire from within, whereas Alfie's were a more faded cornflower. What Alfie wouldn't give to possess even a fraction of the confidence and intensity in that stare. A stare, he realised with a jolt, that was aimed directly back at him.

The weight of Tripner's gaze was warm and heavy like honey, trapping Alfie in place where he stood. Suddenly Alfie had the strangest sense of familiarity, like he knew this man, and had felt this weight before. But that was impossible. Alfie studiously avoided all but the best neighbourhoods in London, and there was no way an obvious brawler such as Tripner could have passed in polite society.

The moment was broken when a man with dark skin and a full beard caught Tripner's attention. The fighter turned away from Alfie to speak to him, and Alfie spent a minute lost in the ripple of his back muscles as he moved. Eventually he realised his cousin had spoken.

"Pardon?"

"I said, I wouldn't want to meet either of them in a dark alley, that's for certain. This Terror fellow should be able to give a good show, but smart money is always on Nunn. Care for me to place a wager for you? Maybe use the winnings to pay for some... *amenable* company afterwards?" Reginald's eyes glinted.

Alfie rolled his eyes. "No, but don't let me stop you," he said with a false smile. He handed over several more bills, hoping they would be the last of his cousin's requests. "Perhaps you can buy me a drink if your intuition proves correct."

Or pay back all my money you've spent tonight, he

thought darkly and without much hope as he watched his cousin elbow his way through the crowd to place his bets.

I wouldn't want to meet either of them in a dark alley.

Alfie tapped the end of his cane against the floor in consideration. Hadn't he just been thinking about potential murderers skulking in alleyways? Perhaps it would do Alfie some good to hire protection. He hadn't before, when he could explain away the other incidents, but a gunshot wound did not leave much in the way of interpretation.

Cold dread spread through Alfie's veins. There was no use trying to avoid the thought any longer. Someone was trying to kill him.

He swallowed. It was a terrible feeling, knowing that someone wanted him dead. Not that they simply didn't care one way or the other, Alfie had lived with that feeling his entire life. But that there was someone out there, who for reasons Alfie didn't even understand, had taken real steps to try and have him killed.

What I need is a bodyguard.

As soon as Alfie had the thought, it seemed obvious in its simplicity. He could not go to the police, he had too many secrets himself to want to draw their attention. No, if he was going to figure out who was trying to kill him and have them stopped, he would have to do it himself.

And he couldn't do that if he was too afraid to leave his house because of rogue gunmen. But if he had a bodyguard, then there would always be someone there to keep an eye out for danger. He'd be able to investigate—and *live*—in peace with someone watching over him. And what a better place to find such a person. Surely some of the men here could use a few shillings, and there were certainly many who were scary enough to fend off any would-be murderers with their looks alone.

Or even better, why not one of the fighters? If they had the skills to compete in the ring, then surely they would have the skills to protect him. He'd simply wait until after the match and ask the winner if he'd be interested. A boxing champion might cost a little more, but Alfie had the money, and surely when it came to one's personal defense, one should hire only the absolute best.

He would not let himself be swayed into thinking about which of the two men in the ring he would rather have by his side at all hours. Such thoughts came secondary to personal safety. He would hire the winner regardless of who that was. Only the absolute best.

A chill ran down his spine. While he would secure himself protection after the match, until then, he *didn't* have a bodyguard. And here he was, alone and defenseless in the most dangerous part of town. He thumbed the latch on his cane again and waited breathlessly for the fight to begin.

CHAPTER 4

The fight was brutal.

At first it had seemed evenly matched. While Nunn had the distinct advantage of size, Tripner was clearly the faster and more agile of the two. He danced around the ring, avoiding Nunn's blows, but unable to land many of his own. Those that did connect were quick, glancing things as Tripner ducked in and out of Nunn's range before the behemoth could strike back.

The crowd was beginning to grow restless. They had been promised a bloodbath, not this lopsided dance.

If Alfie hadn't been watching Tripner so closely, he might have missed the moment it happened. Tripner ducked under a right hook from Nunn that could have cracked iron if it had connected, but instead went sailing well over Tripner's head. In that moment, Tripner took his eyes off his opponent to glance over at the man with the beard he'd been talking to before. The man had a watch in his hand, and at Tripner's look, shook his head in an almost imperceivable movement.

The split second of distraction was all Nunn needed. Moving faster than Alfie could have imagined possible, he drove his knee up, slamming it into Tripner's gut. Alfie swore there was an audible crack of ribs.

The crowd gasped, pressing in around the ring now

that things were finally getting good.

Tripner grunted, but had no time to recover as Nunn rushed him, landing blow after blow to Tripner's body. Each hit sounded like a hunk of meat being slapped down upon a butcher's block. Tripner responded by headbutting his opponent in the face.

Nunn howled, rearing back as blood began to pour from his nose. Tripner took advantage of the distraction to break free and retreat to the other side of the ring. He was breathing heavily and crumpled slightly to the left as if something in that side was torn and could not straighten fully. A line of blood appeared at his hairline and began to trickle down his forehead towards his eyes. He wiped angrily at it with the back of his wrist, red staining the cotton bands wrapped around his knuckles.

A cut like that must have come from teeth, Alfie thought and looked back at Nunn in time to see the man spit teeth onto the floor of the ring. The drinks Reginald had enticed Alfie into lurched unpleasantly in his stomach.

Nunn roared with rage and ran at Tripner who raised a clawed hand and raked it across Nunn's face, missing his eyes but only barely. He had not thought to account for Nunn's momentum however, and was slammed back against the ropes, letting out an animal cry as the full weight of his opponent's body collided with his.

The force of the impact was so violent that the entire crowd on that side was driven back several feet before swarming in again, uncaring of the splatters of blood and sweat that flew off the two locked combatants with every blow.

Tripner landed several more hits, mad uppercuts and

hooks that would have felled a lesser man, but seemed to have no more impact on Nunn than the batting of a kitten. Nunn however, having finally trapped his agile opponent, was giving Tripner all the mercy a hound gave a cornered fox.

A left cross to the temple sent Tripner to his knees, and Alfie began to relax, knowing that would be the end of it. But to his shock, Nunn merely hauled the beaten man back to his feet and, pinning him upright with one massive arm, struck again.

Tripner folded in half, hanging suspended in his opponent's grip. His head lolled, but his limbs jerked as if he was still trying to fight back.

The crowd roared its approval as Nunn raised his free arm in the air, the bindings on his hands nearly soaked to the elbow in Tripner's blood.

In that moment, Tripner looked up. Across the ring his eyes met Alfie's, his face twisted in fear and panic. The din of the crowd faded to a hush as something in that terrified gaze hooked into Alfie's soul.

Alfie tried to move towards him, drawn like a magnet without his mind even willing his body to do so, but found he was trapped. There were too many people surrounding him. The injured boxer gave him one last look, and a small quirk of the lips that might have been a smile, before Nunn struck him again, twisting Tripner's body out of view.

Why wasn't Tripner giving up? All he had to do was call it and the match would be over.

I can't let him die!

Alfie looked around frantically. By the corner of the ring, Tripner's friend kept glancing between the match and his pocket watch. If he was Tripner's trainer, perhaps he could end the match on his behalf.

Alfie forced his way against the tide of the crowd, making judicious use of elbows and knees, every hard-fought step bringing him that much closer to the man with the watch.

In the ring, Tripner had broken free, but collapsed onto his knees. He began to crawl away, body trembling, but still did not tap out. It wasn't over.

Nunn circled him, arms raised again to the cheers of the crowd. He kicked Tripner lightly, toying with his prey, before turning to the crowd like a gladiator of old, waiting to hear whether they wanted him to grant quarter. From the screamed suggestions Alfie could hear, they did not.

Alfie finally reached the bearded man. This close, there were streaks of grey visible in his hair. His hands were clenched around the watch. He paid no attention to Alfie as he stared at Tripner and shook his head slowly.

It's rigged. Alfie realised. *He has to last a certain amount of time in the ring.*

From the look on the bearded man's face, that time was still a long way off.

"He's going to die!" Alfie screamed. The man started, and turned to look at him. In the ring, Tripner had staggered to his feet, only to be dropped immediately by a right hook. He lay gasping on the stone floor, a bubble of blood popping over his lips.

"Nunn's going to kill him! Forget the bettors, he's going to die!"

"You don't understand," the bearded man hissed. "He makes it five more minutes he gets a whole quid. You know what he can do with that kind of money?"

Alfie reeled. There was no way Tripner would make it that long. He was going to die for less than the cost of Alfie's boots. "I'll give you ten times that."

The bearded man hesitated.

"Each!" Alfie continued. He glanced over at the ring. Nunn had stopped his victory lap and was sauntering over towards Tripner's prone form, ready to deliver the killing blow.

"Ten pounds each, if you call the match right now."

In a flash the bearded man was gone, diving into the ring, hands raised. The crowd groaned.

And like that it was over.

The publican came over and raised Nunn's fist in the air while shooting dirty looks down at Tripner and his friend. Nunn smiled his broken toothed smile at the crowd, then spat a bloody gob at Tripner's face before wandering off to bask in the adoration and free rounds of beer. Some men grumbled and headed for the door, complaining about The Body Snatcher not living up to his title, while others ran over to the bar, winning bets clutched in their hands.

Alfie watched as Tripner's friend carefully drew him into a sitting position and helped him work a loose shirt over his shoulders. They had a short conversation. Alfie couldn't hear exactly what was said, but it ended with the friend pointing over at Alfie and Tripner looking over, face first open in surprise, then glaring darkly. He said several more words to his friend then pushed him away, rising slowly to his feet. He wavered there, snapping when his friend reached out to help. The bearded man threw up his hands and stalked back over to Alfie.

"Fecking fool says he could've made time, and the trouble from the bookmakers is gonna cost a lot more than ten quid. So you know, that's his way of saying thanks for you saving his hide. If I was you, I wouldn't go near 'im 'til he's had some time to cool his head. If you want to give me his ten quid too, I'll make sure he gets it."

Alfie hesitated. What concern of it was his if Tripner actually got his money or not? He had spent enough coin and concern on the loser of the fight, when his only thoughts should be on the victor. By all rights he should just hand the bearded man twenty pounds, then go over and secure the services of The Body Snatcher for his personal protection.

He looked over towards the bar. Nunn was leaned back on a chair that creaked under his girth. With one still filthy arm, he had pulled one of the serving women onto his lap, where she looked resigned at best, while the other arm waved a tankard perilously close to the face of a man who was trying to stitch up a wound above his ear. No doubt he was recounting the entire fight from his perspective for the enthralled audience that gathered around him, hanging off his every word. If Alfie had any sense, he would go join them.

Alfie's eyes slid over, just in time to see Tripner hobble out the door into the night.

"Thanks for the warning," Alfie said, pulling ten pounds from his pocketbook and carefully counting them out. "But I believe it's best to always pay my debts in person."

He turned to go, but was pulled up short by a hand grasping his wrist.

The bearded man gave him a long look. "Ten quid is just for the fight. Don't be thinking it gets you any more. You want extras, you pay him for extras, understand?"

Alfie blushed bright red. "I understand what you are implying and take extreme offense!"

"Sure you do." The man nodded and released Alfie's wrist. "Pleasure doing business with you, guv."

Alfie turned on his heel and sped off into the dark alleys of Spitalfields as quickly as his dignity would allow, leaving his cousin forgotten behind him.

CHAPTER 5

Dominick spit on the cobblestones as he shambled back to his lodgings. He squinted to see as best he could through his swollen face. His ribs felt like the devil himself was trying to pry them apart with hot tongs.

He reached up to wipe a hank of sweat and blood soaked hair from his face and hissed. His fingers were numb where they weren't on fire. He cradled his hands protectively against his chest, unable to straighten them from the crooked claws they had become. How in the hell was he going to get the wraps off? He tried tearing at them with his teeth.

I had him! If it hadn't been for fucking Jimmy and that fucking ponce.

Dominick lowered his hands with a sigh. Even as he had the thought, he knew he was lying to himself. If Jimmy hadn't stepped in then, Dominick would be in the back of a cart on his way to a dead room by now. Still, there'd be hell to pay in the morning.

He bit back another snarl of frustration. He should have at least collected the ten quid Jimmy told him about. It wouldn't be enough to cover what the bettors lost on him not lasting the full twenty minutes he'd promised, but it might be enough to earn him time to make up the rest before they started breaking fingers.

He wiped his stinging eyes as best he could as dreams of even the smallest passenger berth vanished before them. At this rate, he'd be dead of old age before he even saved up enough pennies to take the mail coach to Portsmouth, never mind seeing any of the actual world.

So lost was Dominick in visions of ships sailing off to unknown lands without him, he barely noticed the sound of someone following him down the narrow lane. When he finally did, he spun around, his hands raised in a pathetic mockery of his boxing stance earlier in the night.

The man skidded to a halt a few feet from him, fancy shoes sliding on a bit of refuse that almost sent him tumbling. Unfortunately, he recovered his balance at the last moment, depriving Dominick of even that small satisfaction. It took him a moment to recognize the man as the same pretty toff Dominick had seen in the Red Dog, the one Jimmy had pointed out as having "saved your bloody rank hide".

"What do you want?" Dominick barked.

If the man was taken aback, he didn't show it.

"I told your friend to stop the fight with the promise of payment to you as well. Since you did not seek me to collect, I had to seek you out instead."

He held out several bills, folded in half.

"I don't need your rotten money."

The man eyed Dominick up and down. "Forgive me for saying this, but I believe you do."

Dominick spit again, and tried to walk away.

"I wasn't done—" A hand landed on Dominick's shoulder and he saw red. Next he knew, he had the man pinned against the wall, Dominick's forearm pressed dangerously against his throat.

"I said bugger off. Leave me alone."

The man dropped the bills into the filth of the street as he choked and scrabbled at Dominick's arm.

Dominick had noticed the man in the pub, how could he not? He was gorgeous, all fine long lines, high arched cheekbones and wide doe eyes. Maybe it was because he would never taste such finery himself, but there was something about such a rich morsel of fine young gentleman that made Dominick's teeth itch with the desire to gobble him up.

Dominick leaned in closer, the man's aborted breaths panting against his lips. His fingernails scratched ineffectively at the fabric of Dominick's shirt and his eyes were wide with fear. Now that Dominick had a better look at him, there was something eerily familiar about him, his face buzzing at the back of Dominick's brain, like the words to a song he couldn't quite remember.

He sneered cruelly and leaned closer. "Unless this is what you're after is it? Fancy swell like you after a bit of rough? Got scared off by old Body Snatcher but thought you could handle the loser, eh?"

He raised a bruised hand and looked at it contemplatively. "Think my hands and mouth are going to be out of commission for a while yet, but your tenner and a crown extra will get you either my prick or my arse. What's your fancy?"

Dominick brushed the back of his hand against the man's face in a parody of a lover's caress. He then gave a light squeeze to the arm still trying to push him away. To Dominick's surprise, the man hissed like the soft grip had caused him actual pain.

Before he could react, the man's other hand swung out in a wild arc. Dominick hadn't even noticed the cane until it struck him in the shoulder. He grunted, but did not release his grip. The angle of the glancing blow was too poor to cause him much harm, but then the man drove up with his knee, hitting Dominick squarely in the balls.

Dominick dropped like a stone. He heaved, coughing up only air as he fought to swallow down bile. Every breath sent new knives of pain cutting upwards through his guts and slicing at his cracked ribs. He groaned, rolling onto his side and cupping himself. It didn't help much for the pain, but at least provided a little protection should the man attack him again.

The man was still leaning against the wall, cradling the arm Dominick had grabbed with the hand still holding that damned cane, his head back against the brick as he filled his lungs. A band of red was clear across his throat in what little light the moon and distant streetlamp provided.

"Didn't think I'd been beat enough?" Dominick croaked. "Christ, what a rotten night."

At this the man started to laugh, just a hoarse chuckle at first, then building until his entire body shook with hysterics. Wonderful. He was completely mad. Of course he was. Of all Dominick's luck.

"Rotten night, rotten night..." the man panted. "It has been, hasn't it?" He descended into another fit of laughter.

Dominick rolled carefully onto his knees, but didn't seem to be able to get his legs under him enough to stand up.

"You won't try and choke me again if I help you up, will

you?"

Dominick snorted, then regretted it as nausea rolled through him again. He sat very still until he was sure he wasn't going to cast up his accounts. "Only if you promise not to knee me in the balls again."

The man bent to retrieve the fallen bills, then got his uninjured shoulder under Dominick's outstretched arm. By leaning against each other and the alley wall they eventually returned Dominick to his unsteady feet.

They stood a moment, catching their breaths, Dominick's arm still draped over the stranger's shoulders.

Dominick glanced sideways at the man, catching little more than his profile and the side of his head. From this angle, Dominick could see that his hair, short as it was, had a definite curl, the low light picking up on gold undertones to the dark red. With that hair and those eyes, he must have been a terror as a child, surely no one could have denied anything to such an imp.

"Where'd you learn a move like that anyway?" Dominick asked. "I thought you fancy types were all about the gentlemanly art of the sport?"

The man grinned. "Such a move would get me barred from Gentleman Jackson's I'm sure. But no, when I was a child I had a friend who taught me that the only way to win a fair fight—"

"—Is to cheat."

"—Is to cheat."

Dominick's world spun as everything clicked into place. The eyes, the hair, the strange familiarity. He had said exactly those words time and time again when he was a child back in the workhouse to comfort a sweet, crying little boy after the older children picked on him. The same boy he had taken under his wing and taught to survive, teaching him a few moves—bites, kicks, scratches, *knees to the groin*—that would fell even the largest attacker.

The same boy, *Alfie*, who had been his best and only friend until the day he had left Dominick behind forever.

"Dominick?" the man, *Alfie,* asked.

"Alfie?"

The man nodded. Dominick didn't even know where to begin. Little Alfie, his Alfie, all grown up and healthy and rich... and beautiful. Oh, Christ.

Beside him, Alfie gaped, jaw working several times before he finally sputtered out, "How... I mean, Dominick, you..."

He moved to face Dominick, the movement jarring Dominick's arm from around his shoulders, wrenching his side. Dominick yelped.

"Oh Jesus, Dominick, you nearly died." A look of horror crossed Alfie's face as he gingerly reached out towards Dominick, only to withdraw at the last possible moment. His eyes went wide, "And I assaulted you!"

Dominick laughed, wincing. All the nights he'd hoped to get a chance to see his Alfie again, he'd never imagined it would be like this. This was better than anything he could have dreamed.

"To be fair I went after you first. I'm glad you still remember what I taught you, although my bollocks aren't."

He threw his arm over Alfie's shoulder again, like he had done hundreds of times when they were young. He shivered as the night air cut through his thin shirt.

"Come on then, I think this is a longer talk than I want

to have in the street. I've got a room just up ahead. I lead, you help carry."

He rewarded himself with one more look at Alfie's shocked face, then began the arduous task of putting one foot in front of the other.

CHAPTER 6

Alfie glanced around at the tiny set of rooms Dominick had dragged him to. The three flights of stairs had been a challenge, but between the two of them they had managed. The two rooms combined were roughly the size of one of his townhome's smaller pantries. The first held little more than a three-legged stool sat beside a table with uneven legs bearing a dented metal pitcher. Through an empty doorway stood the second room, empty as well save for a small window over a low bed and on the far wall, a tiny fireplace which Dominick probably considered a luxury.

At Dominick's grunt, Alfie carefully eased him down onto the bed. He shivered at the loss of warmth, feeling suddenly awkward and too large to be sharing such a small space with Dominick after all these years.

By God, he'd never expected to see his friend again after the day he'd been dragged away kicking and screaming into a better life. How many times had he cried himself to sleep those first months apart, curled up alone in his empty bed without Dominick there to tell him it would be better in the morning and lull him to sleep with his stories? All the times he had turned to share some funny thought or idea for mischief only to find no one by his side.

And now here he was, face-to-face with the one person he'd always been able to share everything with, and Alfie didn't have the faintest idea of what to say.

"You can get the fire sorted then, if you're just going to gawk."

Alfie did as he was told, kneeling by the hearth and laying in the assortment of odds and ends he found there. Oily newspaper that smelt of fish, a few small lumps of coal, slivers of wood that appeared to have been broken down from larger boards. It took him a while to get the fire going with such scraps, but it gave him time to gather his thoughts.

If the truth came out he would be ruined and probably gaoled. He should lie, or say nothing at all, but he had spent years with his secrets eating him from the inside out and no one to confide in.

And this was Dominick. Whatever may have passed in all the years since Alfie had last seen him, there was no one on earth he had ever trusted more. Still, he couldn't bring himself to reveal everything to a man he hadn't even known was still alive a few hours ago. He cleared his throat.

"You remember that day at the workhouse that the flash couple showed up and we thought they were looking for a kitchen boy or the like? About twelve years ago?"

"Hard to forget, since it ended with them carting you off. And it was thirteen."

Alfie nodded. Thirteen years. Could it really have been half his lifetime since he'd last seen Dominick?

"Thirteen. Well, that was Lord and Lady Crawford, the late Lord and Lady that is. My parents."

The sounds of Dominick settling onto the bed suddenly ceased. Alfie swallowed and kept his eyes on the fire. He didn't think he would be able to get through the rest of it if he had to look at Dominick while he told the story, the official story at least. And the truth would probably be even harder.

"They had spent many years travelling abroad and their return to the ton with a half grown child was something of a shock for everyone, not the least the earl's rather noxious brother and presumed heir. His son is the one who dragged me to the fight tonight. He's as unpleasant as his father was, but I suppose I owe him now."

Alfie risked a quick look back at Dominick, who listened in wide-eyed amazement, one hand raised as if he had started working his bindings off, only to be distracted by Alfie's story and completely forget what he was doing. Alfie couldn't help but smile, it had always been Dominick's tales distracting *him*, not the other way around.

Without thinking, he rose and sat next to Dominick on the bed. He carefully brought the large hand down and set it upon his knee while he worked on picking out the blood encrusted knot. He wrinkled his nose as the blood flaked and gathered under his nails, but this was not the first time he had patched Dominick up after a fight, or vice versa. Indeed, his entire childhood at the workhouse had seemed little more than an endless series of them tending to each other's injuries, be they from the matrons, other boys, or the most dangerous jobs.

"I was shipped off to school almost immediately, after the requisite private tutors to ensure my coursework and behavior were comparable to those of my fellows. At first my accent and etiquette left much to be desired."

"Too busy on all those 'abroad travels' to learn your manners, eh?" asked Dominick dryly.

"Precisely. I continued my studies through university, until the death of my father, at which point I inherited the title of Lord Crawford and returned to London to care for my mother until her death some six months ago."

"I'm sorry for your loss."

"Thank you," Alfie nodded, the words feeling as meaningless as ever.

"You realise I know it's all horseshit. The first half at least, I don't doubt you were a right terror when they tried to scrub some respectability into you."

Alfie could only shrug in return. He so desperately wanted to tell Dominick everything, but fear held his tongue.

"Fine then," said Dominick softly. "A man's past is his own concern. I won't pry."

The room descended into silence then, broken only by the occasional pop from the hearth. Alfie tried to focus on his work, and not think about the warmth of Dominick's hand soaking through to his skin, or the things Dominick had said when he'd had Alfie pressed against the wall.

What Dominick had said about a man's past, did that mean he had things in his life that were dangerous to discuss as well? The *acts* he thought Alfie wanted him for, had those been things Dominick had actually been forced to do in the past? The idea of Dominick, his protector, being so vulnerable as to having to resort to that to survive... His hands shook as he slowly unwound the fabric.

"And what of yourself," he tried to ask nonchalantly. "'Tripner' is new."

He felt more than saw Dominick's shrug. "When I left the workhouse I needed a last name. I got it off a gin bottle."

"Oh."

Alfie tried to think of something else to say that wasn't one of his thousand burning questions about Dominick's past, but came up with nothing.

"My history isn't nearly so mysterious," Dominick sighed, reading Alfie's mind. "About a year after you left I got the choice of moving from the boys' dorms up to the men's or leaving the workhouse entirely, so I left without a second look. Spent a few years running with some Blackguard Children, begging and snatching and the like, then I spent a few years cracking houses. Had one close call too many and didn't fancy a term in Newgate, so I've been finding odd jobs ever since. But it's the usual, not enough work, too little pay.

"I'm good with my fists though, have to be. So I win a few fights, get the moniker 'Nick "the Terror" Tripner'. Which is funny, since the last time anyone called me 'Nick' was you when you were too small to remember the whole thing. I guess publicans and urchins have about the same amount of brains.

"Then tonight an opportunity comes along to make some fast money... Money I *will* take now that I know it's from you. Consider it payment for that time I told matron it was Baz Watts who put that frog in her desk after he threw your shoes down the privy."

"Baz the Badger."

"That's the one."

Alfie was silent a long moment, but couldn't help but ask. "Does he still blame me for—"

"He does," Dominick interrupted, wincing as the fabric

pulled away from his raw skin. "He's as vicious now as he was then, and twice as ugly."

Alfie couldn't help the laugh that escaped him. Dominick himself hadn't changed much either. Still able to draw a smile out of Alfie when his worries began to get the best of him.

He finished unwrapping Dominick's hand and carefully felt it over. Nothing seemed broken, thank goodness, but the bruising was going to be hell in the morning. He wordlessly took the other one and repeated his task. They sat quietly as Alfie worked. It was almost as if the last thirteen years hadn't happened and they had never been apart.

But they had, said a voice in the back of his mind. Thirteen years, during which he had lived the finest life and attended the best schools, was kept warm and fed as a member of the noble class, while Dominick had nothing but this tiny room that he had scraped and fought and… done other things to pay for. It was unfair.

"In the alley…" Alfie hesitated. He didn't really want to know, but some compulsion drew him to ask anyway. "The things you offered to do. You've done them before? For money?"

Dominick's hand tensed in his, but his voice when he responded was steady.

"Not my favorite way to earn a meal, but it's better than starving. I keep taking fights with the likes of The Body Snatcher though, I doubt my face will be pretty enough to draw them in anymore."

Alfie tried to smile at the jest, but it was a half-hearted thing at best. Inside he was burning with pity and anger and some stronger, wilder emotion he couldn't name at the thought of the men who had treated Dominick so poorly. At the sight of Dominick's shoulders hunching defensively he bit back his thoughts as best he could. He hadn't been there to help Dominick then, but he could be useful now.

He let go of Dominick's hand and stomped the few paces over to the pitcher, his anger still not fully controlled. The pitcher was full of water, but he could see no towel. He yanked off his cravat and dipped it in. When the cravat was soaked through, he pulled it out, twisted it tightly, but could not seem to wring out all of his frustrations.

"Move more into the light. I need to see if that head injury needs stitches."

"I don't remember you being so bossy, *milord*," Dominick muttered petulantly as he shuffled closer to the fireplace, but his shoulders relaxed and Alfie took that as an encouraging sign.

"And I don't remember you losing fights, but here we are." Alfie said, stepping in front of Dominick and flicking him on the ear.

Dominick's eyes went wide and his hands came up to his reddening ear. Alfie flushed. What was he thinking? He was no longer a small child playing around with his only friend. He was a grown man. More than that, he was an earl with responsibilities and properties and tenants. He couldn't go around being overly familiar with men he didn't know.

And that was just it. He didn't know this man, this *Mr. Tripner*. Once upon a time, a lifetime ago, a poor orphan boy named Alfie had known another poor orphan boy, but that Dominick hadn't even had a surname. He'd had kindness and laughter, and a shoulder to weep into, and let Alfie tuck his icy feet against his stomach on the coldest nights, and been the one person Alfie believed would always be there for him. But then he hadn't. He had let Alfie go. And while that had given Alfie a life of luxury...

Hell, Alfie thought, looking at Dominick's meager room, *It probably saved my life*.

But it meant that the boy he had been and the boy he had known had grown so far apart that they might as well inhabit different worlds. And any bonds they might have had were long since broken.

Really, it was grossly unacceptable for him to be in the quarters of a strange man, touching his bare skin and tending to his injuries. *However...* Alfie squared his shoulders. It would only be more awkward if he were to stop now and draw attention to his impropriety. Best to continue on as he had begun, then never think of this strange night again.

"Tilt your chin back," he said, reaching out with wet cravat. His hand only wavered a little. Dominick hesitated slightly before complying, closing his eyes as Alfie wiped gently at his face, then scrubbed harder when the drying blood refused to comply.

"Ow."

"Hush," Alfie leaned in closer. He placed two fingers against Dominick's jaw, pointedly ignoring the sharp rasp of stubble under his fingertips. Tilting Dominick's head to best catch the scant light from the fire, he leaned in and hummed thoughtfully.

"It doesn't look deep, but I think you should see a doctor

regardless, that was an awful lot of blood."

"Head wounds always bleed like a stuck pig. It's fine."

Dominick opened his eyes, and Alfie was struck suddenly at how close they were. Dominick sitting on the bed with Alfie leaning over him, just barely touching, the firelight casting a warm glow that didn't reach into the corners of the room. It was like they were all alone in their little pocket of the world.

"For the rest of you then," he whispered. "You took quite a beating. What kind of man takes a fight he knows he'll lose?"

"The kind willing to take the risk." Dominick smiled. This close the effect was devastating. "I got off lightly thanks to you. Only a few bruises and cracked ribs. I know the feel, I've had worse."

"My doctor wouldn't mind. He's already seen me once today, I'm sure he wouldn't mind doubling his fee."

"Oh?" Dominick's hand brushed against Alfie's hip. "And why were you being examined by the good doctor anyway?"

Alfie swayed, closing his eyes. He murmured, "Because I was shot," and leaned in.

Dominick jerked back and grabbed Alfie by the arms.

"You were shot?" he yelled.

Alfie cried out as Dominick unintentionally gripped right over his injury. Instantly Dominick released him and was on the other side of the room faster than Alfie could see him move.

"Shit! Fucking bloody hell! Why didn't you say something? Christ, when I grabbed you before, no wonder you kneed me in the balls." He paced then turned to Alfie.

"What the hell happened?"

Alfie sagged, sitting heavily on the edge of the bed. He was suddenly so very, very tired.

"It's a long story, and it is very late. Suffice to say, it's the reason I followed you out of the pub this evening. I was trying to hire you."

Dominick shook his head. "Hire me for what?"

"For protection," Alfie said. "To watch my back while I investigate precisely who it is that wants me dead."

Out loud, it didn't sound quite as great a plan as it had before. Surely there were agencies one could consult for this sort of thing.

"Oh wonderful." Dominick threw his hands in the air. "First you're a lord, now you're a detective. Will wonders never cease. 'Who it is that wants me dead,' he says. Christ. I'm surprised there isn't a queue."

Alfie huffed and stood up. This was a mistake. All of it. It would be better to cut his losses and put the entire idea behind him. Perhaps his solicitor could suggest a discreet firm. Or Alfie could just leave the country. That plan had worked for others, surely it would be the easiest solution.

"Thank you for your time," he said stuffily, straightening his coat and smoothing down his shirtfront. "I respect that you are uninterested in the—"

He stumbled over his words. "The offer of employment. I suppose the person who placed second in a two-man fight is not the best choice for the position anyway. It was most pleasant catching up, but I won't trouble you again." Alfie walked swiftly towards the door.

"Wait, wait!" Dominick called out. Alfie paused with his hand on the knob. Dominick scrubbed his hands over his face vigorously. Even from across the room Alfie could see him wince as the action hurt both his injured hands and face.

"I didn't say that, just Christ, it's late. Would you be willing to go over this again—*slowly*—when I don't feel like an entire music hall has been dancing on my face?"

Alfie shifted, warring with himself. Really, from the egregious way he'd been acting, the correct response would just be to end this now and never have to face Dominick again. On the other hand...

＊　＊　＊

Alfie watched wide-eyed as Dominick chased off Baz and two other boys. He bent and threw a clod of dirt, hitting Baz squarely in the back of the head. The boy tripped, but kept running as Dominick shouted obscenities at him. Once the other boys had disappeared around the corner of the shed, Dominick jogged back to where Alfie was sitting on the ground, clutching his knee.

"What did I tell you about going around without me, eh? Bound to get yourself in trouble."

Alfie couldn't help the sniffle. He'd known better, but Baz said a frog had tadpoles in the puddle behind the shed, and Alfie had wanted to see.

"Hey now, none of that." Dominick went down to one knee in front of him. "Let me see."

He pried Alfie's fingers gently from around his knee, examining the graze there, before he spit on it, and rubbed in some dirt from the edge of the sadly empty puddle. At Alfie's disgusted expression, he laughed.

8

4

SAMANTHA SORELLE

"That'll make it heal up twice as strong. And this," he pressed a quick kiss to the knee. *"Will take away the pain. Feels better already, don't it?"*

Alfie unbent his leg cautiously, then nodded.

"See, you can always count on your Dominick." He dusted off his hands and stood, reaching down to Alfie. "Come on, let's see if those sad eyes can't con a spoonful of honey from one of the girls on kitchen duty."

Alfie's eyes lit up at the thought of an unexpected treat. He was ready to run off, knee forgotten, when Dominick grabbed the collar of his shirt to hold him in place. He bent over until his eyes were level with Alfie's.

"I can't look out for you if I don't know where you are, Alfie. Next time you want to go off on some adventure, you take me with you. Promise?"

* * *

"I promise," Alfie whispered. He shook himself, trying to loosen the tendrils of the past that clung to him.

"What's that?"

Alfie straightened up, donning the manners of aristocracy like armor. "I said, very well. I'm at 43 Bedford Square. Do you know it?"

"I'm sure I can find it."

"Good. Call on me, let's say tomorrow morning? If that is convenient for you."

"I'll have to reschedule tea with the Duchess, but I think that'll work," said Dominick dryly. "My apologies for not seeing you out, but I think I'd fall asleep halfway down the stairs. When you get to the bottom, there's a drunk sleeping by the door. That's Old Frank, give him a kick and tell him I said to take you somewhere you can find a cab to get home. All sorts out this time of night."

Alfie flushed with warmth at Dominick's consideration. He hadn't even thought about how he was getting back, too flustered from the entire night.

"Thank you... Dominick."

"Goodnight, Alfie." Dominick eased himself down onto the bed and lay back, throwing an arm across his eyes.

Alfie hesitated, the invitation for Dominick to come with him pressing against the back of his teeth. He was momentarily overwhelmed with the desire to take him away from all this, to bring Dominick with him the way he should have found a way to do when he was taken in by Lord and Lady Crawford as a child.

But there was nothing he could have done then. And now, it was best for them both if Alfie kept a measure of distance between them. Two poor children in the workhouse could have a friendship, but an earl and a backroom boxer? It was impossible. Any chance for that had ridden away in the coach with Alfie all those years ago.

"Goodnight," he said, and shut the door behind him as softly as he could. It wasn't until he was halfway home that he realised he'd left his cravat behind.

CHAPTER 7

Dominick groaned as the dawning sun fell into his eyes, waking him. He tried to roll over, only to curse as his entire side erupted in flame. He reversed course and lay on his back, blinking. What had happened last night?

Oh. *Oh.*

He smiled, wincing only slightly at the pull on his bruised and swollen face. After that last day at the workhouse, he'd never expected to see Alfie again.

It was fitting in a way. He had been fighting the day Alfie was taken from him, forced to watch Alfie leave him through blackened eyes. It was only right that he watched him return the same way.

And the years in between had clearly been good to him, in more ways than one. Dominick's childhood friend had grown into a lovely man. Strong too, if the way he'd held his own against Dominick and helped him up the stairs was any indication. Nobility, false or otherwise, suited him well. He looked as if he was born to the part, all lofty and refined.

Over the years, Dominick had hoped that Alfie was somewhere warm and safe, since even those modest ambitions were too often beyond his own reach. But this was more than he could have ever dreamed for his friend.

He didn't regret the decision he'd made that day at the

workhouse for one second. Alfie deserved to have all of the finest things. If Dominick hadn't done what he did then, that rat-faced weasel Baz would have—

Dominick scowled, covering his face with his arm. No reason to ruin such a fine morning thinking about that vermin.

Something soft brushed against his fingers. Even from such a light touch he could tell it wasn't the coarse muslin of his bedclothes. He pulled it down, squinting as he tried to figure out what it was. A long piece of white fabric, very fine, but smeared with dried bloodstains. Alfie's cravat. Dominick flushed at the memory of Alfie taking care of him the night before. He rubbed the fabric between his fingers. The silk glid between them, catching on his many scars and calluses before sliding away.

Alfie's hands were almost as soft, he remembered. An aristocrat's hands that had touched Dominick so gently. For a moment last night, he'd almost thought that Alfie might be like him, but surely not. Alfie was just a good man helping to care for an old and injured friend.

Still... Dominick's prick twitched. There was no harm in thinking about it. All that fine pale skin. Those beautiful blue eyes staring at Dominick in surprise and wonder.

He slid his free hand down over his stomach and under the tie of his trousers. What else might give Alfie a similar look? He raised the hand holding the cravat to his face and breathed in deeply. The smell of copper and iron hit him first, his own blood, but underneath lurked some fine cologne, spicy and warm, and beneath that, just the faintest hint of clean, masculine sweat. He wrapped his hand around his slowly rising cock then tugged hard, the way he liked.

He yelped, his hand flying out of his trousers.

"Christ," he hissed through clenched teeth.

Apparently there was plenty of harm in thinking about it. Especially if the man doing the thinking was trying to pleasure himself with busted fingers on a bruised cock. Dominick groaned as pain rolled through him on waves of nausea. He might not regret his actions Alfie's last day in the workhouse, but he certainly regretted whatever day it was he'd taught the little fuck to aim for the crupper.

After taking several minutes to regain his breath, Dominick gingerly rolled up to sit on the side of the bed. He could have used a few more hours, days, weeks of sleep but he was awake now. And he had promised to meet with Alfie again today.

He winced. Maybe if he left now, he could walk slowly enough to not be limping too badly by the time he arrived.

Spying the cravat still lying on the bed, Dominick folded it as neatly as he could before painfully climbing down onto his knees in the middle of the room. He pulled up the loose floorboard, and felt around for the little tin box hidden underneath.

Pulling the box out and placing it on the bed, inside were only the few coins he'd managed to scrape together and his ring. He pocketed a few of the coins to pay for breakfast, then a few more. He was getting ten quid from Alfie today after all, and maybe more work besides; he had earned a treat after the excitement of the day before. He picked the ring up too and examined it.

A cheap and poorly made thing, the little bird and leaves that had once encircled the band now lived more in his memory than on the chipped and worn pewter. Made for a man's hand, it was some token given by his mother to a father he didn't remember, and left with him after both his parents died.

At least, that was the story he told himself.

In reality, all he knew was that it had been left behind by whoever dropped him off at the workhouse as a child. There had been a system in place where someone abandoning a child could leave a token, something worthless but unique. If they ever wished to have their child back, all they had to do was describe the token to prove they had a rightful claim and the child would be returned to them immediately.

No one had ever come for Dominick.

On the day he left, the warden had handed him the ring and wished him good luck. It was the one thing that had come with Dominick from the workhouse and had stayed with him all the years since. For all that it wasn't even worth the price of a hot meal, it was his only real treasure.

He set the folded cravat down in the bottom of the box, then after a moment's hesitation, left the ring and remaining coins on top of it. He'd grown into being able to wear the ring when he was in his teens, but with his knuckles as swollen as they were, he didn't want to risk getting it stuck and damaging it. It would be safe enough in the box until the swelling went down and his hands returned to normal.

He closed the box and tucked it back into its hiding place, making sure to kick some of the dust and dirt on the unswept floor over the replaced board so any potential thieves could not tell it had been moved.

Satisfied, he swapped out his shirt for his slightly cleaner one. The bruises on his torso weren't as bad as he had feared. As long as he didn't push himself too hard for the next few weeks, he'd be right as rain.

Whistling, he grabbed his coat and headed out in search of breakfast.

* * *

"Didn't expect to see you this morning," Jimmy McVitie boomed when Dominick finally shambled into The Barge.

His beard and hair were far too neatly groomed for the early hour, but Dominick supposed that being a married man and business owner would do that to you. Long gone were the days when he was up till all hours teaching Dominick to crack houses or sneak into unwatched stores.

He was downright respectable now, when he wasn't getting Dominick into and out of illicit boxing matches.

Jimmy snorted, but didn't stop wiping down the bar when Dominick sat gingerly on one of the stools.

"I suppose that answers the question of if that dandy knob ever caught up with you."

"That's none of your business," Dominick retorted. "And his money was fine enough for you wasn't it? Besides, can't a man be moving a little slow after a go in the ring with The Body Snatcher? Christ, I feel like I've been beaten with an oaken towel."

Jimmy laughed and patted Dominick on the shoulder, not as carefully as he could have.

"For that, there's a half pint on me. Want me to see if the missus has anything left she'll let me give you for cheap?"

"No," Dominick said, pulling the coins from his pocket. "I'll take the drink, we both know you owe me that and more, but I'll have a full breakfast to go with it, sausage, eggs, the whole lot. I've got a line on some work, want to be at my best."

Jimmy raised a knowing eyebrow, but said nothing, pouring Dominick's ale, then heading into the kitchen. Dominick sipped it slowly, lost in thought.

"Oy there, Tripner! And aren't we looking gorgeous this morning?"

A hand slapped against Dominick's back, and he coughed, choking on his beer. He wiped frantically, trying to keep the worst of the spills from staining his shirt.

"Baz." Dominick said. The warning edge to his tone might have been more effective if he was in any shape to do anything about it.

"Saw Nunn just about knock your block off last night. Good show."

"Really? I didn't see you there. You should have said hello. I'd have let you in the ring first for practice."

Baz Watts, known as Baz the Badger ever since he'd been picking on the younger lads at the workhouse, had only grown more into his nickname as the years went on. A nuisance with sharp teeth and beady eyes, he'd been bigger than Dominick for the first fifteen years or so, and made his life a living hell. But over the course of one summer, Dominick had gone from cowering from Baz, to towering over him.

Alfie must be bigger than him too now, or taller at least, Dominick thought. *I'll have to tell him later. He'll be sure to get a laugh out of it.*

Baz now barely came up to Dominick's shoulder, his small cruel eyes in a pitted face only adding to his rodent-like appearance. His pale hair already thinning on top. All and all, it was probably better that the nickname "Badger" had stuck as a child, because anything based on his adult appearance would have undoubtedly been worse.

The man had never lost his vicious streak, and all these years later Dominick was still wary of him. He had threatened to kill Dominick that day at the workhouse, and just because he hadn't yet, didn't mean he had forgotten.

"Really Tripner, not all of us can make a living by taking a pounding from other men one way or the other. Some of us got to make it honest-like."

Baz sat down on the stool next to Dominick. He swiped Dominick's tankard and took a long sip. Dominick gritted his teeth, but in the end did nothing. He still had to go meet Alfie today, and didn't want to get blood all over his only clean shirt.

Well, he glanced down at the spreading beer stains. *Mostly clean at least.*

Besides, Baz was faster with a knife than any man Dominick knew, and always had a few of them hidden around his person. The man was as thin and sharp as his blades, more weasel than badger. Dominick eyed Baz's bulky coat, elbows patched and long hem caked in mud. He wasn't about to press his luck.

The man swallowed and wiped his mouth with the back of a greasy hand. "Besides, don't I come here today with kindness in my heart, hoping to share some of my good fortune with my fellow man?"

Dominick snorted, "What do you want, Baz? And make

it quick, some of us got places to be."

Baz scowled and glanced around the empty pub. He leaned in, voice dropping to a froggy croak. "Rich bloke, needs some things done, you know? Things that might be a bit... unsavory. But I've got no such qualms do I? And you for sure don't. What do you say? A man of your reputation could make my job a lot easier."

"And what reputation would that be?"

Baz gave Dominick an incredulous once over.

"I'll leave you to figure that out for yourself. Tell you what, I'll give you three shillings a day from what he's paying me, any day I need you."

Dominick laughed. The money Alfie promised him already was more than two month's wage at that rate, and that was without whatever pay he would be getting from this bodyguard business Alfie had been talking about. Surely he'd been exaggerating though. Who could actually want his Alfie dead?

At the thought, he glared over at Baz. Dominick hadn't been the only one he'd sworn to kill that day.

Dominick stood and yelled toward the kitchen. "Forget that breakfast, Jimmy."

He turned to Baz. "I've suddenly lost my appetite."

Dominick couldn't resist the petty urge to knock Baz with his shoulder as he walked out, but the other man didn't react.

"Tripner," he croaked, still sitting facing the bar, rolling Dominick's tankard between his palms. "Saw that molly chase you after the fight last night. Near panting for it he was, so I'm guessing you don't need the money right now.

"But I'm not the only one who's seen that from you

and more besides. Might be a day where your reputation as a fighter don't outweigh your reputation for other things. Someday soon maybe. So when that happens, you just remember I offered you a chance to be on my side."

That warning ringing in his ears, Dominick stepped out of the pub. He had better places to be.

CHAPTER 8

It took Dominick over an hour to make his way on foot to the address Alfie had given him.

He spent most of the walk cursing Baz's name and glowering at anyone who stepped too close. He shivered and pulled his much-mended coat tighter around him. It might be nearly April, but London still clung to the wet miseries of winter. The icy wind cut through the worn fabric, letting in the persistent damp. He was chilled to the bone before he'd even passed Moorgate.

He stuck his stiff hands deeper into his pockets and thought about Baz's words, which brought a flush of shame to his face. Most folk in Spitalfields turned a blind eye to anyone, man or woman, boy or girl, who took the occasional coin for going down an alley with a man. That the act was a crime bothered few, and a sin even fewer. Everyone knew how hard money was to come by and didn't begrudge those whose looks—or desperation—granted them another way to earn their supper.

But now Baz was threatening Dominick. If he went to the constables, it could be a hanging offense. But that was unlikely. It would be almost as bad for Baz as it would be for Dominick if he squealed to the coppers and word got around. More likely, he'd just use the knowledge to make Dominick's life hell.

Dominick sighed. Nothing new there.

At least it wasn't something he was forced to resort to often. He was strong and hale enough that he was usually able to make his living by his back, rather than on it. But when there was no good work to be had and the choice was prostitute himself or starve?

He'd made that choice before, and doubtless would again. His size and rough looks meant he didn't attract the same kind of men who'd gone for him when he was a skinny youth, never able to earn or steal enough to keep himself fed, but there would always be those sorts of men —rich men—who came down to the stews looking for a bit of rough.

Rich men like Alfie.

Dominick groaned. The first time he'd seen his best friend in thirteen years and what had he done? Propositioned and then attacked him. Of course he had. Act first, think second, that was him. Christ.

At least Alfie had handled it like the gentleman he now was. Well, he did knee Dominick in the bollocks, that was true, but he hadn't turned away in disgust for the way Dominick had... accosted him. No, instead he'd helped Dominick get home and patched him up. There'd even been a moment where he thought Alfie was going to kiss him, of all the absurd notions.

Dominick shook his head and muttered at his own stupidity. A clerk, no doubt on his way to work, gave him an alarmed look and hastily walked past.

The moment had just been in his head. Alfie wasn't like that. Hadn't Dominick done everything he could to make sure he would grow up good and right?

He hadn't felt that way towards Alfie when they were children of course. He'd loved Alfie, still did love the memory of him. His best friend, so sweet and brave, who'd made Dominick want to do the right thing just to see the pride in Alfie's eyes, looking at Dominick like he was King Arthur and Robin Hood and Nelson himself all rolled into one.

But last night hadn't felt like that. No, whatever tension in the air he thought he'd felt as Alfie stood over him, hands on Dominick's skin, those beautiful blue eyes Dominick had missed so much locked with his own, that was just wishful thinking on Dominick's part. He'd been overwhelmed was all. The touch of a beautiful man paired with the joy of reconnecting with his old friend turning his head.

Dominick laughed. Not that his head needed anymore turning. The Body Snatcher had just about twisted it right off with that last hook. He gingerly touched the bruises he could feel blossoming across his face. With his senses as addled as they had been, maybe Alfie hadn't been much to look at all. Or maybe it hadn't even been Alfie, just the strange dream of a confused mind.

"Well, someone left their cravat behind, I didn't make that up," Dominick said aloud as he entered Bedford Square. "One way or another, I'll have my answers soon enough."

Dominick followed the edge of the park around to number 43. He took a look at the row of elegant townhouses with their carved archways and decorative railings and then a look down at himself. There was no chance he could walk in the front door of such a fine home looking as he did. Alfie's footman or butler or whatnot would slam the door in his face before he even got two words out. And rightfully so.

That in mind, he opened the little gate in the railing to the side of the front steps and descended down to the servants' entrance.

Even the service door was nicer than anything in his part of town. Its paint shone fresh and unmarred by any crude words carved into the wood. He knocked and as he waited, he ran his fingers through his hair, pushing it back into some kind of order. When he heard footsteps approach the door, he smiled as best he could without splitting his swollen lip. Hopefully, he still had enough charm to impress whatever timid little scullery maid was sent to open it.

The door wrenched open and a grey-haired woman with the forearms of a young Hercules glowered at him.

"What do you want?" she barked.

"Begging your pardon, ma'am. But I have an appointment with Al—" Dominick tried to remember the title Alfie had given him, something silly sounding. "With Lord Crawford?"

She snorted. "Sure you do, and I got my lovely bonnet right off of Marie Antoinette's head."

Dominick looked up at the plain cap the woman wore. "I'm sure it looks much better on you, ma'am," he said soberly.

She began to close the door in his face.

"Wait, please! I did have a meeting, but I figured the butler wasn't going to let me in by the main door. If you could just have him check with your lord, you'll see. Tell him it's Mr. Tripner here about the job."

He hesitated, "And to collect my payment for the fight last night."

She paused, "What fight was that?"

"Boxing, ma'am. A most noble sport."

"Mmm. That's what happened to your face then."

"The parts I wasn't born with, yes, ma'am."

She crossed her arms. "And who'd you fight, in this noble sport?"

"A Mr. William Nunn."

Her eyes widened, "Blood and 'ounds! You took on The Body Snatcher and you're still walking? I'll be damned. At The Red Dog, was it? Ah, the mister will be sorry he missed it."

She eyed Dominick up and down. "Well, I don't know about any jobs. Can you peel potatoes?"

"I'm told I'm a quick study."

She rolled her eyes, but stepped back so Dominick could enter. "Come on then, I'll let you work off the price of a hot meal at least, until his lordship wakes up. Still early for the kinds of hours his set likes to keep."

Dominick ducked through the door and sat on a stool by a long kitchen table. The cook bustled off, and he took a moment to look around. The kitchen was large and clearly well kept, but empty. Wasn't a lord supposed to have an army of servants for every need? The woman returned and dropped a basket of potatoes in front of him before pulling a small jar out of her apron pocket.

"Arnica," she said. "There's a mirror just up the stairs. Go rub some of that on your face, then come back here and wash your hands. I don't need you getting who knows what all over my vegetables. And you won't even think about lifting any trinkets while you're up there; I know the look on a man's face when he has something in his pockets he shouldn't."

Dominick did as he was told. He marveled at the change as he walked up the short flight of stairs to the ground floor. Alfie's home was beautiful. The walls on this level were painted a pale yellow, the colour of freshly churned butter, and paintings of rolling hillsides and people in strange clothing hung in ornately carved frames. On a table under the mirror sat a vase painted with roses that looked so delicate, Dominick was afraid the whole thing would shatter to pieces if he breathed on it too hard.

He looked in the mirror. It had been a long time since he'd seen a clear image of his reflection. No wonder the cook didn't want to let him in. One eye was almost swollen shut and his entire face was mottled black and blue. He rubbed in the sharp-smelling paste as quickly as he could without looking at himself too closely, then went back to the kitchen.

* * *

Half an hour later, Dominick had earned himself a fresh scone with jam and the cook's name, if not her trust. He noticed Mrs. Hirkins kept a good deal of knives and pans between the two of them, although based on the silence from the rest of the house, he didn't blame her. He also wouldn't want to be alone with a man looking like he did.

He jerked as a bell over the doorway rang. It was one of several, all unmarked, but Mrs. Hirkins seemed to know exactly what it meant.

"That'll be Master Alfie up then. You wait here, and I'll go see about this job business."

She picked up a large tray laden with a tea set, scones, toast, butter, and jam. Dominick stood to help her, but she shook her head.

She knocked the kitchen door open with a hip, "And don't be thinking of stealing the silver while I'm gone. All that's under lock and key."

Dominick sat back down and waited for her return. He didn't have to wait long.

"Strike me dead, you weren't lying. Go on, up the stairs to the hall, second right, he's in the dining room. Here, take this." She handed Dominick a second tray, this one loaded with eggs, sausages, and some of the potatoes he'd peeled, fried up in sausage grease.

"Try to see he gets some of that into him. Skinny thing's got legs like cat-sticks."

Dominick took the tray and followed her directions.

The stairs were tricky to navigate with such a burden, and he wondered how Mrs. Hirkins handled it every day. Surely there should be someone else to help her?

Fortunately, the door to the dining room was open and Dominick walked in, careful not to over-balance the tray. He kicked the door shut behind himself, wincing at his thoughtless action only after it was too late to undo it without dropping everything. He had a moment to take in the simple opulence of the room, nothing gilded or frilled but clearly all of the finest craftsmanship, before his eyes landed on Alfie and his apology died on his lips.

His memory of last night certainly hadn't exaggerated

how beautiful Alfie had become. If anything, it hadn't done him justice. Alfie by dim and smoky firelight was pretty, but in the bright morning sunlight he was dazzling. He rose from his seat at the head of the table and stepped forward into a sunbeam that caught the reds and golds in his hair and glowed like a halo around his head.

He was in his shirtsleeves, no coat, but wrapped in a banyan embroidered with flowers and birds that glimmered and caught the light. Dominick was reminded of the adventure stories he used to tell Alfie about grand sultans and maharajahs, or the tales the sailors told of the far-off lands they had visited and the fantastical sights they had seen. Alfie looked like that; alluring, exotic, and completely beyond Dominick's reach.

Then he smiled, and Dominick had to sternly remind himself why he was so out of reach. Alfie had made it out, had a good clean life. He didn't need Dominick dirtying him back up.

"I see Mrs. Hirkins put you to work already. You can set that here." Alfie indicated a clear space on the table.

Dominick set the tray down, then found he had nothing to do with his hands. Alfie made an aborted half step forward, hands rising to shake Dominick's? Give him a hug, even? Before he clearly thought better of it. They stood a moment in awkward silence until Alfie cleared his throat and waved a hand at the chair to the right of his own.

"Please, sit. I apologise for keeping you waiting, I didn't think you'd be by this early. Have you eaten?"

Dominick squinted at the carved clock on the mantle. "It's nearly nine."

Alfie gave a self-deprecating laugh. "Ton hours. I could be abed until noon and still be considered an early riser. I didn't sleep very well last night, however." He took a slice of toast.

"Mrs. Hirkins says you don't eat enough."

Alfie rolled his eyes. "I eat plenty. She's been trying to fatten me up since I first came here, but it hasn't taken. That said, I don't want either of us to incur her wrath. Split this with me."

He took a second plate that Dominick hadn't noticed out from underneath the one on the tray, and divided everything out onto both.

They spent a few minutes eating silently. The quiet felt good though. Comfortable. Dominick's shoulders eased down from a hunch he hadn't even noticed, the familiarity of eating together with Alfie relaxing him. They'd shared a meal plenty of times before. He just didn't have to pick gristle or weevils out of this one.

While Dominick spread the jam thick on his second scone of the morning, Alfie poured himself another cup of tea, squinting a little in the morning light.

Dominick's curiosity finally got the better of him. "I thought you dukes and such were supposed to have people to do that sort of thing for you. Butlers and footmen in shiny buttoned uniforms, pouring your tea and saying 'Yes, sir,' every time you belch. But all I've seen is Mrs. Hirkins, and I'm pretty sure she'd hit you with a spoon first."

Alfie smiled around the rim of his cup. "You're more right about that than you know. She can pretend, though. You should feel honored. The less she likes you the more formal she is. She treats my cousin as if he was the king himself. And I'm not a duke, only an earl."

"Only an earl, he says," Dominick mocked. He glanced towards the door and then lowered his voice. "At least as far as they know."

Alfie set his cup down and spoke slowly. "I find myself in a position with few people I can trust. It has always been a danger, my being not exactly who I am supposed to be. As the years have gone on, there's been less risk of being caught, or so I thought."

He turned the cup around and around on the saucer, then sighed.

"But still, it's simpler this way. After my father died, my mother stopped throwing parties and being invited to few herself, gradually began to cut down the staff. All pensioned or given stellar references at their preference of course.

"By the end it was just her, Mrs. Hirkins and myself. I do not socialize much and have, for reasons you understand, never found much in common with my peers. In fact, I could honestly say the only real friend I've ever had was a grubby little boy I never even got to say goodbye to."

There he faltered and took a moment to collect himself. "I haven't seen you for thirteen years, Dominick, but I'm hoping I can trust the man that boy grew into. Because honestly if I can't, I have nowhere else to turn."

Dominick's heart lurched at the look on Alfie's face. He ached to go over and hold him, shush his fears and smooth back his hair. It's what he would have done had they still been boys. But they weren't, and men did not have the same luxury to provide simple comfort to one another.

Instead he moved his chair closer to Alfie's, and slid one of his sausages onto his plate.

"Eat up, then tell me everything."

CHAPTER 9

Alfie toyed with his food, not eating more than a few bites. Tossing and turning in bed the night before, he'd decided to tell Dominick all of it.

The risk was enormous. He *didn't* know Dominick. Not really. And if he was wrong, if Dominick was no longer as trustworthy and good as he had been, if the last thirteen years had twisted him into someone else, someone worse? He already knew enough to ruin him if he so chose. But someone was trying to kill Alfie, and if it came to it, he would choose ruin over death any day.

"I am not of noble birth, as you well know. My parents —that is, the Lord and Lady Crawford—were considered extremely scandalous. For example, there's a portrait of them in the front hall in full Eastern dress. Quite shocking. They were adventurers, you see, and spent much of their lives abroad, going to the sorts of far flung places where a child would have only been a hindrance in their travels.

"By the time they decided to return to London, they were past both age and interest in begetting an heir. They did not think it would much matter; my father had a younger brother who could inherit. But when they arrived, they quickly discovered that my uncle had squandered what money, responsibility, and reputation he had. I'd rather not list his crimes, but believe me when I say that his son, my cousin Reginald, is a vile wastrel of a man but only a pale imitation of his father."

Alfie paused to take a sip of tea. He shouldn't speak of his cousin like that, even if it was true. But he needed Dominick to fully understand.

"My parents decided that under no circumstances should my uncle inherit and that rather than risk the entire earldom falling to shambles and destroying the lives of all who depended upon it for survival, the morally though not *legally* correct thing to do was to find themselves an heir. So they went to the least-reputable workhouse they could find, where a child might be acquired off the books…"

"And found you."

Alfie nodded. Dominick didn't need to know that Alfie had been his parents' second choice. As they were fond of reminding him when he misbehaved. It would have been Lord Baz Crawford if the other boy hadn't been stupid enough to tussle with Dominick before they made their final decision.

As guilty as that made Alfie feel sometimes, he tried to make up for it by being extra diligent with his investments and correspondence with his land managers, to make sure the earldom had the best care and that his tenants were as prosperous and contented as possible.

Baz and Reginald would probably have got on like a house on fire, and burned the earldom to the ground around them.

"And found me," he continued. "Of course an adopted child can't inherit a title, so they claimed I'd been born in Egypt years earlier and they simply hadn't written about me because of a local superstition that said it was bad luck to do so.

"Utter nonsense naturally, but it gave them an excuse to suddenly have a child no one knew about. After that it was merely a matter of private tutors to train the Spitalfields accent out and the manners in, and they had an heir. All I had to do was keep my mouth shut and act the perfect little gentleman."

Alfie laughed darkly, "And if I made a mistake, they could always blame my foreign upbringing. You can't imagine all the wondrous places I have supposedly been."

He couldn't keep the wistfulness from his voice. He risked a glance up at Dominick.

When Mrs. Hirkins had announced that Dominick was waiting for him, Alfie had intended the first words out of his mouth to be an apology for his unforgivably familiar actions the night before, but when he'd actually seen Dominick walking into his dining room, bruised and battered but real as life and with such a fierce look of concentration on his face as he tried to keep the tray from spilling, Alfie couldn't help but smile. His heart warmed at the sight, and he remembered why he hadn't slept well the night before. Each time he'd drifted off to sleep, he'd dreamed of being a small child, nestled up in bed, surrounded by warmth and protection. It had felt so real that he kept waking up, reaching back for someone behind him, and blinking confused in the dark when he wasn't there.

It wasn't hard to decipher the reason for those dreams when it was literally right in front of him.

He cleared his throat.

"And that was that. To no one's surprise, my uncle died of overindulgence well before my father, and I inherited instead of Reginald. I told myself at first that I would just keep up the charade until my mother died and then hand everything over to the rightful heir. I even tried to bring Reginald more into the running of the earldom, so that the transition would be easier.

"I gave him one of the smaller estates, thinking it would give him a purpose if he had something to manage, as well as serve as a pleasant escape from the city and its temptations.

"Within a fortnight he'd lost it in a game of cards to a man who wanted to clear-cut the forests for timber and sell off the farmland to his friends. Dozens of families would have been forced from homes that they had lived in for generations. It took me nearly a month to convince the man to sell it all back to me, and even then I had to pay twice what it was worth. Financially it was a terrible decision, but I knew what poverty would mean for those families and I could not bear the thought of being in some way responsible."

Alfie jumped as a warm hand wrapped around his wrist. He looked up at Dominick who was smiling fondly at him.

"You always had a good heart, Alfie. Even when it got you into trouble. Don't start apologising for it now." Dominick gave his arm a friendly shake. Alfie could feel the warmth of his hand even through his shirt and banyan.

"So I kept the title. And now someone is trying to kill Alfred Pennington, Earl of Crawford."

Dominick's grip on Alfie's wrist tightened almost to the

point of pain, his face darkening. Alfie hissed as the bones of his wrist ground against each other. Dominick's glower changed to a look of contrition and he let go. Alfie missed the feeling immediately.

His injured arm throbbed in sympathy with his wrist as he methodically went over the shooting the day before. He could scarcely believe that it had been less than a full day since the shooting, finding Dominick, everything. Life could turn so suddenly on the smallest things.

As he described the dizzying realisation of what had happened, he saw Dominick's hand twitch, like he wanted to reach out and touch him again. He didn't, instead twisting his napkin between his hands, but the fact he had wanted to at all gave Alfie the perseverance to keep going.

"...and that is why I want to hire you to be my bodyguard," he finished. "To keep an eye out when I'm distracted. I assumed there was nowhere in London safer than Mayfair and look what happened. I doubt you would make the same mistake."

Dominick didn't respond for a long moment, then said softly, "You said there were other attacks?"

Alfie leaned back in his chair. "I think so. At the time I just chalked them up to accidents or coincidences. A stone from nowhere striking my horse causing her to rear up while I was out riding. A jostle on a crowded walkway nearly pushing me in front of a speeding mail coach. That sort of thing."

Dominick nodded slowly, then put his elbows on the table, face in his hands.

When no further response seemed forthcoming, Alfie said tentatively, "You always said I needed a keeper."

Dominick groaned, and scrubbed his face.

"I should have known," he muttered, in a voice low enough Alfie had to lean in to hear.

"You were trouble enough when you were little. Of course the trouble grew with you. Right, someone is trying to kill you. I suppose I'd better make sure they don't. Why though?"

"Why... do you have to make sure they don't kill me?"

Dominick rolled his eyes. "Because I don't want to waste the effort I put in keeping you alive when we were little. No, I mean *why* does someone want you dead?"

Oh. Alfie hadn't actually thought about that. The realisation that it was happening at all was as far as he had gotten.

"Well, out with it," Dominick said. "No use keeping secrets now. I already know you're a lowborn, flea-bitten orphan posing as a lord. How much worse could it be? Sleep with a married woman? Fell in with anarchists and revolutionaries? Spit champagne on the wrong person at a ball or whatever it is you rich coves do for fun?"

Alfie smiled faintly. "No, no, and definitely not. I mean, I suppose it could be revolutionary republicans after me, *liberté, égalité, fraternité* and all that, and I am just the first on a very long list of targets. But it seems unlikely."

"How about your cousin then? That seems the likely answer to me. Is there any way he could have found out that he's the rightful Count of Cuckold?"

Alfie rolled his eyes. He knew Dominick was doing it on purpose to distract him from the fact they were discussing who wanted him dead, but couldn't resist correcting him anyway. "Earl of Crawford."

"Ah yes, of course." Dominick's face was blank, but his eyes sparkled with suppressed mirth. "I associate with so many lords and ladies, it's hard to keep them all straight."

"I'm sure. And I hate to think it, but..."

"But it does make sense."

"It does," Alfie admitted. "But why kill me? If he knows he's the rightful heir, then why not just take me to court? It's not like he's ever given a damn about scandal before. It would be less risky than taking a shot at me, or even hiring someone else to do it.

"And if he doesn't know, that means he's trying to kill his own flesh and blood in order to inherit. I would like to say that for all his faults I don't think he has it in him, but I just don't know."

Alfie stood, no longer able to be confined to a chair. He paced angrily over to the window. "I should just give it to him, just find some way to hand it over and disappear. Go to one of those faraway places from your bedtime stories that I'm already supposed to have visited. Just go and never return."

He looked out the window. The dining room was along the front of the house with views into Bedford Square Park. New leaves were budding bright green in the trees, and in the grass a few brave crocuses sprung out in bright yellow and purple. He'd always wanted a chance to see real nature, but his parents had firmly put their travelling days behind them when they returned to London, and the furthest he'd ever been out of the city was to Cambridge for his schooling.

"Did you know, the Earl of Crawford hasn't set foot in the earldom itself for over forty years? It's somewhere on the coast of Scotland. I do the best that I can from here, but I've never been. My parents visited shortly after their marriage, then boarded a ship in Edinburgh and never returned. A beautiful family seat from what I'm told. Several hundred years old. And even though he went everywhere else, my father never bothered to go back."

"It sounds lovely." Alfie hadn't heard Dominick move, but there he was, leaning against the other side of the window frame, his body turned towards Alfie, watching him across the expanse of glass. Alfie leaned his forehead against the cool pane and exhaled, watching it fog up with his breath.

"Maybe I should go there. I had thought about doing it before this all started, after my mother died. But now..."

"Now it would feel too much like running away." Dominick crossed his arms across his chest and ducked his chin.

Alfie nodded. He met Dominick's eyes, and there it was again, no doubting it this time. That pull he'd felt the night before. The undeniable feeling of connection. From the look in Dominick's eyes, he felt it too. It was too palpable to ignore. Alfie felt his chest tighten and pulse flutter. He had never felt such an immediate spark to another person before. Maybe it was because he already knew Dominick and this was just the feeling of their friendship clicking back into place after so many years apart.

Or maybe it was something baser. Lord knew, even with his bruises, Dominick was easily the most attractive man Alfie had ever seen. Despite the open view onto the street between them, where any passerby could look up and see, he felt a physical pull towards Dominick. The light touches he'd had the night before while bandaging him up were nothing, a few drops of water to a man dying of thirst. He wanted, *needed* to touch Dominick all over, and be touched by him in return.

He opened his mouth to say something, although he didn't know what, when there was a knock at the door.

He smiled ruefully at the look of annoyance on Dominick's face, and nodded towards the table. "I'll get it. Go finish your breakfast so she doesn't fuss over the both of us."

He walked to the door and opened it. Mrs. Hirkins stood on the other side with a collection of papers in her hand.

"Beg your pardon, but the morning mail just arrived and I thought I'd see how you were getting on."

"I haven't stabbed you with a table knife and made off with the fine china, if that's what she's asking," Dominick called out cheerily.

"Yet," muttered Mrs. Hirkins under her breath.

"We're fine, Mrs. Hirkins, thank you," Alfie said, taking the mail from her and pretending he hadn't heard either of them. "Mr. Tripner was just telling me how much he enjoyed your excellent scones. He said they were the best he's ever had. He's agreed to my offer of employment for the foreseeable future, so I'm sure we're all looking forward to having an amicable relationship."

Mrs. Hirkins looked like she'd bitten into a lemon and gave an aggrieved sigh. She pulled a small canister from her apron pocket.

"In that case give him this, I don't want to have a heart attack every time I turn a corner and see his face." With that she bustled off, back to the dominion of her kitchen.

Alfie handed the canister to Dominick and sat back in his seat with the mail.

"More arnica," Dominick said. "That means she likes me, doesn't it?"

"I'm sure she'll be asking to go for a turn with you next half day," Alfie said distractedly.

He flipped through the letters. Invitation, invitation, he set those in a pile to either ignore or politely decline. A quarterly update from his solicitor, that would need responding to later. Odd, this last one had no return address. He opened it, and read the single line it contained.

It was as if someone had thrown open all the windows at once and let in the sharp chill of morning air. A shiver ran down his spine. Distantly he heard Dominick calling his name. He read the line again and again until his hands began to shake so hard the words blurred.

I know what you are.

CHAPTER 10

Dominick looked up at the rough gasp. Alfie bolted upright, knocking his chair back, a look of absolute terror on his face.

"What's wrong?" Dominick asked, immediately on alert. He rushed to Alfie's side, then hesitated, torn between the demands of society that he keep a proper distance and the clear distress on Alfie's face.

To the devil with it.

Dominick threw an arm over Alfie's shoulders, and felt the fine tremors running through his body. He tucked Alfie securely against his side, and reached for the letter.

Alfie sagged, knees going out from under him, and Dominick cursed, taking a moment to maneuver him back onto his chair. He kept his hand on Alfie's shoulder, hoping to ground him with his touch. Finally confident that Alfie wasn't going anywhere, he turned back to the letter.

The paper was high quality; even Dominick's uneducated eye could tell that. There was a weight to it and a softness, almost like cloth. It was far from the near-translucent newsprint or coarse pamphlets he was used to. The top edge was rough, but not like it had been torn away, more like whoever made the paper wanted you to see all the rich layers of pulp that had gone into it, so everyone would know how fine it really was.

The handwriting on it was not of the same high quality. The letters were large and blocky in a way that Dominick would have called childish, if not for the fact he could write little better himself.

Their message however, was clear.

I know what you are.

"Well," he said slowly. "I guess that answers the question of if anyone else knows you're a fake." He squeezed Alfie's shoulder companionably.

"That's not my cousin's handwriting."

"If it was, I'd say those swish schools were an even bigger waste of blunt than I thought. Paper's quality though, did you notice?"

"Did I notice the paper?" Alfie looked up at Dominick. It was a good angle on him. Dominick pushed that thought to the back of his mind and focused Alfie's incredulous look instead.

"Do you have ice water in your veins? No, I can't say my first thought when opening a blackmail letter was to take note of the excellence of the stationery!"

Dominick huffed and chucked Alfie lightly under the chin before going to sit back in his own chair. "No need to be like that about it, just because I figured out the first clue to our blackmailer before you."

"Our... *what*? And how is that a clue?"

"Well," Dominick leaned his chair back on two legs. The delicate wood gave a faint groan at the strain and he thought better of it. "For the first, you don't send a letter like that for no reason. It's to get the mark good and scared. When he thinks you're at your wit's end, he'll send another letter with his terms.

"For the second, you'd know if someone in your set wrote like that, wouldn't you? All you lot do is write back and forth from what I can see."

"The alternative is meeting in person, and we're all equally insufferable, I assure you. But I see your point. No, in the peerage everyone has the same overly ornate hand drilled into us by equally indistinguishable tutors and schoolmasters."

"Right, and this looks like it was written by a coster's wife. So that means that whoever's been trying to kill you is either lower class, or has at least contracted out to someone lower to do their dirty work for him."

"And is paying him well enough that he wastes money on paper?"

Dominick shrugged. "Maybe it was all he had. Or since he had to pay to post it anyway, perhaps he felt like splashing out? That might explain it if he was expensing it. Would also explain why he tried cheaper ways to off you first, rocks and shoves and the like. A pistol is the first thing a man pawns when money is tight, and the last thing he buys back."

"If you say so." Alfie frowned. "So we have a poor man, working for a wealthy one. But if he's being paid to kill me, then why the letter?"

That was a good question. Dominick turned the letter over in his hands, looking for some sort of answer.

"Unless..." A fire lit in Alfie's eyes, and his gestures grew more animated. "The other two attempts could have passed as accidental. Even I thought they were at first. But he has to know an earl being shot in the street would be investigated, not to mention the headline on every paper between here and Bombay. He's not trying to hide it anymore."

Alfie got up and started to pace down the long side of the table, the silk of his banyan fluttering behind him. Dominick felt a pang in his heart every time Alfie mentioned the shooting. The thought that someone had come so close to snuffing out this bright flame of a man was unbearable.

Dominick had a vision then of what could have been. Alfie lying somewhere cold and alone, a slowly growing pool of blood forming under him and running out into the indifferent streets as the spark in those luminous eyes dimmed forever. And Dominick, never even knowing Alfie was in danger, going on with the same dreary routine of his daily life, working, fighting, fucking. Never even knowing that he'd failed to protect the only good thing he'd ever had.

He was shaken out of his morbid reverie when Alfie reached the end of the table and spun around, snapping his fingers.

"I'll bet he's trying to double his profit. He expects me to pay the blackmail, then after I have, he'll take the reward for killing me."

A dark thought overtook Dominick. "Or the next letter he sends asking for payment is a trap to lure you somewhere nice and secluded."

"Or that." Alfie turned on his heel, beginning another long lap of the table. "I don't see how this gets us any closer to finding him."

Dominick watched Alfie pace, but doing that got him no closer to discovering who was threatening him. He looked back down at the letter, hoping to find something else to lead them to the blackmailer.

"How many places in London do you think sell this fine a paper?"

"Not very many," Alfie said. "Why?"

"And all in only the most exclusive neighbourhoods, I'm sure. Not a lot of call for them elsewhere. Think about it, if someone who looked like me walked into a store like that, you'd notice, wouldn't you?"

"Absolutely."

"So all we have to do is go to these fancy shops, and ask if they remember any dirty and disreputable types buying paper from them."

Dominick couldn't help but grin, smug at the cleverness of his reasoning.

"Dirty and disrep—oh. Oh! Dominick, you're a genius!" Alfie ran to the door and pulled a braided cord that hung beside them. Faintly, Dominick could hear the echoing of a bell ringing somewhere in the empty house.

"When she comes, please give my regards to Mrs. Hirkins for the excellent breakfast and ask her to send word that I'll need my carriage and a driver for the day. I need to go finish dressing, then we can get started."

Alfie was halfway out the door before Dominick asked, "Aren't you forgetting something?"

Even down the length of the room he could see the furrow in Alfie's brow. "What?"

"I never *actually* agreed to work for you. And you still owe me ten pounds."

"Oh. Of course. I just assumed… But of course you can't be expected… One moment and I'll fetch my pocketbook."

Alfie's shoulders slumped and Dominick could kick himself. Christ, he'd just meant to tease him a little. Either he was too out of practice with giving a bit of ribbing, or Alfie was too out of practice receiving it.

"Of course I'll take the job, you muttonhead. Clearly someone's got to look out for you. I did it for free long enough, might as well let you pay me for the privilege this time around."

"Thank you, Dominick," Alfie said softly. "There's no one I'd rather have at my back than you." Then a look of confusion passed over his face. "How much does one pay a bodyguard anyway?"

Dominick laughed. "I wouldn't know. It's not like I'm a *real* bodyguard. I guess it depends on who he's guarding."

"An earl?"

Dominick considered, "Well now, that would be expensive. I'd need at least two castles, and a cart full of gold that takes eight horses to pull."

Alfie smiled impishly over his shoulder as he walked out the door. "Then I suppose it's a good thing I'm not a *real* earl."

CHAPTER 11

By the fifth stationer, Alfie was beginning to think that their plan was flawed. The near permanent scowl on Dominick's face suggested he felt the same way. The carriage slowed as it turned onto Clifford Street then came to a stop in front of a store window with finely made quills, ink pots and stationery sets on prominent display.

"Once more into the breach?" Alfie asked.

Dominick sighed heavily in reply and did not move from his slouch. They sat at diagonals, the only way to keep from bumping knees in the confined space, but Alfie still found the proximity to the other man to be stiflingly close. Funny, he had shared a carriage with several people at a time before and it had never been an issue, even when he was escorting her mother and her lady friends somewhere and risked drowning under their endless shawls or losing an eye to an overly feathered bonnet.

"You don't have to come if you don't want to."

Dominick sighed again, then slowly unfolded himself and reached for the door handle. "I can't exactly keep an eye on you if I'm hiding away in here. Come on."

As they exited the carriage, Alfie took a quick moment to surreptitiously check that all of his buttons, seams, and sleeves were in place and flicked a bit of lint from his cuff. Out of the corner of his eye, he watched Dominick spread his arms and arch his back obscenely before cracking his neck to either side. A bolt of lust shot through Alfie and he quickly averted his eyes.

How beautifully aware and comfortable in his body Dominick seemed, although on reflection he had winced a little and leaned more heavily to one side than the other. Probably his severely bruised if not cracked ribs from the night before. Alfie would have to keep an eye on him and make sure he didn't over-exert himself.

Still, he was envious of Dominick's freedom to move in such a manner in public without caring who saw. To better maintain his role as the perfect earl, Alfie was aware of his appearance at all times and worked hard to constantly uphold the image of an immaculate gentleman. He doubted his tight jacket and even tighter waistcoat would allow him to bend in such a way even if he dared attempt it.

He tapped his cane on the pavement and strode into the store. The smell of ink and paper hit him immediately, the comfort of the familiar smell relaxing his shoulders just a little. Perhaps this experience would not be as unpleasant as the last four. If they were extraordinarily lucky, then perhaps the shopkeeper would remember selling the paper to someone outside of his standard clientele and they would have a general description or even a name.

Within a few hours, Alfie might have the entire situation handled. The blackmailer would be found and with Dominick at his side for a bit of intimidation, dissuaded from pursuing any further actions against him. Then Alfie could retire to his study, put his feet up by the fire, and free himself of these ridiculously confining layers.

Dominick would be there too, of course, sprawled in his chair like a king. The firelight would catch the invitation in his eyes, and Alfie would rise, cross over to stand between those spread thighs before—

"Can I help you, my lord?"

Alfie shook himself and addressed the small bespectacled man just quickly enough that the moment didn't stretch into awkwardness. "Yes, I was hoping you could tell me—"

The man, who had been smiling serenely as Alfie spoke suddenly cut his eyes over to the door, his entire demeanor changing to one of extreme umbrage.

"You! Out! This is a respectable business! Be gone!"

Alfie exhaled heavily. He didn't even have to turn to know the man was addressing Dominick, who occupied the doorway behind him. The same thing had happened at every other stationer they had visited today. The shopkeepers would fawn all over Alfie the second he walked in the door, but the moment they laid eyes on Dominick, they acted as if a leprous dog had wandered in to defecate on the floor and then die.

It had been so long since Alfie had lived without the mantle of wealth and privilege that he barely remembered what it was like. Was this how the poor were regarded everywhere—with immediate hostility and suspicion? Alfie was ashamed of his ignorance.

"He's with me," he said.

The shopkeeper glanced swiftly back and forth between them. "My lord?" he said tentatively.

Alfie sighed. It looked as if he wasn't going to be as lucky as he'd hoped after all.

❋ ❋ ❋

Less than ten minutes later found them back in the carriage as it slowly made its way through the busy streets. That store had been the last stationer on the list Alfie had been able to come up with. He'd tried at the first two stores to get the names of others, but the owners had been reluctant to share the names of their competition, especially after Dominick's presence soured their demeanors.

His stomach grumbled. He had thought earlier that it might be nice to treat Dominick to a luncheon at one of his clubs, but based on the agitation his presence had caused in a simple paper shop, he wasn't sure the idea was worth the potential uproar and embarrassment. Not to mention the gossip. The Earl of Crawford bringing a commoner to Boodle's—or even worse—White's? The entire ton would have been informed in time for the evening rush.

As a result, he'd put off suggesting they stop for anything to eat at all, and now his hunger only added to his irritation.

"Well, that went about as well as expected," said Dominick not at all helpfully.

"I told you that you didn't have to come in," Alfie snapped.

"And I told you that yes, I did. It would have been nice if you hadn't acted so shocked every single time they tried to throw me out on my ear."

"How was I to know?"

"What did you think they would do? 'Oh here,

milord. One moment, milord. Let me just set some more easily pocketable things over near your friend with the bloodstained trousers, milord.'"

"This was your idea in the first place!"

"I know!" Dominick shouted, then slumped back, the wind seemingly gone from his sails. "I know. And it seemed like a good idea at the time. I'm sorry, I'm being an oaf. It just wears on you. It's one thing to be nothing and spend all your time with other folk who are the same, but to come over here…"

"You're not nothing, Dominick."

"Sure. Then tell me why we haven't stopped for luncheon when I've been listening to your stomach crying for the last two hours."

"W-well of course we could get something to eat." Alfie stuttered, caught off guard at how closely Dominick's thoughts matched his own. "I was only thinking to wait until we had finished our errand is all, but there must be a pub? Or a cart nearby. I'll have the driver…"

"Or we could just go down to the Thames and catch the eels in our teeth. That's how common folk eat, don't you remember?"

The guilt Alfie felt earlier redoubled under Dominick's words. He knew that he had forgotten a lot of things from his childhood, but he hadn't forgotten the pain of going hungry, or of being so cold in the winter that he couldn't feel his feet, or the bone deep exhaustion that long hours of grinding work did to a body, only to be unable to sleep because your muscles were so sore.

He also remembered who had been there to sneak him an extra crust of bread or rub his feet until feeling returned even though he was just as tired and miserable as Alfie was. It was the same person he was now treating so shamefully that he couldn't even face taking him out for a hot meal.

"I'm sorry," Alfie said in a voice as small as he felt. "I've treated you very poorly today, and even worse, allowed others to do the same. Please accept my apologies. I'd say that it's been a rather trying few weeks, but that's no excuse when you've done nothing but try to help me."

Dominick was silent for a long time. "Well, that's not true. I did try to choke you yesterday."

Alfie nodded, "When you've done nothing but try to help me, excluding one incident of attempted choking."

"Apology accepted," said Dominick, his innate good nature showing through the dark cloud that surrounded them both. Alfie made a note to himself not to take advantage of that nature, and to be especially careful of Dominick's feelings in future.

"Now by God, I really could eat a live eel." Dominick thumped his fist on the roof of the carriage to tell the driver to stop. "Hand over some of that that ten quid you owe me, and I'll treat you to the finest meat pie the first pub I see has to offer. You wait for me here. I don't need some barmaid 'milording' all over the place when I'm just trying to get a bite to eat. Would put me right off my food."

Alfie laughed and handed over the money. A pie wouldn't cost more than a few pence, but if he added an extra few pounds to the full ten, neither of them said anything. He did have to pay Dominick some kind of wage after all.

As Dominick disappeared into the colourfully named The Bear and Staff with a waggle of his eyebrows, Alfie dropped back into his seat with a sigh. He had no idea what their next steps should be. The paper had been their one clue. Unless they could think of something else, there was nothing to do now except await the delivery of a follow-up letter listing demands.

Or another attempt on my life, he mused.

Nothing to be done about it now though. Perhaps an idea would present itself once they had sated their appetites.

Alfie flushed at the images the idea brought to mind. He forced himself to look out the window on the opposite side of the carriage from the pub that held Dominick. There was always something going on in the streets, surely he would find distraction there.

He glanced across the throngs of people going about their daily lives, but there was unfortunately little to interest him. An old woman was ladling steaming bowls of salop for waiting customers, but neither spilled a drop of the fragrant drink nor had any customers disinclined to pay. A stray dog wandered into the path of a group of young boys, but they barely paused long enough to give the mongrel a quick pat on the head before allowing it to continue on its way without distress. Even the wind refused to blow a single bonnet off a single lady's head!

He was about to give up his perusal in disgust at the downright civility on display when his eye happened to catch on a strange man lounging in a doorway a few buildings down. There was nothing in his appearance that warranted particular note, short men with pale hair and long shabby coats were two-a-penny in London after all, but he seemed to be staring directly across the street, either at the pub or Alfie's carriage, but made no attempt to approach either.

A prickle of unease traced down Alfie's spine. The longer he looked at the man, the more he seemed vaguely familiar, but Alfie couldn't quite place him.

The coach door opened with a bang. Alfie started, knocking his head against the low ceiling.

"Sorry about that, hard to open the door balancing these," Dominick clambered his way inside with a paper wrapped package in either hand.

Alfie looked back out the window, but the man was gone.

"See something interesting?" Dominick asked, passing Alfie one of the savory smelling parcels.

"I'm not sure. There was a man across the street looking this way, but he's gone now. It was probably nothing, but it did seem odd."

Dominick leaned across him to get a better look. Alfie pressed himself as deeply into the cushions as possible.

"Don't see anyone odd now. Odder than usual at least," Dominick sat back and began to tear at the wrapping on his lunch. "Still, we can't be too careful. You let me know the second that someone else catches your eye."

Alfie nodded mutely as he watched Dominick lick a drop off gravy off his thumb. He didn't think someone else would be catching his eye anytime soon.

❊ ❊ ❊

It was barely a blink before the two perfectly serviceable steak and kidney pies Dominick had acquired at the pub were gone, devoured with the fervor of men who had had a very unpleasant day. Full and content, Alfie was on the edge of drowsing as the motion of the carriage rocked them on its steady way back to Bedford Square.

"Are you sure you won't stay for tea?" he asked. "I'm not going out this evening so I won't need your services later, but you're more than welcome to refresh yourself before heading home."

"Thank you, no," Dominick said, equally soporific. He kept raising his feet like he wanted to put them up on the seat cushions and fully stretch out but caught himself each time. "If you don't need me, there's errands and such I need to run."

His sleepy eyes caught Alfie's. "Maybe another time."

"Tomorrow for sure," Alfie said firmly. "And you have to take the carriage back. I still can't believe you walked all this way."

"The horses would be missing and the driver stripped naked before we even made the Whitechapel Mile," Dominick laughed. "The walk will do me good, helps the digestion."

"Have it your way," Alfie smiled as they pulled into Bedford Square and his townhome came into view. "Same time tomorrow? I'll tell Mrs. Hirkins to expect two for breakfast."

"I'd love to hear what she says to that." Dominick exited the carriage with a groan. He stretched again in the same vaguely obscene fashion before offering a quick wave. "Until tomorrow, Alfie!"

Alfie watched Dominick round the park until he disappeared at the corner of Gower Street headed south.

Then he reluctantly turned away. After advising the driver he might be needed the following day, he walked up the stairs into the house and tried to think of some way to fill the long, empty hours before bed.

* * *

Alfie was restless and distracted all evening. He tried to read, but never got more than a few pages in before he found himself staring out the window, wondering when the next attack would happen and if Dominick would be able to save him when it did. Had Dominick made it back to his lodgings safely? How could he bear to live in such an awful place? Had he built all that muscle intentionally for fighting, or was it merely a byproduct of a life of hard labor? Had his smile always been so dashing?

He shook his head. Those were not the sorts of thoughts he should be entertaining. Dominick was not some anonymous gentleman who Alfie met at a discreet club where they could disappear into a backroom for a time, then never see each other again. He knew Dominick, or at least, *had* known him, and he was enjoying renewing that friendship.

And that was all it would be, a friendship. He remembered all too well the look of disgust on Dominick's face in that alley when he'd assumed that Alfie had wanted to buy his services. He couldn't bear to see such a look from him again.

Alfie threw his book down in revulsion. His own encounters with men may have been brief, dispassionate affairs, but both parties had always enjoyed themselves and gone away satisfied. That desperation had forced Dominick into such acts when he clearly abhorred them made the gorge rise in his throat.

An image rose in his mind of Dominick as he had first seen him, bleeding and exhausted, being happened upon by some unscrupulous man with coin to spare. The type who didn't care if his partner was unwilling.

Would Dominick drop to his knees there in the alley? Or would he turn, raising an arm as high as his injured ribs would allow, to brace against a wall, wincing while his other hand painfully loosened his trousers enough that—

Alfie jumped to his feet, momentarily dizzy as the pain from his wound mixed with the feeling that such an image provoked in him. Wine. That was what he needed. Something to numb the senses.

He strode over to the sideboard, crossing his study in quick, angry strides. There was a new bottle amongst his usual decanters. Mrs. Hirkins must have brought up the gift Reginald had left him. He read the label. Port. Excellent, the evening called for something fortified. His cousin might be a mean, conniving, uncouth lout who was potentially trying to have Alfie blackmailed and killed, but at least he was generous with his intoxicants.

He picked the bottle up and was searching for a corkscrew when another thought occurred to him. Immediately upon seeing Alfie, Dominick had assumed —and not incorrectly—that Alfie was the sort who took pleasure in other men. Reginald had been making sly comments that fell just short of insinuating the same thing for years. Naturally Alfie was cautious in his manner and made all the appropriate noises in conversation about the fairer sex, his life depended on it. But clearly there was something about him that gave away his unnatural desires. What if his attacker had seen it too?

One only had to pick up a newspaper or set foot in a church to know that there were plenty who would be happy to save the courts a trial and the hangman a rope. Perhaps he had caught the eye of one of these vigilantes, intent on cleansing the world of immoral men.

I know what you are.

That could apply just as much to being a sodomite as to being an imposter. He would have to discuss it with Dominick and see what he thought.

And what a fun conversation that would be.

I say, Dominick, it's entirely possible someone isn't trying to kill me for being an imposter lord, but for being buggerer instead! Isn't that better? Quite the weight off my shoulders. What's that? Indeed! Those acts you find utterly repugnant, I rather enjoy them. You know, we have some time before Mrs. Hirkins comes back to collect the breakfast service, would you care to...? Why yes, bent over the table would be just fine.

He set down the port with a heavy thud and picked up the decanter of scotch instead. Much stronger. He wasn't going to need a glass.

※ ※ ※

Alfie lay in bed that night, lulled into a soft haze by the effects of the drink. Well, *drinks.* A noticeable amount of the decanter really. His thoughts were still running in circles but at a much more leisurely pace and he found he didn't mind at all now when they invariably came back around to Dominick. He was so much more pleasant to think about than the rest of this mess.

He shifted to bury himself more deeply in the many feather pillows, nestling down into them with a happy sigh. The linen of his nightclothes skimmed pleasantly across his skin and ignited the ember that had been glowing steadily all day. It had flickered to life when he had first gotten into the carriage in the morning and realised he'd be completely alone with Dominick in the dim, intimate compartment, and had grown hotter with each moment spent in his company. Even so long after Dominick had left, it was still burning him from the inside out.

He groaned. This was exactly why he had picked up the scotch in the first place, to drown these feelings out.

What harm could it do? a voice inside him asked. *You're going to be seeing him every day until this is solved. There's no reason to torture yourself with denial. After all, it's not like he's here.*

Alfie wavered, his hands picking at the quilting of his heavy bedspread. If Dominick *was* here in his bedroom though...

His composure broke and he groaned aloud at the thought. His hands flew under the covers, rucking his nightshirt up under his armpits. He hissed as his hand, chilled from the night air, wrapped around his prick. He felt like he'd been half hard all day, and the cool touch was as much a balm as it was a shock to his tender skin.

What if Dominick really was here? What if he was leaning against the wardrobe with that brash smirk on his face watching Alfie touch himself?

He closed his eyes. In his fantasy it was warm enough that he had the covers thrown down, and lay atop the sheets, completely naked and bared to Dominick's eyes.

His cock twitched at the thought. Dominick would be fully dressed in quality clothing, boots, coat and all. His arms would be crossed over his chest, emphasizing the span of his shoulders and the solid bulk of him hidden from Alfie's view. He'd look happy but a little bored. Indulgent. Yes, that was it. He was indulging Alfie.

His hand, now warmed, began to work faster, the slight burn of the dry skin only heating him further.

"Ah, ah now, why the rush, sweetheart?" Dominick would say, merriment dancing in his eyes, before they darkened and his voice dropped to a gravel command. "Hands off."

With effort, Alfie pulled his hands away, twisting them tightly in the sheets to resist the urge to touch.

"That's better. Now go slowly, I want to see all of you."

Alfie's legs spread wider of their own volition, and he could see the satisfaction writ across Dominick's face. There was no shame to be had in this fantasy, only pleasure. He placed his hands on his hips before sliding them down to caress his inner thighs.

"Look at you, all spread out for me. You look so fine, Alfie. So fine. Is that where you want me to touch you?"

Alfie nodded, eyes still closed. He pinched hard right where the skin was most tender, and let out a cry.

Distantly, he was glad Mrs. Hirkins went back to her own home in the evenings and he had no night staff. He was free to be as loud as he wanted with no one to raise any awkward questions.

Dominick clucked his tongue. "The noises you make. Make more noise for me. Where else feels good?"

Alfie ran his hands up his torso slowly, wriggling a bit as one passed over his navel. He spent a minute running a finger around the edge, and dipping it in, less for his own pleasure than for the look it got him.

"Tease," Dominick growled. Alfie hummed and moved his hand higher. He hissed as the movement pulled at the stitches in his injured arm. He left that hand slowly stroking the soft skin of his belly as his right went higher, brushing first over one nipple, then the other. Alfie was fully hard and leaking copiously by now, drops of liquid dripping down onto the back of his left hand. But instead of giving in to relief he continued to tease himself for the benefit of his imagined lover.

He couldn't help the moan that escaped him as he scraped his thumbnail over the bud of a nipple. He continued to torment it, pinching it hard and rolling it between his fingers, until the slightest touch sent shivers of pleasure mixed with pain rippling through his entire body before pooling in his groin. When he thought he could take no more, he moved his hand over to the other nipple and repeated the same rough treatment.

"Imagining they're my hands? Got a good feel for them last night, did we? But maybe not as good as you wanted. That's what you're thinking about right now. How rough they are. How the burrs would catch and scrape. I bet you've only had soft little noblemen's hands on you. You can't even envision how much better mine would feel."

Alfie sobbed, the sensations, the words, the heat he imagined in Dominick's gaze as he calmly lounged there, as at ease as the master in his own castle, watching as Alfie writhed wantonly before him.

"Please," Alfie whispered aloud. "Please, Dominick, let me..." His words cut off in a groan. He ran a hand over his sensitive collarbones, then up over his lip, nipping at the pads of his fingers, before sucking them wetly into his mouth.

"More," Dominick said lazily.

Alfie's cock jerked at the command and he complied, licking his palm thoroughly and running his tongue over each finger, twisting between them and lapping at the knuckles. He tried to bring his left hand up as well, but could barely crane his neck enough to sample the very ends of his fingertips, sighing at his own taste that had collected there, salty and bitter.

"Do it, then."

Alfie didn't have to wait to be told, his right hand flying down to grip his cock firmly, the wet slide of spit and precome a sensual relief.

"And the other one."

Alfie reached down with his other hand between his legs and rubbed his fingertips gently around the pucker of his opening. He couldn't bring himself to stop long enough to find the oil he used for such a treat, so he didn't go any further in, but even just that light touch was enough to leave him panting. He imagined how he would look to Dominick.

Warmth rose in his cheeks and spread downwards. If he looked in a mirror, he knew his face and chest would be flushed red, but he felt no embarrassment, only a wild joy at appearing this way in front of someone he could fully trust with his body, his secrets, and his life.

He cried out, hips jerking off the bed. By this point, Dominick wouldn't be able to stay away. He'd come over to him, the heat in his eyes an inferno that threatened—promised—to burn Alfie alive. He'd sit on the edge of the bed mere inches from Alfie's side.

He ran his thumb down the delicate vein along the underside of his shaft, then twisted his hand as he stroked upwards. So close. Dominick would sit so close to him that Alfie would feel the warmth of his body. But it wasn't enough. With his other hand, Alfie pressed more firmly against his entrance, but still it just wasn't enough. Maybe if Dominick would touch him.

Suddenly, Alfie remembered the way Dominick had grasped his wrist that morning. How strong and unrelenting his grip had been, and how Alfie could feel the heat from his palm through his sleeve.

His back arched as he came with a choked off howl. He kept his hand moving, imagining that Dominick was making him do it, holding onto his wrist and moving his hand back and forth, milking every last drop from him. Spend flew over his chest, a few drops even landing on his abused nipples. He shuddered, and his cock twitched again, sending more come over his hand and dripping down his wrist.

It would be all over Dominick's hand, he thought, breath hitching at the very idea.

He kept stroking until he was well past sensitive. He rolled his hips as the ecstasy of his release slowly began to transform into something heavier.

"That's it, gorgeous. Well done," Dominick would say,

his hand finally stilling but staying wrapped around Alfie's wrist.

Alfie lay there, catching his breath, content to bask in the afterglow. He took a moment to imagine what might come next.

Dominick would get into bed with him, laughing as Alfie's tired fingers fumbled with his buttons. He'd take Alfie's hands then, and kiss the palms of both, not minding the taste of Alfie's spend in the slightest. He'd then strip, and lovingly prepare Alfie before taking him. He would melt into the mattress as Dominick's body moved powerfully over his own.

When he reached his climax the second time, it would be like the rolling of a wave crashing over the shore —unavoidable, unstoppable. When Dominick came, he would drop down over him, kissing Alfie and wrapping him in his arms, Dominick surrounding him completely as he filled him from within.

Alfie took one more second to imagine that perfect moment, his lips tingling with the feel of Dominick's phantom kiss.

When he opened his eyes, his bedroom was cold and empty once again.

With a sigh, he sat up enough to get his nightshirt off, although not without difficulty. He wiped himself down with it as best he could. The few steps to the wash basin seemed as distant and impossible as crossing the Himalayas even though he was sure in the morning he would regret not cleaning up more fully. He kicked the nightshirt to the bottom of the bed and hoped it got tangled enough to not be noticed in the pile of bedclothes until after the laundress finished with them.

In the morning.

In the morning he would have to face Dominick over the breakfast table. He'd have to make idle talk and figure out the next steps in their plan all with the knowledge that he'd brought himself to climax the night before just from the memory of Dominick's hand on him. Under no circumstances could he let such thoughts show if he wanted to keep their tentative friendship. Maybe it would even be safer to pull back further and keep their interactions strictly as bodyguard and employer until they caught Alfie's attacker.

And after that…

And after that nothing, he told himself forcefully.

"After that" wouldn't change Dominick's inclinations in any way. "After that" would only mean that Alfie no longer had an excuse to keep Dominick in his employ. He hardly needed to hire a bodyguard to keep away the matchmaking mamas at balls, or ensure that no one in this theatre box attempted conversation in the middle of a play.

You could hire him for other things, said something deep and dark. *Just because he's not inclined that way doesn't mean he wouldn't take your money for it. He's already said as much. A crown, wasn't it? And you have so very, very many crowns to spare.*

"No." Alfie said aloud to the darkened room. He would not be that sort of man. It didn't matter if that was the only way he could ever actually have Dominick. Alfie would rather never have Dominick in his bed at all than have him be indifferent, or god forbid, unwilling. The very idea was abhorrent and against every moral Alfie held dear.

Most of those morals being ones Dominick had taught him himself.

No, after they discovered who was plotting against him and had the villain firmly behind bars, Alfie would thank Dominick for his help, pay him a generous bonus, and then let him go. If Dominick asked, Alfie could help find him some employment. One of Alfie's many estates must surely be in need of an overseer of some sort. Or if Dominick wanted to stay in London, Alfie could ask around at his clubs. Someone was bound to be in need of a man who was strong, smart, loyal, funny, compassionate... and many other desirable qualities in a worker as well.

Perhaps they could even see each other now and then. They could take in a show, or even get that luncheon that Alfie had been too afraid to attempt today.

To have Dominick back in his life, to have his friendship, was more than Alfie had ever dreamed possible. He wouldn't waste his sighs on wishing for a lover. He had never had a real one of those before anyway, just his fleeting encounters, so at least he didn't really know what he was missing. No, instead of pining for something that couldn't be, he would rejoice in having his friend.

He relaxed into the pillows, contented until he remembered the reactions of the shopkeepers upon seeing Dominick with him.

Hell. They'd never be accepted in public together. A lord and an illicit boxer? A friendship between them was just as out of reach as a romance. The stationers had proved that today. There was no place at all in the city where a man dressed in superfine could be seen with another dressed in rags. Anywhere Alfie took Dominick, he'd be sneered at, and anywhere Dominick took Alfie, he'd be a mark for every cutpurse and throatslitter in the rookeries. Alfie might have been from the slums, but he no longer belonged there. There was no way he could ever pass in that world.

Although...

He pulled the covers higher over his bare shoulders as a truly marvelous idea came to him. Dominick would probably hate it at first, stubborn, proud creature that he was. But the more Alfie thought about it, the more it seemed like a brilliant solution to all of their problems. Well, perhaps not all of them, they did have quite a few after all. But several at least.

With that thought in mind, Alfie fell asleep grinning, eagerly awaiting the morning and Dominick's return.

CHAPTER 12

"Good morning, Mrs. Hirkins." Dominick nodded as his repeated knocking on the kitchen door was finally answered. He waited for her to step aside and let him in, but she remained rooted in the doorway.

"You're back."

"I am indeed." Dominick smiled sunnily at her, but his charm seemed to have no effect. He tried his next weapon in his arsenal: flattery. "I look forward to working in the lovely home you've maintained here, and may I thank you again for the arnica salve? I'm sure I'll be fit to shine everyone else down in no time."

"Hmm."

She didn't budge.

Dominick sighed. "I did accept Lord Crawford's offer of employment, you know."

"I know."

"So he's expecting me."

"He may be."

Dominick cocked his head to the side, taking in the elderly woman with even greater respect.

"I could just move you out of my way."

"You could," she agreed. "You won't."

"No. I won't."

Dominick wasn't sure if there was something about

him in particular, or if it was strangers coming into her domain in general that she disapproved of. Alfie had said she liked him, but clearly that wasn't the case. To be fair, in her place, he wouldn't have been thrilled to be told that some scrubby-looking man off the streets was going to be keeping Alfie company either.

He thought of the way she was the only one Alfie had kept on to look after him in his big empty house, and the way she'd fussed at Dominick to make sure Alfie ate enough breakfast.

"I shouldn't have tried to butter you up. I see that now. May I speak plainly?"

At her nod, Dominick continued. "You and I have the same aim, and I see no reason to be at odds. You've been looking after Al-Lord Crawford for some time I believe. I'm here to try to do the same. He's hired me to be his bodyguard for a while, and I want you to know that that is not a task I take lightly. If something happened to him on my watch... If something happened, I'd willingly let you take a frying pan to me or whatever else you're plotting, because it couldn't possibly hurt more than failing to protect him."

She regarded Dominick for a long moment, long enough that he began to wonder if he'd have to bodily remove her from the doorway after all.

"Wipe your boots," she said, turning back into the kitchen, already checking the stove and bending over to pull fresh bread from the oven. "Tea's on the counter there, take that in before it goes cold. I'll be along shortly with the vittles."

Dominick carefully lifted the tea service and noticed

that there were already two teacups waiting upon it.

* * *

"Does Mrs. Hirkins know? About your... questionable origins?" Dominick wiped a bit of egg from the corner of his mouth as he spoke, and wondered idly if he had room for one more sausage. He decided he did, and added another to Alfie's plate as well.

Truly, if Alfie just wanted to pay him in Mrs. Hirkins' cooking, Dominick would probably be fine with it. Not that he needed payment of any sort to look after Alfie really. It had always been his duty after all, and he was pleased to find he enjoyed Alfie's company just as much now as he had as a child. But he did have to think about the long term. Alfie wouldn't need him after they caught his attacker, so Dominick would take the money in his pocket, as well as the fine food and better company for as long as they lasted.

"If she's ever wondered why a noble child supposedly born in Egypt showed up several weeks after his parents' return and had an accent straight from the stews with the vocabulary to match, she's never said anything."

Alfie sipped his tea, a small smile tugging at the corner of his mouth. "She was quite helpful actually. My parents correctly assumed that my lack of education and general knowledge would mark me as different from my chums and hired tutors accordingly, but they were so used to foreign dialects that they never considered what a marker my mouth was.

"Mrs. Hirkins was the one who taught me the 'proper' way to speak, having had to learn herself when she entered service. My parents didn't think it was an issue at first, but after I called the family cat a poxy whore for stealing my cheese, they conceded she might have a point."

Dominick laughed. He couldn't take credit for Alfie's colourful vocabulary, he'd come to the workhouse with a mouth on him that could make a sailor blush, but he'd never discouraged him from speaking that way either. It had been helpful more than once. A bully generally didn't expect the small, sweet child Alfie had been to have such a blistering mouth. By the time their shock had worn off, Alfie had the precious few seconds he'd needed to get away and find Dominick.

Dominick glanced over at the mouth in question, then quickly looked away. Perhaps sausages had not been the best idea after all, at least not for his own composure.

He cleared his throat and searched for another topic. "Where did you want to try today? I was thinking, some booksellers sell paper as well, so we might go 'round some of those."

Alfie shook his head. "A good idea, but I was doing some thinking as well, and I have a different sort of errand I think we need to run before we do any more investigating."

"What's that then?"

Alfie's lips twitched before smoothing into an overly bland expression. Dominick didn't trust the look in his eyes. He knew that look, and it never boded well for him.

"I'd rather not say until we're there. Think of it as a surprise."

Christ.

CHAPTER 13

Alfie smiled to himself as the carriage pulled up in front of the exclusive address, relishing Dominick's look of confusion. He'd worried that that after his *imaginings* of the night before, he would be too mortified to meet Dominick's eyes over the breakfast table. But the moment the man had walked in, delicate tea tray in hand, all unease had melted from Alfie, replaced with the growing fondness that was swiftly reaching excessive levels. There was something about Dominick that made his constant fears dissolve, or at the very least, seem manageable.

They alighted from the carriage and Alfie could see the exact moment when Dominick's curiosity got the better of his patience.

"Getting a new pair of gloves is more important than catching your attacker?" Dominick asked dubiously, staring into the shop windows where several evening suits of the finest quality were displayed on wooden figures.

"Don't be ridiculous," Alfie replied. "This is a tailor's, not a glovers. Although thank you for the reminder, we will be sure to visit there next. And I'll have you know, this *is* a part of the plan to catch him. Or at least, a way to make the process easier and far less irritating."

With that, he strode inside, biting his lip to keep his smile from giving the game away.

"Lord Crawford! It is an honor to see you again so soon! What can I get for you today? Another waistcoat perhaps? I just yesterday received a bolt of silk in an exquisite fern green that would compliment your complexion wonderfully." An old man in a somber, but impeccably tailored suit came over and shook Alfie's hand.

"Perhaps another time, Mr. Bonheur. I'm afraid we're on a most urgent mission. My friend here has recently had an accident resulting in the loss of his luggage and requires an entirely new wardrobe."

Alfie had been watching Dominick in one of the shop's many mirrors, so as not to miss his reaction. He wasn't disappointed. Dominick choked on nothing and began to cough. As if by magic, a tailor's assistant appeared at his side with a freshly poured cup of tea. Dominick waved it off and the young man vanished as if he had never been. But Mr. Bonheur himself was not so easy to dismiss.

He turned from Alfie as if only just now noticing Dominick's presence and clasped a dramatic hand to his chest. The gesture, combined with the man's bald head and prodigious side whiskers that seemed to fly away from his face like two startled doves, reminded Alfie of a music hall caricature of the obsequious shopkeep. Despite his antics, he was one of the best in London and had a reputation for both fine work and absolute discretion, both of which Alfie valued extremely highly.

"You poor man!" Mr. Bonheur gasped. "Waylaid by ruffians were you? Gracious. You must have put up quite the fight! Oh, but you are lucky to have escaped with your life! Please, please come this way. I have several suits in need of just a few alterations that might suffice for the time being, but I must get your measurements first. Just behind the curtain there if you please, thank you."

Alfie watched as a still speechless Dominick was herded over to the measuring area of the store. Just before the curtain to the section was pulled closed, he looked over his shoulder and glared daggers at Alfie. Alfie smiled cheerfully in response, although certain parts of his anatomy took careful note of what Dominick looked like angry and stern for later contemplation.

He sat on one of the plush chairs provided for waiting customers and took a moment to look around the shop. *Bonheur et Fils Tailoring* was the only place Alfie ever visited for the many, many pieces of clothing that being a lord required; each designed for a different set of social circumstances, activities, or time of day. It was exhausting. Frankly, he didn't see how the more outgoing of his set found the time to be social in between all the wardrobe changes.

What made Alfie so fond of Bonheur was not just the excellent craftsmanship and privacy, but also that while the address was in one of the finest areas in town, it had not yet been discovered by the beau monde. As a result, the garments created were actually wearable, unlike most of the latest frippery that would be fashionable one week and laughable the next.

He was admiring bolts of brightly coloured velvet leaning against the nearest wall when a commotion broke out behind the curtain.

"Oy! Watch where you're putting those!" came Dominick's unmistakable shout. Mr. Bonheur darted out from behind the curtain looking uncharacteristically flustered.

"Is something the matter?" Alfie asked.

"Ah, I'm afraid my lord, that there was a bit of trouble taking your friend's measurements. My apologies, all my fault entirely." He dropped his voice to a confidential whisper, despite Alfie and Dominick being the only patrons at this unfashionably early hour. "I assumed your friend, Mister…?"

"Mr. Tr-Trent. Mr. Trent." Alfie caught himself.

"Mr. Trent," continued Mr. Bonheur, wringing his hands. "I assumed that he had come dressed in the appropriate undergarments for a fitting. I know the continental style has become modish, but most of my clientele is of a more traditional nature. A gross overstep on my part not to inquire directly however. My apologies again."

Alfie was so unsettled by having to make up a nom de guerre for Dominick on the spot that it took him a moment to parse the man's words.

"The appropriate? Oh. Oh I see." Or rather, Alfie tried very hard not to see.

Dominick wasn't wearing anything under his trousers. Had he ever? This morning at breakfast, with Dominick sprawled out in his casual way, could Alfie have just gone over, flicked open the buttons of his front fall and been rewarded with Dominick's cock? Or in the carriage earlier, it would have been so easy in the dark confined space to slide a hand in. Had just one worn layer of fabric been all that covered Dominick this entire time?

Alfie coughed. "I-I believe you have… appropriate garments for sale, do you not? If you could kindly retrieve a pair and add them to the bill. And half a dozen more, to replace the ones he lost."

"Yes, my lord. Those items are not on display of course, so allow me just a moment. And my apologies again."

As soon as the tailor had scurried off into the back rooms, Dominick's head and bare shoulders popped out from behind the curtain. Alfie bit his lip to keep from laughing at the expression on his face. He looked as displeased as a cat who'd missed the fish and fallen in the pond.

"This isn't funny."

Alfie nodded insincerely.

"I don't know who was more startled, me or him." Dominick opened his eyes and mouth wide in an exaggerated expression of surprise, then flashed his hands either side of his head. The effect was so like Mr. Bonheur's expression and wild side whiskers, that Alfie burst out in laughter, which set Dominick off as well. Each time one of them started to taper off, they would make eye contact again and start all over.

Several minutes later, Alfie was hiccupping for breath, and wiping the tears from his eyes with his handkerchief, while Dominick clutched the curtain for modesty and support.

"Ow, my ribs," complained Dominick finally. "He's sure taking an awfully long time back there, don't you think?"

"I'm sure he doesn't want to be alone with a pair of madmen and is waiting for us to come to our senses."

Alfie folded his handkerchief and tucked it back into his pocket. He looked up at Dominick, and the two shared a fond smile. All of a sudden, Alfie felt relaxed, peaceful for the first time in years. Something had shifted between them, and he could tell Dominick felt it too. It was almost like old times again, Nick and Alfie against the world, sharing all their laughter, friendship, and adventures.

"So, 'Mr. Trent'?" Dominick finally inquired.

He shifted behind the curtain, and Alfie fought a blush as he realised that their situation was almost an exact reversal of his fantasy last night. Him fully dressed and at ease while Dominick was completely naked behind the curtain. He felt his cock twitch at the idea, and swiftly crossed his legs.

Alfie dropped his voice, "I thought it would be easier for us to find my attacker if we were able to travel in the same circles without notice. Hence, the new clothes and the 'Mr. Trent'. I don't want any boxing fans to look too closely if they hear your real name and make the connection. Especially as you're still clearly injured."

Dominick nodded. "I don't know how I feel about wearing macaroni clothes, but I see your point. What about the accent? Can't put 'appropriate garments' on that."

"I thought about that," said Alfie. "If anyone asks we'll say you're from Cornwall."

Dominick furrowed his brow. "I sound like I'm from Cornwall?"

"I have no idea. I've never been."

"And if the bloke I'm talking to is from there?"

"He'd never admit it."

Dominick opened his mouth to say something else, but just then Mr. Bonheur returned, red faced but with a folded garment that he handed to Dominick with as much grace as possible before turning his back and giving the man some privacy. This unfortunately, left him facing Alfie. There was a sudden pressing need for the tailor to rearrange some of the display items on the other side of the shop.

Alfie turned to Dominick, and in a moment of playfulness, made the same surprised face with his open hands either side of his head. Dominick laughed, the sound warming Alfie to his core as Dominick disappeared behind the curtain with a wink.

The rest of the fitting went well enough, with Mr. Bonheur finally assured there would be no more—Alfie suspected rather large—surprises to be had, and was able to take Dominick's measurements with the practiced efficiency his shop prided itself on. There was some muttering to be had as to how much extra fabric would be required across the shoulders, but remarkably, while new garments would require at least a week, Mr. Bonheur let slip there was a finished suit in the back that would be a near fit that they could take that day.

Alfie pinched the bridge of his nose as Mr. Bonheur simpered about it being so out of character for him to usurp another customer's garments in this way, but for a peer of the realm he could be persuaded. Doubtless, the owner of the suit had ordered it and failed to pay, but Alfie's stomach was beginning to rumble, and if using his title got them out of there faster, he would do it.

"I appreciate that, Mr. Bonheur, and I'll be sure to

mention how accommodating and helpful you were today the next time I attend one of Lady Darrish's salons." He felt a prick of guilt that he had never actually attended one of the fashion setter's famed gatherings. But he would make an effort to do so now, to appease his conscience if nothing else.

That seemed to spur the man into action, returning from the back room with the aforementioned suit in hand, as well as a shirt, and a flash of blue that Alfie suspected was a waistcoat. There was a great deal of amusing grumbling from behind the curtain as Mr. Bonheur assisted Dominick in getting dressed.

"The highwaymen stole everything," Alfie called out, feeling mischievous. "So he'll need stockings, cravats, and anything else you can think of as well."

Mr. Bonheur emerged from behind the curtain and scuttled around the shop, acquiring a flurry of items before disappearing again. Finally he re-emerged. Dominick however, did not.

"How do you look?" Alfie called out.

There was a long beat of silence.

"Fine."

Mr. Bonheur wrung his hands again. Alfie wondered idly if that was the best habit for a man who made his living from their dexterity.

"My apologies once more, this will not be my best work. Once I am able to tailor a suit to Mr. Trent's measurements exactly, I'm sure he will be much more pleased with the result."

Alfie waved the man's concerns away. "Come on then," he said, with impish glee. "You can't stay in there forever.

We have much more to do today."

When no answer was forthcoming from behind the curtain, Alfie stood and with silent steps crossed the shop and flung it open.

"I'm sure you look..." he trailed off mid-sentence. Dominick looked... He looked... Well, he didn't look like an orphaned boxer from Spitalfields, of that Alfie was certain. He had fantasized about what Dominick might look like in finer clothes the night before, but his imagination was clearly lacking.

The dark grey coat was perhaps a touch too tight, but the effect only broadened the look of Dominick's shoulders even further. Its high collar hid a great deal of the bruising, leaving only a few dark areas remaining visible around his eyes and on his cheekbone. It gave him less the look of a ruffian that he had worn before, and more that of a corinthian who had been overzealous in a bout at Gentleman Jackson's, or perhaps some noble hero who had come to fisticuffs over the honor of a lady.

A snowy white cravat was tied in a crisp knot against his throat, the pure colour setting off the golden tones in his tanned skin. The coat was open, and Alfie numbly congratulated himself on being correct, the blue he'd noticed was indeed a waistcoat, the bright hue muted with pinstripes of either grey or a very pale green. The garment brought out the colour in Dominick's eyes to devastating effect, even more so once Alfie realised those eyes were looking into his own, awaiting his approval. He was helpless to say or do anything, however, save continue his perusal of Dominick in his new wardrobe.

The coat was long in the back, but cut only to the waist

in the front, leaving the entire length of Dominick's lower body exposed. Thankfully, for the sanity of both Alfie and the greater female population of London, Mr. Bonheur still favored a cut of a trouser that was looser in the front. If he had given in to the new fashion of inexpressibles, Alfie would probably have been under arrest within minutes for unnatural acts.

However, Alfie went from wanting to thank Mr. Bonheur to wanting to shoot him as his eyes traveled further downward. The trousers had been cut on a bias, and clung to Dominick's legs like a second skin, showing each swell of perfectly defined muscle as he shifted from foot to foot. Stirrups that went under his feet kept them pulled perfectly taut the great length of his legs.

Dominick began to fidget with the buttons on his coat; real silver, Alfie could tell, not the cheaper pinchbeck. There was silver threading along the pockets of the waistcoat as well. Whoever they were stealing this suit from, he had opulent tastes.

"Quit that," Alfie murmured without taking his eyes off Dominick's body. He knew he was staring but he couldn't help it. Whether it was that the fineness of the outfit finally matching the fineness of the man or just a reaction to the tightness of the material, Dominick looked more handsome than any man Alfie had ever seen. Despite his nervous fidgeting, the way the coat pulled Dominick's shoulders back implied an unquestioning authority, and the sleek fit of the suit displayed all the reasons why such authority was deserved. With his old shapeless and dirty clothes replaced with these fine new ones, Dominick wasn't so much a man transformed, as a man *revealed*.

No matter how dry-mouthed his appearance made Alfie, he was still the same Dominick, and Alfie still couldn't help teasing him a little.

"I suppose you'll do."

He then turned and took pity on Mr. Bonheur. "He looks quite well; I applaud your ability to do such excellent work under such adversity. We'll take this now, and perhaps two more suits to order?"

Out of the corner of his eye, he saw Dominick startle, but pressed on. "Perhaps one in black and the other a dark brown?"

"That should suit all occasions, my lord."

"Excellent." Alfie couldn't help himself. "Throw in one in navy as well. Also I believe half a dozen waistcoats should be variety enough. I trust your judgment when it comes to fabric and colour. And as many pairs of stockings, shirts, and the like as you deem necessary. Mr. Trent will be in London some time before returning to Cornwall, and I would like him to be comfortable."

"In that case, I would recommend a night shirt and an overcoat as well."

Alfie nodded. "Very sensible. Does that work for you, Mr. Trent?" Alfie turned to Dominick who just spluttered, before turning back to Mr. Bonheur. "He's right, practicality over fashion when it comes to the overcoat if you please. Those coastal winters are rather frigid."

"Very good. It should take me no more than ten days, perhaps two weeks at the most. That is, if my sons and I are able to focus exclusively on your order."

Alfie sighed. Would Dominick even be around in two weeks? Or would they have found the blackmailer by that time? He was swiftly realising that he would do anything to keep Dominick with him in whatever way he could, but if he wanted to leave Alfie and go back to his old life, Alfie couldn't stop him.

"Have the pieces delivered as they are completed then, and add the express fee to my bill. I think that should be all." He nodded at Dominick. "Don't forget your boots."

Dominick scrambled to put his old boots on. They looked completely out of place with the rest of his ensemble. Alfie checked his pocket watch. Almost time for luncheon, but if they were going to buy Dominick boots and gloves to match his new wardrobe, it would be better to do it before the afternoon crowds.

He closed the watch. He'd have to get Dominick one of those as well at some point. And cufflinks. Perhaps to celebrate Alfie's attacker being put behind bars. Or for their first Christmas together.

He could just imagine it. The holly over the mantle in his study. The bemused look on Dominick's face when Alfie pulled out the small box, protesting that Alfie shouldn't have gotten him anything. The way his face would light up when he saw the silver—no gold, to match his hair— cufflinks.

He'd extend his arm, clad only in shirtsleeves but wrapped up in one of Alfie's robes against the cold. And Alfie would carefully attach the cufflink for him, teasing Dominick only a little with a few brushes of his fingers against his pulse.

Dominick would growl and pull him in for a kiss that began fierce but melted into tenderness. Alfie would kiss him back, not with the desperation of a man who must take such things if he could get them, but with the sweetness of one who knows his affections are returned and has all the time in the world to enjoy them. He would start whispering things about tie pins and watch fobs just to hear Dominick laugh, then Dominick would push him onto the couch and give Alfie his own Christmas gift in return.

He came back to himself when Mr. Bonheur held out a paper wrapped parcel towards him. Alfie had a moment of panicked confusion. It couldn't be Christmas already? Surely it was still spring.

"My lord? What would you like me to do with Mr. Trent's old clothes?"

As tempted as Alfie was to burn them, he knew his dream of Christmases to come and a life together was just that, a dream. Dominick would return to his old life eventually. There would be nothing left to tie him to Alfie, save money. But Dominick was too independent to want to lounge about like some sort of mistress, waiting for Alfie to give him funds. And when he did go back to his life, he would need his old clothes.

"We'll take them along, thank you," Alfie said, and looking over to make sure Dominick was ready, took the bundle and walked out the door.

❋ ❋ ❋

"You're uncharacteristically quiet," Alfie said as they bounced along in the carriage.

Finding Dominick boots, gloves, a hat, and the small frivolities that every gentleman needed to maintain his appearance had taken visits to several shops. Alfie took great delight in picking out items that were not just functional, but were of the highest quality available and would keep well for as long as Dominick wanted them. And when the time came, the fineness of the items would make them easy for Dominick to pawn, ensuring his comfort long after he had left Alfie's side. He liked knowing that he'd still be able to help Dominick, even if he wasn't with him. But Dominick had hardly said a word the entire time.

"I'll never be able to repay you for these," Dominick whispered to the floor of the carriage. He had an expression on his face, not quite sadness. It took Alfie a moment to realise what it was. Shame.

"Dominick, no." Alfie leaned forward, crestfallen. This was the opposite of what he had wanted. The tall, regal man who had stood in Mr. Bonheur's shop was gone, replaced by the boy who had only one pair of trousers and a shirt to his name. Alfie hesitated, then took the risk and reached across the coach, taking one of Dominick's hands in his own. Dominick finally looked up at him.

"I'm not buying you these because I expect any sort of repayment. I'm buying them because you need them if we're going to be able to work together to find my attacker without drawing unnecessary attention. If it helps, think of them as a uniform. A footman doesn't have to buy his own uniform, his master does that for him."

Dominick glared at him and tried to pull back his hand. Alfie clutched it tighter. "I'm sorry. Poor choice of words. A constable doesn't have to buy his uniform either."

Dominick still looked dubious, so Alfie tried again. "Fine. You do need the clothes for my plan to work, but I also bought them for you because you are my friend and I can. I have been blessed with a very fortunate life, and if I can spread some of that good fortune to those who are close to me, I will."

Dominick was silent for a long time, long enough that Alfie began to feel awkward still sitting there holding his hand. Surely this was not within the acceptable bounds of men's behavior. But he refused to let go unless Dominick pulled away.

"You still consider me your friend? I thought you were just saying that to Mr. Bonheur because it was the easiest lie."

Now it was Alfie's turn to be shocked. "Of course you are! That is, I assumed…"

"No, no," Dominick smiled and gave Alfie's hand a gentle squeeze. "I like it. I'm honored to still be your friend, Alfie."

Alfie squeezed back. They sat like that for another moment, before a wheel struck an especially deep pothole and they were forced to break apart to brace themselves against the sides of the carriage. Once they had settled, Dominick leaned back as comfortably as he could in the seat.

"Am I supposed to feel like a sausage with too much stuffing?"

Alfie laughed, "You see why I stay in as much as possible."

"Mm," Dominick agreed. "And why you're always in that robe thing, it looks much more comfortable."

Alfie didn't know that Dominick had even noticed his banyan. He decided to test the waters. "I'll have to buy you one then."

Dominick waved a hand. "You've spent enough. Even for a friend."

"Very well, you can just borrow one of mine," Alfie agreed. Dominick hadn't seemed upset with the idea of Alfie buying him more things, just dismissive. Good. They rode several more blocks in silence, but while he had been waiting for Dominick to try on all his new garments, Alfie had remembered something that had been bothering him for years. Now, in the friendly quiet of the carriage as it trundled along, seemed as good an opportunity to ask as any other he would get.

"Dominick, all those years ago, did you start the fight with Baz on purpose?"

Although he made no outward movements, Dominick' posture, which had been relaxed, went rigid. When he finally spoke, it was in a voice devoid of all emotion.

"What makes you think that?"

"Because if my parents hadn't seen the two of you fighting, I know they would have chosen him over me, and I was wondering—*have* been wondering for quite a long time—if you did it on purpose."

Dominick shook his head slowly. When he finally looked up at Alfie, the humor and light from earlier was gone.

"You think you owe all this to me. You don't. I'm not that good or that clever, Alfie. That fool was just a stupid bastard who didn't know a good thing when he almost had it. You don't owe your life, your money, or any of this to me."

"I do, though!" Alfie shouted, frustrated. Just when

he thought he was starting to know Dominick, the man pulled back again, and claimed not to be the person Alfie thought he was.

"Fine! Baz was an idiot and it was just my good fortune to take his place. Good fortune that I wouldn't have been around to receive if it hadn't been for you! Who kept me from freezing to death? Or starving? Or being beaten to death by the other boys or falling into the machinery? You did that. You may claim not to be good, Dominick, but that is a bald-faced, beef-headed, fuck-faced bastard of a lie."

"You still sound like the slums when you're angry."

Alfie slammed his cane against the carriage floor. "Go be hanged! You think any of this is worth anything? My life. Would you trade that suit of clothes for it?"

Dominick looked at him as if he was mad, a fool, or both. "Of course not."

"What about for all those other clothes today then? And the fine boots? And a silk banyan with water lilies or dragons or fancy women dancing on the sleeves if that's what you want. Would you trade those for my life?"

"Never."

The rumble of Dominick's voice as he said the word sent a chill through Alfie at the same time as it gave him the courage to finish what he had to say.

"Then I'm still in your debt. You may not think you're good, Dominick, but you are. Everything in my life I owe to you, and the good you did. So if I want to call you friend, or buy you a dozen shirts, please, *please* let me. Because I wouldn't be alive to do those things if it wasn't for you."

Eventually Dominick nodded, but there was something in his eyes that Alfie couldn't understand. Maybe it would just take some more time. Alfie had said what he needed to. Dominick would either come to believe these things for himself or he wouldn't.

"With all that in mind, if I invited you to my club for lunch, would you go?"

"Yes."

"Would you hate it the entire time?"

"Yes."

Alfie huffed. "Would you hate it if Mrs. Hirkins made us sandwiches at home instead?"

"No." Dominick hesitated. "But only if I can borrow a banyan."

Alfie smiled. "There's an extra one in the closet of the blue bedroom upstairs. You can keep all your extra clothes in there, if you'd like. And if you're too tired from being a living doll, feel free to take a nap as well. The room hasn't been used in years, it can be yours too."

"Don't push your luck."

CHAPTER 14

The next few weeks were the happiest of Dominick's life.

Each morning he walked the few miles from his lodgings to Alfie's townhouse, arriving just in time for Mrs. Hirkins to sigh wearily at him and tell him to make himself useful and carry in the breakfast tray. And each time he walked into the dining room with the tray, Alfie looked up at him and smiled. Even on the most wet, cold, and miserable days it was like watching the sun rise just for him.

After a leisurely breakfast, Dominick would go up to the blue room to change into what he and Alfie had started calling his "dandy duds" before making their plans for the day. Most of those days involved going out to follow whatever leads they came up with.

Some leads were more useful than others. Dominick had been proud of his idea to have Alfie go to his solicitor's office to see if any of his business contracts matched either the paper or writing on the letter, on the chance that the attacks were related to those. They hadn't found anything, but it still felt like progress. Alfie's idea to go for a ride in Hyde Park seemed more like an excuse to show off his driving skills in his phaeton than it was to try and flush out the villain. It had been fun though, clinging to the side, whooping like a bedlamite while Alfie raced the horses faster and faster until they were nearly flying down the paths.

And each night Dominick changed back into his regular clothes and retraced his steps to his lodgings, going over the day in his mind and tucking the most precious moments away for later, after Alfie didn't need him anymore. But even thoughts of that eventual future couldn't dampen his spirits, and he fell asleep each night smiling and eagerly awaiting the day to come.

In all that time, a handful more letters arrived, all saying the same thing, *I know what you are.* Even before Alfie said anything, Dominick could tell when another was delivered by the worry that creased his brow. He spent those days sticking even closer to Alfie's side, his hand clenched into fists, ready to fight.

But when no demands were made, nor any more attempts made on Alfie's life, they both began to relax. In all those weeks, the greatest danger Alfie was in occurred when his doctor, a man named Barlowe, came to remove his stitches.

Even then, the danger had not come from the medical man himself, who seemed imminently competent, but from the risk that Dominick, seeing Alfie without his shirt for the first time, might be unable to restrain himself. Alfie was lithe and lean, his chest pale from being kept hidden from the sun—which was an absolute crime.

Dominick had been doing well at keeping his baser impulses in check until the point when Alfie turned a bit to give the doctor a better angle, and the light slid down his smooth chest and caught, glittering on a trail of dark red hair that started just above his trousers and disappeared tantalizingly below. Dominick had turned tail and woodenly walked away with a mutter about fetching something to settle both doctor and patient. But when he reached the sideboard, he found himself unable to remember why he was there at all and the doctor unfortunately left without his drink.

Afterwards, Alfie had smiled at him as he rebuttoned his shirt, and suggested that since there was too little time left in the day to accomplish much detecting, they could wander over to Montagu House to see the new Egyptian busts instead.

Dominick was almost able to trick himself into believing this was his life now, spending every day in the company of a warm, funny, irresistibly beautiful man and never having to worry about where his next meal was coming from, or whether his next fight would be his last, or what degrading things he would be forced to do in order to pay his rent. He got to go all over London in his fancy clothes with his charming friend by his side and without a care in the world. It was not a life he could ever actually have, but for those few weeks, he could pretend.

It was the happiest time of his life, so of course it had to come to an end.

✳ ✳ ✳

Dominick woke early, and decided to go by The Barge and see how Jimmy was doing before making the long walk over to Alfie's. He hadn't seen his friend since the morning after the fight, and any time he went too long without saying hello, it seemed like Jimmy's wife Maeve had another baby in the interim. They had four of the little ones by now, and Dominick worried if he waited too much longer, the number might grow to five.

"Well, look what the cat drug in!"

"'Morning to you too, Jimmy."

"Get over here by the light, let me see your face."

Dominick let Jimmy turn his face this way and that. Dominick knew from the many mirrors in Alfie's home that the bruising had finally faded to almost nothing, just a slight yellowness if someone looked at him in the wrong light. Jimmy hummed, seemingly satisfied, before poking Dominick sharply in the ribs.

"Fuck was that for?" Dominick flinched, grabbing his side and backing away.

"Ribs aren't quite healed up then, that's a shame. I've got a line on an Irishman looking to book fighters. A bob each the pay would be."

"Find somebody else and get your shilling that way. Being mauled by The Body Snatcher tends to put one off of going in the ring."

"It's not like you to turn down money, Tripner," an unpleasant voice crowed from the back of the pub.

Jimmy winced. He looked at Dominick to ask if he wanted him to try and run Baz off, but Dominick just shook his head. No reason to get Jimmy on the Badger's bad side. He tilted his head toward the kitchen, giving Jimmy his out. He didn't blame the man for not wanting to tangle with Baz, he had a wife and four or five children to provide for after all. Besides, Dominick was pretty sure he didn't want Jimmy to overhear whatever Baz was about to say.

"Funny running into you again, Baz. I'd say it's a pleasure, but..."

"Likewise. I've been looking around for you, but no one seems to know where you've been. You think any more about that job I offered? I got word the work's about to get serious. There's good money in it. I'd even up your pay to four shillings a day."

"The answer was 'no' the first time and it's not going to change. You can keep your four shillings a day or give them to someone else. I wouldn't work for you even if you offered four quid a day."

"Is that so?" Baz smiled his sickly, black-toothed smile. "And what kind of service does four quid a day get from you, I wonder? Even Covent Garden whores don't charge that much."

Dominick reacted before he could think, grabbing Baz by the throat and slamming him against the side of the bar. He raised his fist, ready to silence his filthy mouth once and for all, when he felt a sharp prick in his side. He looked down. Baz had the point of one of his many daggers pressed just between two of his ribs. The razor-sharp blade had sliced through Dominick's shirt, and a thin line of blood was already beginning to seep down the metal. Baz adjusted his grip and angled the knife more sharply up. Even if Dominick killed him with a single blow, a knife entering at that angle would slice cleanly through his lung and straight into his heart. He'd be dead before he even finished his swing.

Dominick snarled, years of Baz's torments finally coming to a head. He'd take the risk. He drew his arm back to end things between them once and for all, then paused.

If he died today, Alfie would never know what happened to him.

The thought stopped him cold. He'd be lying there dead on the floor of The Barge and Alfie would never know. He'd sit in that big dining room all by himself, waiting for Dominick to arrive. At first maybe he'd just assume Dominick was late. He'd read his paper. When he finished that, he'd start to pace. When would he know that something was wrong? Would he worry, and as the hours ticked by, decide to come looking for him? He might be able to find Dominick's lodgings again, but by the time he did, the scavengers would have heard of his death and taken everything from the room. No one would talk to Alfie, and he'd go back home, never knowing what had happened.

Or would he just assume that Dominick had tired of his company? It wouldn't be the first time they had parted ways without a chance to say goodbye.

Dominick pushed Baz away, sending the man skittering halfway across the pub. The blade never left his hand, and even in the dim light, Dominick could see his fingers itching for a second one tucked up his sleeve. It wasn't a risk Dominick could take. He himself might not be worth much, but Alfie certainly was.

"I don't want to hear from you again. I don't want your wretched job and I don't need your filthy money." Dominick headed for the door.

"You might not today, with whatever mysterious job you have now. But tomorrow always comes, Tripner. And you've been spending like it won't, haven't you?"

Dominick froze in the doorway. There was no way Baz could know about Alfie and his lavish suits and fancy meals.

"That's right. I hear things. I hear you bought two blankets at market last weekend. New ones too. And a bar of soap. Your landlady says she never had a single tenant buy so much coal for their fireplace either."

Dominick left the pub without turning back. His blind anger carried him halfway to Alfie's house before he even stopped to think. His steps slowed as he actually considered what Baz had said.

He'd sworn years ago he'd never work for the pale, venomous little toad. He knew the man was just biding his time, childhood hurts only adding to years of adult grudges. Whatever this job he was trying to entice Dominick into, he wasn't offering it out of the kindness of his heart. But the fact that he had noticed how much money Dominick was spending was worrying.

Flashing blunt around was a sure way to attract all sorts of attention, none of it good. All he needed was to round the wrong corner and have the last thing he see be a cosh coming down on his head. If he was lucky he'd wake up later, boots and purse missing. If not...

Dominick willed himself not to check the inner coat pocket where he kept his money. He hadn't been paid a set wage yet, but he still had most of the original ten Alfie owed him, and every time Alfie gave him money to buy something, he told Dominick to keep the change. Dominick realised with a start that he must be carrying over fourteen quid. Fourteen pounds in his pocket, when he'd seen men's throats slit for pennies.

He turned abruptly, startling a woman and her young son who had been walking behind him. He murmured a quick apology and headed back towards his lodgings. He had been a fool to carry so much on him at one time, and an even larger fool to be spending it the way he had. Not only was it likely to get him noticed, but he had no idea how long he would have to live off it after Alfie was done with him.

Fourteen pounds was enough to get him set up nicely somewhere, maybe even somewhere out of the great stink of London, but what would he do after that? He was still just a rough, uneducated piece of street trash whose only real skills lay in his fists or his mouth. And someday he'd be too old to get anyone to pay for either.

He climbed the stairs and unlocked the door to his lodgings. Better to go without those extra comforts and save his coin. The worst of the cold weather was past, so he could pawn one of the blankets he'd just bought, and he didn't really need the coal. He did some calculations as he pulled up the floorboard and removed his tin box.

If he went back to living the way he had before he'd met Alfie again, he could stretch the money he had for a year or two if he was careful. Longer even, as long as he kept working when he could and only turned down the most repugnant jobs. Not spending it would keep from raising suspicions as well. Let everyone assume he had wasted whatever coin he'd earned and had nothing more worth stealing.

Decided, Dominick opened the box. Underneath a scattering of coins, Alfie's cravat still lay there, folded neatly and perfectly white, save for the ruddy brown stains of Dominick's dried blood.

But his ring was gone.

CHAPTER 15

Dominick sighed heavily as the coach pulled up in front of Alfie's club. Alfie shot him another worried look.

"We really don't have to—"

"It's fine." Dominick snapped.

He'd spent over an hour scouring his rooms looking for his ring, but it was nowhere to be found. He knew that he had left it in the box—there was nowhere else safe enough for it—but if it wasn't there, where else could it be?

The only option was that someone had broken into his lodgings and stolen it, but that didn't make any sense either. Nothing else in his room had been touched, and the box itself was still beneath the floorboard. Any thief determined enough to search his rooms so thoroughly as to discover his secret hiding spot would have taken everything in the room. His spare clothes, his pitcher... Even the bent poker by the fireplace was worth just enough for a desperate thief. And even if a thief had somehow found the box's hiding place, why leave the coins and just take the ring? Alfie's cravat was worth more than its few ounces of pewter if someone managed to rinse the bloodstains out.

Besides, Dominick had worn that ring since he was a child. It would be impossible to sell. Every pawnbroker and rag-and-bone man in the East End would recognize it as his. Even though he had lost to The Body Snatcher, Dominick still had enough of a reputation that none of them would risk crossing him just for the sake of a few pennies.

By the point he'd finally given up searching, it had been well past the hour for him to head over to Alfie's house. He'd run nearly the whole way but even then, by the time he'd arrived Alfie had long since finished his breakfast and was pacing the length of the dining room. The relief in his eyes when he saw Dominick brought back that morning's encounter with Baz, and how close Dominick had come to never showing up at all.

But there was no way he could explain any of that to Alfie. Especially not with how knowing Alfie had been worried about him, had actually cared if Dominick showed up or not, warmed something in Dominick that had been cold for years. To cut off any questions, he'd suggested it might be a good idea for them to spend what was left of the morning planning, then finally go to Alfie's club and see if anyone there seemed suspicious.

It was a thin excuse, but he knew Alfie had been trying to find a way to invite him back since the last time Dominick refused. And if the way Alfie's eyes lit up at the suggestion made Dominick feel guilty for keeping things from him, then that was Dominick's own problem to deal with.

"It's fine, Alfie," he said again.

His sour mood had only worsened as he'd changed into his dandy duds. So much money gone to waste and for what? A shirt that he would only get to wear another few weeks at most? A pile of cravats, each worth at least a week's rent? Enough stockings to wear a new pair every day for a fortnight, and yet not a one would stand up to a single day of hard labor.

Then the carriage driver sent over from the stables seemed to be the worst one yet, seemingly intent on hitting every single pothole between Bedford Square and St. James. By the time they finally arrived, Dominick's mood was as dark as the storm clouds that had begun to threaten overhead.

Still, there was no reason to take it out on Alfie. He glanced up at the worried look on his friend's face, and tried to put on a reassuring expression.

"Don't mind me. I'm just worried about making a fool of myself is all. Now remind me, how do I remember which fork is for fish and which is for scratching my balls?"

Alfie's look of concern vanished in a burst of laughter. "The fish fork only has three tines," he said with a grin. "The general rule is to work from the outside in."

"Outside in, got it."

They dashed out of the carriage through the first heavy drops of rain, to have the front door opened by a stone-faced doorman even before Alfie's fingers even brushed the knocker.

"Good afternoon, Lord Crawford," the man said. His wig and knee length breeches were highly decorated, but several decades out of fashion. Dominick supposed this was not the sort of place where things changed very quickly, if at all.

He tried not to be overwhelmed as Alfie signed *Mr. Dominick Trent* in as his guest and they were led up a wide staircase into a dining room that could have held his lodgings fifty times over.

Christ. His eyes followed the tall mirrors and gilt-framed paintings up to an elaborately carved ceiling. It could probably fit the entire lodging house.

They had arrived towards the end of the luncheon rush and were seated at a small table near the edge of the room. The sight of so many nobles and wealthy men of business had Dominick itching to escape. He'd even thought he'd recognized one or two men from prints in the newspaper, and not from the crime section. The smell of leather and cigar smoke hung heavily in the air, mixing with the smells of roast potatoes and braised pork. His head began to spin.

He felt a swift kick against his shin and then a foot pressed against his, hidden by the long tablecloth.

"You don't have to do this just because I wanted to," Alfie said warmly. His hands betrayed the confidence in his tone, fluttering to straighten the already militarily aligned silverware. "I'd be just as happy sitting in a pub or eating pies from the back of a cart as long as it was with you, Dominick."

Dominick's heart stuttered in his chest at the sincerity in Alfie's voice. Alfie smiled at him and he felt the fears that had been weighing on him all morning slide from his shoulders. This man. He really was too gorgeous and kind to be believed. Alfie could have anything he wanted and would deserve every bit of it, but all he wanted was to share a meal with Dominick.

"Even eels fresh from the Thames?"

"Even if we had to catch them with our teeth." Alfie laughed, and in that moment, Dominick knew he was completely, irredeemably, and inescapably in love.

＊ ＊ ＊

The meal was one of the finest of Dominick's life, but later he would have been hard pressed to say whether he had the lamb or the pork, the fruit or the pudding. Afterwards, they sat sipping coffee and observing the other members and their guests, looking for suspects.

"What about that one by the window?" Dominick whispered, leaning in.

"Which one?"

"The one who looks like Old Harricutt the fishmonger, if you stuffed her into her grandson's pants and shaved her bald."

Alfie looked at him in horror.

"That's Lord Wicksteed! He's Deputy Speaker in the House of Lords!" he hissed.

"You knew who I meant though," Dominick couldn't help but tease. "Perhaps he really is Mrs. Harricutt in disguise. She knows you're the one who stole her pickerels to feed the alley strays when she wasn't looking and has been trying to destroy you ever since."

"You're being ridiculous." Alfie rolled his eyes. He took a sip of coffee and scanned the room. "What about that one in the red waistcoat?"

Dominick surreptitiously looked in the direction Alfie indicated with a nod to see a man with skinny legs in a brown suit and a red waistcoat that distended over his potbelly. His face was flushed from too much wine in too warm a room. He appeared to be in the process of nodding off into his soup as his tablemate told some unending story, his head bobbing up each time before it hit the table. The overall effect reminded Dominick of a cheery little robin, hopping along and pecking at seeds.

He leaned in and motioned for Alfie to do the same. "You shouldn't jest about such things. I recognize him. He's a very dangerous man."

Alfie's eyes went wide, darting over to the man in question then back to Dominick.

"He is?" Alfie whispered. His breath gusted over Dominick's lips as he spoke. They were close, almost too close for even the companionable atmosphere of a gentleman's club, but Dominick couldn't find it in himself to pull away. He nodded, face grim.

"One of the worst men in all of England, I'd wager. He was a captain under Nelson, but they say the admiral's death drove him mad. He turned pirate, and has been the terror of the West Indies ever since. Stealing women and gold, and burning any ship that can't provide him with both. Captain Crinkums, they call him."

This close, Dominick could see Alfie's lips twitch suppressing a smile. "Oh dear, that does sound dreadful. But why is he after me?"

"You don't remember?" Dominick shook his head sadly. "You were one of his pirate crew, but developed a conscience. In the middle of the night, it was you who slipped off in a rowboat and warned Kingston of the coming attack. You saved the entire colony, and the governor offered you the hands of both his daughters in marriage—it being the New World and him being the one to make the laws and all—but your one true love was the sea.

"So you left the weeping sisters behind you and sailed off. Never knowing that Captain Crinkums had not gone down with his ship, but survived, marooned on an island, kept alive by his desire for vengeance. And now he has returned to do battle with the man who destroyed him."

Across the room there was a clatter as the man in the red waistcoat finally lost his battle with sleep, falling face first into his soup bowl and knocking half the table to the floor as he spluttered awake.

Alfie chortled and Dominick nearly snorted out his coffee, but their laughter was lost in the raucous chaos that ensued. The man hardly had time to leave the dining room, puffed up with humiliation and bellowing drunkenly as a small army of the club's staff trailed after him, sopping up the soup that still dripped from him as they went. They had gotten their laughter down to wheezing when a hand smacked Alfie in the middle of his back.

Dominick tensed immediately, hand reaching for the spot on the table where the knives had been, to come up with only a coffee spoon.

"Freddie boy! We haven't seen you in ages! Weeks at least. How have you been?"

A flicker of dislike crossed Alfie's face before he rose and shook the hand of the man who had attacked him. Dominick rose too. The back slap may have been meant as a gesture of friendship, but he wasn't letting his guard down. He ignored the twisting feeling in his gut that was too close to jealousy. Alfie was allowed to have friends other than Dominick. Just because he hadn't spoken of any during their weeks together meant nothing.

"Lord Boyle, a pleasure as always. And I believe I see Mr.

Stockton on his way over as well. How delightful it is to run into you both."

The flatness of Alfie's voice made it clear that it wasn't.

"I say, is that Freddie?" A skinny man so pale he was almost blue joined them, shaking Alfie's hand before taking a spot next to his portly companion. Dominick thought immediately of the nursery rhyme about Jack Sprat and his wife.

"It's been absolutely ages," said the skeleton in a nasal whine that had Dominick's hair standing on end. "Since that night we all went out together with Reggie wasn't it? God, what a night that was! I remember almost none of it, but I woke up the next morning in Greenwich with an unsigned IOU in my pocket for a thousand pounds! It's not yours, by any chance?"

A thousand pounds. Someone wagered and lost more money than Dominick could even imagine in a single night's gambling and this Mr. Stockton didn't seem to care if he collected on it one way or the other!

"No, not mine, I'm happy to say." Alfie said, shifting on his feet. "Wonderful to see you both, of course, but we were just leaving."

"Now that would be intolerably rude," said a voice from behind Dominick.

Every street-raised fiber of his being wanted to spin around and confront the man at his back with raised fists.

"You *must* introduce us to your friend, we so rarely see you with any."

Alfie's eyes went wide with more than a trace of fear. Whoever the man behind him was, Dominick decided he would very much like to rearrange his face.

"Reginald," Alfie said haltingly. "I didn't know you were a member here."

Reginald. The cousin. The man who was threatening to send Alfie to an early grave all for the sake of a fortune he'd likely fritter away on a turn of the cards. White hot anger clouded the edges of Dominick's vision as he turned to face his foe. He fought to keep the satisfied sneer from his lips when he discovered he towered over the red-faced man.

"Well, they do allow most anyone in now," St. John drawled. He flicked a glance up and down Dominick. "Clearly."

"Reginald, Lord Boyle, Mr. Stockton, allow me to make introductions. This is my friend Mr. Trent."

A pallid, fish-like hand was thrust into Dominick's range of vision. He turned to face the other two interlopers, but kept St. John in the corner of his eye.

"Call me Stokes, and this one's Batty," the skinny one said, laughing at his own joke as Dominick shook his offered hand gingerly so as not to break him. From the look on Lord Boyle's face, this was not the first time Mr. Stockton had made that jest.

"Any friend of Freddie's is a friend of ours," Lord Boyle said. "I swear, you look familiar. Have we met?"

"Yes, do tell us where our Freddie met such a gentleman as yourself," said St. John. "I'm sure I would remember if I'd seen him with such a... memorable *friend* before."

The insinuation in his voice was barely veiled. Across the table, Alfie flinched. From the panic in his eyes, Dominick guessed this "night out" Mr. Stokes had mentioned was likely the night he and Alfie had met. Bless the vice of overindulgence that they didn't remember

Dominick's face. If St. John knew who he was, it would be easy enough for him to find out about his past and his more unsavory occupation, which would be all the ammunition he needed to destroy Alfie. An earl parading a male prostitute at his fancy club? Even a whiff of such a scandal would be ruinous.

He cursed silently. Why had he let Alfie convince him to come here? It was a ridiculous risk and for what? A meal that now sat like lead in his stomach. If he was really Alfie's bodyguard, it was time he started treating this like the dangerous situation it was, not some grand adventure story.

"I'm sure I'd remember a man of your stature as well," Dominick said evenly. "I'm just up from Cornwall."

At that pronouncement, Mr. Stockton looked about ready to flee or reach for his smelling salts, but his infernal friend persisted.

"I'm sure I've seen you before. Perhaps at school?"

Dominick faltered. If he agreed, it might stop Lord Boyle before he actually remembered, but if the man tried to reminisce, Dominick would be sunk.

"Mr. Trent went to Oxford, I'm afraid," Alfie piped up. "Unfortunately he's not a Cambridge man like ourselves. Perhaps you met in a scrum?"

Dominick very much doubted any of the three would have lasted more than five minutes on a rugby pitch, but they appeared flattered that Alfie seemed to believe otherwise. Even St. John relaxed a little, his eyes on Dominick not quite so sharp.

"Oh, we would have graduated well before either of you I'm afraid," Mr. Stockton sniffed, making no comment on if he had ever spent any time on the field. "But perhaps at an alumni game. We do donate heavily to the alma mater after all."

"That must be it," Dominick agreed with a forced grin.

He was suddenly very tired. For a moment there, he'd almost felt like he'd belonged in this world, or at the very least, by Alfie's side. But listening to these men talk casually about their universities and vast sums of money, he realised he was only fooling himself. The sooner they could find proof against St. John or whoever Alfie's attacker was and stop him for good, the sooner Dominick could return to the life he was meant to live. Never seeing Alfie again would feel amputating a limb, but he'd survived their separation before. He could do it again.

Something of his thoughts must have shown on his face, because Alfie was making their excuses again, more forcefully this time, and herding Dominick out of the dining room and back down the stairs to the foyer. Dominick took a last look over his shoulder.

Mr. Stockton and Lord Boyle were already wandering deeper into the club, animatedly discussing whatever trivialities they deemed important, but St. John stood stock still, watching Alfie and Dominick depart with an unreadable expression on his piggish features. When Alfie tugged Dominick's sleeve to keep him moving, a slow grin crawled across St. John's face. He raised a silent hand in farewell.

Dominick shuddered. It wasn't until they were in the carriage on the way back to Bedford Square that he finally felt free of those knowing eyes and greedy smile.

* * *

When they were in front of Alfie's door again, Dominick could see him hesitate. Outside the coach's windows, the rain was pounding the cobblestones, one of the harsh London spring rains. In the morning, the city would be as beautiful as it could possibly get, the soot washed from walls and the filth from gutters. The air would be fresh and pure. The sweetness of it would last for a few days, but then dogs would die, horses would shit, men would piss. The factories would bellow out their smoke and soon the city would be its dirty, stinking self once more. Dominick thought about the long walk back to his lodgings, the way the wind rattled through cracks in the chimney and the roof leaked over his bed. It wasn't hard to guess what Alfie was about to say.

"I'm sorry the visit to my club didn't go as well as I had intended, so I hate to ask you to do something else you've refused, but the weather is too foul to walk in. I'd happily lend you the carriage, but that means the driver would have to sit in the rain all the way there and back, so—"

"Yes." Dominick interrupted. "I'll stay in the blue room tonight. Thank you."

Why not? His day had been miserable enough already. He might as well trade the physical torture of the long journey home for the mental one of having Alfie just down the hall. So close and yet so completely out of reach. He couldn't look at Alfie right now, he could practically feel the joy radiating off of him, and so he leapt from the carriage, waiting under the slight overhang of Alfie's front door while Alfie gave the driver his instructions to return to the stables.

Even with that little protection, they were both soaked to the bone by the time Alfie finally got the door open.

"Watch your step, it'll be slippery." Alfie's hair was plastered down against his skull, the auburn dark with rainwater and beginning to curl at the ends. He shivered. "Go get changed. There should be some towels to dry off with in your wardrobe. I could heat some water in the kitchen if you need to wash. I have to put the kettle on for tea, anyway."

"Mrs. Hirkins isn't here?"

"Oh no. I imagine she departed shortly after we did. Never fear, she'll have left the fixings for a cold supper behind her. She has quarters here of course, but prefers to be home, especially when the weather is this bad. Doesn't like to leave her husband alone."

Alfie tapped his leg. "She has a gammy knee. It's never been wrong about the weather. Always gets her home right before the storm itself starts."

So they wouldn't even have the token supervision of Mrs. Hirkins's presence. Dominick shuddered, and not just from the cold. His body was aching for him to take this opportunity, to go to Alfie, to have him while he still had the chance. Strip him down in front of a roaring fire, see all of that long, beautiful body pinken with warmth and desire. Dominick would reveal him slowly, adoring every bit of skin as it was brought to light, then follow that trail of hair he'd glimpsed before to the treasure it promised. Would Alfie just lie there and let Dominick worship him, or would he take control?

Dominick would be fine with either. But the idea of Alfie pushing him down onto the rug, then preparing himself while Dominick watched, pinned under that piercing blue gaze, before sinking down onto Dominick's cock and using him for his own pleasure?

He wrapped his overcoat tighter around himself, not trusting the clinging material of his trousers to hide his reaction to that particular thought.

"A bath won't be necessary," Dominick said, before nearly sprinting up to his room.

Not his room, he reminded himself, slamming the door closed and dropping back against it. *Just the blue room.*

Where all of his clothes were hanging in the wardrobe, and his boots were tucked away in the corner. Where he had his own washstand, upon which the shaving kit he had brought from his lodgings sat, since the light here was so much better to shave by and Mrs. Hirkins made sure the pitcher was filled with hot water each morning.

He kept the set of cufflinks Alfie had loaned him in the same drawer each night, and had a stack of books on the dresser to read on days when Alfie had too much work to go out in the morning and Dominick needed something to fill the hours before he could resume his bodyguard activities in the afternoon. In fact the only thing that he didn't really do in the bedroom was use the bed, but tonight he would.

For sleep, he told himself firmly. Nothing else. Because even with the faint airs and hints Dominick thought he recognized that suggested Alfie might be open to his advances, it wasn't worth the risk. If he was wrong and Alfie kicked him out, there would be no one to protect Alfie from the attacker. And even if he was right...

If he was right, it would be even worse. He had fallen. Dominick could admit it. He had fallen in love with Alfie. He had loved Alfie his whole life in one way or another, he'd known that. But as a child it had been the love of two friends with nothing else in the world but each other. This was different. Those feelings were still there, but the last few weeks they had increased a hundredfold and mixed with desire.

But even if Alfie wanted Dominick like all those other men had wanted him; for an hour, or a night, or even several nights if he was lucky, it didn't matter. There was just no way for them to be together after this was over and that was it. Now, the pain when he had to finally walk away would be bearable, if only just. But to walk away after being with Alfie, body and soul, knowing it could never happen again? That would destroy him.

Dominick sighed, stripping off his wet clothes and wrapping himself in several of the plush towels. He couldn't help but give one a sniff. He inhaled the same clean lavender scent that Alfie smelled of each morning at breakfast, before the scent from his freshly laundered shirts and cravats faded, leaving behind only the sharp smell of Alfie's cologne and the warmth of his skin.

He dropped the towel and buried his face in his hands. He should leave now while he still could. But he really had fallen, and all of the ways out of the abyss were even more painful than staying. At least if he stayed, he could be around Alfie for as long as he still needed Dominick. And then?

He sagged down onto the bed, too dejected to even notice the way it pillowed around him. It really had been the most wretched day.

CHAPTER 16

Alfie clenched and unclenched his hands with nervous anticipation. It helped if he had something to do with them, so while the water heated over the kitchen fire, he went to lay out all the implements for tea. He had watched Mrs. Hirkins do it enough as a child when he was still small enough to not be in the way. That done, he cast his eyes about the kitchen looking for something—*anything*—else to do.

Enough of that. Just because Dominick had agreed to stay the night didn't mean there was anything to be nervous about. Well, there was someone trying to blackmail and kill him, but nothing had really happened on that front in weeks. For now, everything was fine. Alfie was just alone in his home with his dearest friend whom he secretly desired carnally and who was going to be spending the night just down the hall from his bedchamber. Nothing to be nervous about at all.

When the kettle whistled he took it off the heat and carefully poured the water over the leaves in the teapot. Had he been too forward offering to warm some water for Dominick? He honestly hadn't meant it in any sort of lecherous way. Of course, he wouldn't have turned down the opportunity to watch if offered, but he had just wanted to help his friend warm himself after their brief drenching.

He reordered the contents of the tea tray one last time and carefully lifted it. He supposed he'd find out. If Dominick locked himself in his room and refused to come down for tea or whatever supper they could scrounge, then that would be answer enough. If so, in the morning he would pay Dominick for all his time, give him an excellent recommendation, and promptly go about finding himself a new bodyguard. Despite the fact the idea of replacing Dominick, even if after only knowing him again for a few weeks, seemed impossible.

He shook his head, careful not to jostle the tray as he navigated the stairs. He was overthinking things. He had just been thrown off-kilter by seeing his cousin and his odious friends at White's. Thankfully, they had not recognized Dominick as the boxer they had seen nearly killed just scant weeks before, but still, it was a closer call than he was comfortable with.

He took a small mote of pleasure in the fact that his disguise of Dominick as a gentleman seemed to be working. But it was probably only a matter of time before someone either did recognize him, or at the very least realised that that was *not* a Cornish accent.

There was something in the way Reginald had looked at Dominick too that worried him. Nothing so specific that he could put a name to it, just a vague sense of unease. The sooner they resolved this mess, the better.

He had the tea laid out in his study, and was busy coaxing the fire in the fireplace to life when he heard the door open behind him. Still on his knees, he turned and was, not for the first time, stunned into silence with Dominick's appearance. He was in just his shirtsleeves with the cuffs unbuttoned, and his stocking feet flexed against the oriental rug that had been the pride of Alfie's father's collection.

He had obviously attempted to dry his hair, but it was still damp and fell in wild golden waves about his face. The complete image was like some romantic hero from a novel, there to save the day and rescue the damsel. Even the blanket Dominick had clutched around his shoulders didn't look ridiculous, the way it would on Alfie, but more like a kingly mantle. Alfie gestured towards one of the chairs.

"I did promise to loan you one."

He saw the moment Dominick's eyes landed on the banyan Alfie had laid along the back of the chair. He had promised, and they were such cozy garments. Dominick snorted, but to his credit, folded the blanket and wrapped the banyan around himself instead. Red with orange stripes, it was less ornate than Alfie's usual one and so he wore it less often, but it was just as fine. Dominick held out his arms for inspection.

"Very smart," said Alfie. "You look every inch the Cornish gentleman at ease."

"Perhaps I can start a series of rumors. All bootblacks are secretly from Cornwall and that's why they talk that way."

"All Cornish men laugh disruptively in clubs."

"All Cornish men use only one spoon."

"All Cornish men are giants."

"There's enough people already that believe that one," Dominick grinned, pouring himself a cup of tea and then another for Alfie.

As Alfie finally got the fire crackling merrily away, Dominick added just the amounts of cream and sugar that Alfie liked and passed him his cup. Alfie seated himself in the armchair that mirrored Dominick's in front of the fire and smiled softly at the sweet domesticity of the action. He wanted to say something about it, but Dominick had acted like it was a completely common occurrence, like he had made Alfie's tea for him a hundred times before. Alfie decided to say nothing. He took a sip instead. It was perfect.

They enjoyed the silence for a long while, listening to the rain hitting the windows, its ceaseless tapping on the glass blurring with the sounds of the fire crackling in the hearth.

Each chair had a matching footstool, and they both took advantage, stretching their legs out towards the fire and warming their soles. The slight angle of the chairs meant their feet ended up mere inches apart. Alfie was debating whether it would be too much to give Dominick a friendly kick, like he'd done at luncheon, when he found himself being kicked lightly instead.

He glanced over and found Dominick pointedly not looking at him, staring into the fire with a small smile playing about his lips. Alfie nudged his foot back in return, the slide of silk on silk far too intimate. But perhaps here in this little bubble of the two of them, cut off from the world, the rules of proper society that had been beaten into Alfie did not need to apply.

He closed his eyes, indulging in the feelings of warmth and companionship. The worries he'd had earlier dried up like a pool of rainwater on a hot hearth. Whatever his feelings for Dominick were, Alfie knew he was safe with him. That had been true when he was five and it was true now.

It had been a long day. Perhaps he would just take a short rest now while they warmed up. Distantly, he felt Dominick's presence shift and the teacup and saucer being lifted from his slackening fingers. Then there was the faintest brush against his forehead. In his half-awake state, Alfie let himself pretend it was a kiss as he drifted off into his dreams.

※ ※ ※

He awoke slowly. The fire had burned down, and while the embers still glowed, the study was beginning to get the slightest chill. The rain still beat against the windows in a steady tattoo. Alfie rubbed his eyes and looked at the clock on the mantel. He'd been asleep for nearly three hours. Glancing over, Dominick was fast asleep in the chair next to his, banyan wrapped tightly around him and chin tucked into his chest. The tea on the table between them was no more than half drunk and ice cold.

Dominick had never been a graceful sleeper. In their childhood, Alfie had often been kept awake half the night by Dominick snoring directly into his ear. Dominick said it was in revenge for Alfie's icy feet keeping him awake the other half. Alfie shivered in pleasure at the thought of sharing a bed with him now, and out of curiosity leaned in. Sure enough, after a moment, he heard it. Not nearly as loud as when they were children and much deeper in tone, Dominick's soft snores sounded like a basset hound contented after a long day's hunt.

He got up as quietly as he could and added more logs to the fire. One slipped, making the embers hiss and snap, and when he turned around, Dominick was watching him through sleepy, half-lidded eyes.

"I didn't mean to wake you." Alfie whispered. There was something in the air that required hushed voices and soft tones.

"It's fine," Dominick rumbled, voice still heavy with sleep.

"Are you hungry at all?"

"No," said Dominick, stretching his powerful arms high above his head. "Still full from luncheon. You?"

"I'm the same." Alfie sat back down in his chair. "You know that's the thing I remember most about the workhouse? Not the fleas or the cold or that awful matron. I just remember always being hungry. It must have been worse for you, getting the same rations as me and being twice my size."

Dominick hummed and shifted in his chair.

"It was hard," he agreed. He paused, but seemed to come to a decision. "Both then and after."

Alfie turned to face him, but Dominick just stared resolutely into the fire.

"Do you want to talk about any of it?"

Dominick shrugged. "Not much to tell that you haven't already guessed. I told you I stayed in the workhouse until I aged out, and then I was on the streets. No money, no food, no real skills. So I did what I had to do to survive. I stole, I fought, and when the choice was that or starve, I sold my body. There's always a market for that."

A wave of pity swept through Alfie, followed by a wave of anger. That Dominick had been so badly abused by life yet still remained such a *good* man made him rage. Men like his cousin could drink and gamble and raise all sorts of hell and still be granted the utmost respect, but men like Dominick could do nothing but try to survive and were treated worse than dogs.

"I was lucky though," Dominick continued. "My friend Jimmy—you met him at the fight—he came into a little money and bought himself a pub. When things are real bad, he lets me sleep on the floor in there, or sweep up for a few pennies if he can spare them. He'd been through the workhouses too and remembers what it was like."

Dominick took a sip of his cold tea and made a face, but drank it anyway. "To be honest, I'm surprised you remember any of it, least of all me. I tried to forget that place as much as I could the moment I walked out those gates."

Alfie closed his eyes and cast his mind back. His memories of that time existed in flashes. Cold and hunger mostly, thundering machinery and backbreaking work, boredom in the rudimentary school lessons. There were good things too; the coloured illustrations in his favorite storybook, splitting a bag of stolen sweets with Dominick, going all together to the church each Sunday and singing the hymns before having the rest of the day free to play. Tucking up in bed each night with Dominick, the older boy wrapped around his back, spinning stories of far off places and magical adventures in Alfie's ear until he went to sleep.

"I'm not sure how much of what I remember was real, and how much just my imagination." Alfie admitted. He watched the flames eat at one of the logs until it split in half with a hiss.

"I was never able to tell anyone about it, so my memories may be a bit confused. I do remember you though. I remember the wonderful stories you used to tell. You know, I had almost convinced myself that you weren't real? That having such a-a good friend was just my wistful imagination. I was very lonely here."

He reached for one of the biscuits on the tea tray, crumbling it between his fingers as he spoke. It didn't hurt to admit that as much as it once did. "My parents weren't cruel, understand. I think they may have even loved me in their own way, but they never really knew what to do with me once they had me."

Dominick made a small noise at that. Alfie risked a glance over. His friend had his lips pressed together in a look of distaste, but said nothing.

"Will you tell me about that day?" Alfie asked.

"What day?"

"You know what day. The last day. I know you said you didn't start the fight with Baz on purpose, but for years I thought you had. That day changed my life, so I'd like to know what other memories I have that are wrong."

Dominick didn't respond immediately. Alfie tried to read his face but couldn't. There was sadness there, unsurprisingly, but something else he couldn't quite place. When Dominick spoke, there was a strange apprehension in his voice.

"What do you remember?"

"Only a little, it was all rather traumatizing for me at the time," Alfie said slowly, confused by Dominick's reaction. "A man and woman in fancy clothes came to look at us all. We had to line up but you dragged me to the end of the line and made me tuck in my shirt and stand up straight. We all had to recite the alphabet and get tested on sums, then they let us out in the yard to play."

Alfie frowned, "Looking back, I suppose that was a test as well."

"It was," Dominick whispered. "That's why I raced you to the top of the woodpile, no one was better at climbing than we were."

"Then... you were gone somewhere and Baz was calling me names. He said he was going to go be rich and live with the fancy man and woman because he was the biggest and strongest. I think he punched me then, but the next thing I remember for certain, you came flying out of nowhere and tackled him into the mud."

That got a small smile out of Dominick, "He made a noise like a goat. Go on."

"Then all the adults were there, shaking their heads. I think the Governor said something to the...to my parents. Someone grabbed me. By the time I realised what was happening, I was already in their carriage on the way here."

Alfie exhaled. There was more he wanted to say, but he didn't want to make Dominick uncomfortable.

Hang it, he decided. *If I can't tell him how I really feel, I can at least tell him this much.*

"I cried for three days straight and couldn't sleep for a week. I missed you, Dominick. I never even got to say goodbye. And I didn't know where you were or how to find my way back. Finding you again now, it means more to me than I could ever say."

And that was true enough. He could never tell Dominick that these last few weeks had been the happiest of his life, or that each morning when Dominick walked into the breakfast room, Alfie fell a little bit more in love with him. And that every night, he fell asleep to thoughts of touching Dominick, kissing him, their bodies coming together in shared passion and joy.

I love you, he thought, reaching over to place his hand atop Dominick's. But aloud he said, "I'm so glad to have you back."

"And I you," said Dominick, turning his hand so they faced palm to palm and curling his fingers around Alfie's.

Alfie's heart felt like it had turned into a flock of birds, swooping and soaring all about the room. To an outsider, it might have just looked like two old friends sharing a moment of companionship and connection, but it felt so much more profound than just that. Even if Dominick left him tomorrow, Alfie knew he would remember this for the rest of his life.

But he wouldn't let thoughts like that darken his mood. He'd worry about Dominick leaving when it happened. No reason to let it spoil this moment.

"Well?" He finally asked. "How did I do?"

Dominick let go of Alfie's hand gently. He picked up another biscuit off the tray and put it in Alfie's upturned palm. Alfie laughed and gathered the crumbs of the biscuit he had crumbled to pieces, tipping them delicately onto his saucer.

"You got most of it. They made you sing too, when we were all lined up. But you did that all the time anyway so I'm not surprised you don't remember. A little wren you were back then, always chirping and warbling."

Dominick grinned at the memory and Alfie blushed, looking for a way to change the subject.

"What about Baz the Badger?"

"What about him?"

"The night we met, you said he still blamed me for being chosen instead of him. I can't help but wonder what would have happened if he had. I don't think I would have lived very long on the streets in his place, but I can't help but wonder how he would have fared in mine."

"Well…" Dominick seemed to think about it. Alfie offered him a biscuit to help the thought process and he took it with a nod.

"If your parents wanted someone better than your cousin, they couldn't have made a worse choice than Baz. He's still a cheat and a bully and I think money and power would have only made him worse. He likes knives now, would happily stick a man as soon as look at him. I don't know how that would translate if he was an earl. You lot like your duels, don't you? So maybe he'd be good at that, although I don't think he has any honor to challenge."

"What about looks?" Alfie thought about the portrait of his parents in the front hall. "I grew into my father's height and then some, so they stopped complaining about that, but I never did look as much like them as they wanted." He tugged at a short lock of his hair. "My eyes were acceptable at least, but they always regretted this colour. And my nose was never quite right either."

"Well, let's see. He's barely grown since you knew him so they would have been sorely disappointed there. For the rest? You know those white, long haired puppies all the society ladies coo over? The ones that never stop yapping?

Alfie nodded, he was well acquainted with the hateful creatures, the dogs and their owners both.

"And how sometimes, the ladies get tired of all the noise giving them a headache and dump the poor beasts in the gutter? And they turn feral and get those nasty yellow coats that're all greasy and mangy?"

Alfie nodded again.

"Well, that's what Baz the Badger grew into. Frankly Alfie, not to speak ill of the dead, but if your parents told you they'd have preferred a cruel, nasty child like that to a sweet little songbird like you just because your hair was too red and you hadn't grown yet? Then they were the damnedest of fools, and are very lucky they are not still around for me to tell them exactly what I think of them calling you their second choice."

He paused, "God rest their souls."

Alfie couldn't help but chuckle. It didn't hurt quite so much to think of them being gone any more. They had been his parents, but he was starting to realise that they had never really been his family.

"Is there anything else I'm missing about that day? Aside from my parents nearly making a terrible mistake instead?"

Alfie meant it as a jest, but Dominick froze, just a fraction. Just long enough for Alfie to think there might actually be something.

"Dominick?"

"No, nothing," Dominick snapped. "Or I don't know. It was a long time ago, Alfie. You can't expect me to remember every second of it. I wasn't the one who ended the day in a fancy mansion, remember? It gets mixed in with a lot of other miserable days."

Alfie couldn't help the hurt, it felt like Dominick was keeping something from him. But he was right. That day had given *Alfie* a new life filled with every comfort and opportunity, not Dominick. He shouldn't be the one getting all maudlin. What was a little loneliness compared to the things Dominick had endured?

"I'm sorry," he said sincerely.

"No, *I'm* sorry," Dominick replied with a sigh, sinking further into his chair. "You have a right to ask about your past. I shouldn't be such a bear about it. I've just been worried that we haven't been doing enough to catch your blackmailer and it's wearing on me."

Alfie felt like he still owed Dominick more of an apology, but if his friend was going to be gentlemanly enough to change the topic, he could follow suit.

"Do you have any ideas?"

"I might, but you're not going to like it."

"I can hardly like it less than I like someone trying to kill me."

"Fair enough." Dominick grinned wolfishly. "How do you feel about housebreaking?"

"Excuse me?"

"That's what it's called when you break into someone's house."

"I know what it means!" Alfie exclaimed. "And how exactly does us committing a felony help?"

"Ah well, I'd be the only one committing a felony. You'd be tucked up safe in your bed at the time."

Dominick tilted his head. "Although I will need some

information from you on the house. And I suppose providing that information, when you know what I'm going to do with it, does count as a crime. Not that you need to worry a single curl on your head about it, they'd never arrest an earl for something like that."

Alfie reached up self-consciously and patted his hair. Damn. The rain must have undone all his careful arranging. And then he'd fallen asleep in his chair with it still wet? Even as short as it was, he could feel curls and tufts sticking out all over his head. He must look an absolute fright. Wonderful.

"And whose house do you need to break into anyway?"

Dominick gave a pleased little smirk. Alfie dropped his hands from his hair, caught in the act, but that only made Dominick smile wider.

"Your cousin's."

Alfie opened his mouth to protest, then paused. He knew intellectually that his cousin was the only person who made sense. It still hurt to think that he could be behind all of this, but he was one of the few people close enough to Alfie to have possibly guessed his secret, and if Alfie died, the estate and title would go immediately to him. He'd have plenty of money to waste in whatever gambling hell he favored.

For a few months at least. Then he would start raising his tenants' rents to cover his debts, or selling off parcels of the earldom one at a time until nothing was left, and all of the people who trusted Alfie to manage the land they worked would be homeless and starving. Killing Alfie might be a fast way into wealth for his cousin, but Reginald would lose it just as quickly.

He considered Dominick's logic.

"You want to see if you can find any of that special paper there."

Dominick nodded. "And see if there's anything else to find. Plans, maybe a payment note for whoever actually wrote the letters. Like you said, he probably wouldn't try to shoot you himself, so I'd wager there's someone else doing his dirty work. If we can find proof of that, then maybe we can turn one against the other. I imagine that the threat of deportation or hanging would probably get the whole story out."

"And what if you don't find any evidence?"

"Do you think your cousin is careful enough to plan something like this and not leave proof?" asked Dominick immediately. He must have already put quite a deal of thought into this plan before bringing it up.

"No," Alfie answered honestly. "He's not nearly that clever. He was nearly challenged to a duel once, because he stupidly decided to comment on a lady's rather unfortunate appearance without checking to see if her husband was standing directly behind him at the time. I think he's more likely to have left a note saying 'Pay Alfie's killer twenty quid' directly on top of his desk. That is, assuming he is the one behind it."

"Assuming he is," Dominick agreed. "And if it helps at all, I wouldn't kill you for less than thirty quid, at least."

"That does help, thank you. But if you would please not inform Mrs. Hirkins of your price, I would appreciate it. I know she has savings."

Dominick clapped his hands. "It's settled then. You give me the lay of the house, maybe invite him over for dinner to be sure he's out. I'll break in, have a look around. If I find anything, we can confront him or go to a magistrate, whichever you'd prefer. And if I don't, we assume he's not the one as wants you dead, and start over."

"A good plan," Alfie agreed. "There's only one problem."

Dominick's face twisted in confusion. "What's that?"

"There's no way this side of hell I'm letting you take a risk like that for me." He held up a hand before Dominick could protest. "Consider: If you're caught in Reginald's house, what do you think happens?"

"I dance the hempen jig."

"Exactly. Whereas if I'm caught?"

Dominick scratched his chin. "I suppose you say it was some sort of prank, and the constable gets reprimanded for bothering you."

"Exactly. Besides which, I have quite a bit of experience with a gentleman's papers and will be able to spot anything out of the ordinary much more quickly. Which is why I will be breaking into my cousin's house instead."

The words sounded even more mad aloud than they had in his head.

"Ah, of course. They teach you locking-picking in Cambridge then? Or how to break a window without making a sound? Or to tell the footsteps of a vagrant in the street from those of a runner come to nab you?"

"Fine. We'll go together. But if anything happens, it was all my idea, understood?"

"Understood." Dominick smiled, and stuck out his hand like they had just agreed to some sort of business proposition, instead of breaking and entering with a possible side of burglary. Alfie shook it anyway, not willing to miss an opportunity to touch Dominick, however fleetingly. The moment was ruined when Dominick let out a jaw cracking yawn that set Alfie yawning as well.

"I guess that's off to bed with me then," Dominick said. "No use sleeping in a chair when there's a good mattress waiting. You should rest too. Busy day tomorrow, and thievery is a lot more tiring than people think."

He winked. "Or so I'm told."

They both rose, and Alfie started to panic. If he was going to proposition Dominick, now would be the time to do it. He could say something about how they had shared before, so there was no reason to dirty up two sets of bed sheets. Or perhaps he could blame the weather. Wouldn't those beds—with their feather downs and piles of blankets —be far too cold to sleep in on a cool spring night? Best not to risk it, they would just have to share. And wouldn't you know, Alfie just couldn't remember where he kept his nightshirts... How long could Alfie keep up the charade before Dominick grew fed up and threw Alfie on the bed and had his way with him just to shut him up?

Or maybe the direct approach would be better. All he had to say was, "Dominick, fancy a tumble?" and see what happened. They might even laugh about it in bed later that night, or even years down the road, shaking their heads at Alfie's boldness before falling back into each other's arms.

Summoning all his courage, Alfie opened his mouth to speak.

"You go on ahead. I'll take the tea tray back to the kitchen and make sure everything's locked up."

He cursed himself for a coward and picked up the tray just to have something to do with his hands.

It was for the best, really. *Years down the road.* What a ridiculous notion. As if Dominick would want to have him even once, never mind to keep him for years and years. He swept out the door before he could have second thoughts. A faint "Goodnight, Alfie," followed him out.

After he had emptied the tea pot and set everything in the sink, Alfie went around and checked the latches on all the doors and windows, and made sure that the fire in the study would not accidentally catch the house ablaze. Then he went and checked it all again. Only when he was finally certain that there had been plenty of time for Dominick to go up to bed and fall fast asleep did he finally let himself go upstairs.

His feet dragged over the lush carpeting and stopped of their own accord at the door to the blue room. He forced himself to continue down the hall, locking his bedroom door behind him.

It was several long hours of staring at his darkened ceiling, listening to the rain wash in sheets against the glass, before he was finally able to fall asleep.

CHAPTER 17

When Alfie awoke, he felt more rested than he had in years. He was astonished to discover that he had slept through most of the morning. Drawing back his bedroom curtains, the rare sight of a sunny day greeted him. The rain seemed to have washed away the last dreary greys of winter, leaving behind a bright world full of possibility.

As he lathered his neck to shave, Alfie realised he was singing. *Rosemary Lane.* Well, no question of where his mind lay this morning. Although he hoped he hadn't been singing too loudly. Doubtless Mrs. Hirkins had heard worse, but he would rather not face her judgmental looks if she had heard him singing such a bawdy ditty. Or Dominick's teasing if he had. Soaping his face, he switched to humming instead. Much harder to overhear, and far safer while wielding a razor.

He was mildly surprised to find the dining room empty when he went down. Surely Dominick was not still in bed? *The Times* lay by his seat and he flipped through it while he waited for the lazybones to wake up and bring in the breakfast tray like he had done every morning for the past few weeks, barring whatever delayed him yesterday.

On the third page of the paper was an advertisement for a bear baiting that night. Alfie couldn't believe their luck. He detested the cruel sport, but his cousin was all but guaranteed to attend. The fact that it was to take place in Covent Garden meant that he was unlikely to return before the early hours of the morning, if at all. Alfie heard the dining room door open, and looked up beaming.

"Good news! My cousin..." His open smile fell when he realised it was Mrs. Hirkins in the doorway instead.

"What's this about your cousin? I'm not sure I'd consider any news of him 'good'," she said, setting the tray down and beginning to offload the dishes.

"Oh, he... the last time I saw him he said it looked like spring was finally here. It appears he was correct."

"Well there's a first time for everything, isn't there?" She slid two pieces of toast onto a plate with some eggs, then pointedly added two more, and a brace of sausages to boot. "That is if you don't mind my saying so, Master Alfred."

Alfie minded that she kept forgetting to call him "my lord" and instead addressed him as if he was still a child, but decided that discretion was the better part of valour when dealing with the person who prepared his meals.

Once the plate was finally weighed down to her satisfaction, she set the tea pot and a single cup alongside it, before picking the tray up again to leave.

"Is Dominick not joining me?" he blurted out.

She turned and rested the tray against the sideboard as she spoke. "Mr. Tripner left about an hour ago. He said he had some errands to run before you two went to the theatre this evening."

"The... of course, the theatre, yes." Alfie applauded Dominick's ingenuity. There were any number of theatres in town, each packed to the rafters. No one would be able to prove for certain that they had *not* been at one of them, if it came down to them needing an alibi.

He made a note to take Dominick to see something at a later date. Merely so they would be able to keep their stories straight about what they had seen. No other reason.

"We'll probably have supper out after, be back late. No reason for you to stay here after tea. If we're hungry when we return we can fend for ourselves."

"That's exactly what he said, too." She raised an eyebrow, "He also said to let you sleep, you'd both had a few too many at the pub last night and you were unlikely to be up much before noon."

Alfie frowned. Why had Dominick said that they'd been drinking, unless... Oh, he really was a very clever man. Alfie's heart swelled with fondness. He began to butter his toast with a feigned nonchalance. "Yes, I let him sleep it off in the blue room. In his state, I didn't want him wandering the streets in that storm."

"Good," Mrs. Hirkins replied with a decisive nod. "You should do that more often. Poor thing. I don't know where he lays his head each night, but he shows up in my kitchen every morning looking worn as an old sock and twice as fragrant. Perks right up after he gets cleaned and fed, of course, but a few decent nights' sleep would do him a world of good."

She sniffed. "Might even make him tolerable enough to look at."

Alfie laughed out loud. Mrs. Hirkins was the most sensible woman he knew and a grandmother a dozen times over, but it seemed even she wasn't immune to Dominick's charms.

"Oh hush," she scolded him in a manner that didn't seem particularly servile. "Do you a world of good too, it would. Don't like to think of you puttering around in this empty place all by yourself at night. Makes me lonely just thinking about it."

She gathered up the tray and called out over her shoulder as the door swung shut behind her. "He needs the bed like you need the company. Seems like a match made in heaven to me!"

Alfie was so shocked he dropped his toast.

*　*　*

It had been full dark for several hours. Alfie found his way down to the kitchen as soon as Mrs. Hirkins left for the day, but was growing more impatient with every hour that passed without a knock at the door. Finally, he heard footsteps coming down the servants' stairs and threw open the door before Dominick even reached it.

"Where have you been? I've been cooped up in this house all day."

Dominick sauntered in with a laugh and hefted the bag he was carrying higher up his shoulder.

"I needed to pick up some things, it's been years since I've done a proper housebreaking. Do you know how hard it is to find a well priced jemmy or glim on such short notice? Never was able to find a round-about, so let's hope I'm still as good with a screw as I think I am."

Any reply Alfie wanted to make died on his tongue.

Dominick dumped the bag on the kitchen table and began to rifle through it. "Did you find a way to get him out for the night?"

"I didn't have to. There's a bear baiting at Covent Gardens tonight. Gambling, violence, liquor, and whores? He won't be home before sun up."

"Sounds like the night we met," Dominick said with a wink. "Here, go put these on."

Alfie took the bundle that Dominick held out to him. It looked like a rough shirt, trousers and coat such as a laborer would wear. The coarse fabric of the material was rough against his hands and he couldn't imagine how it would chafe against more delicate skin. It was hard to believe that these were the sort of garments he'd worn every day as a child. Of course then, he'd never had anything to compare them to and had no idea how soft and luxurious clothing could actually be. What was more unbelievable was that Dominick changed back into these clothes every night with the knowledge of what silks and linens felt like against him.

"Don't wrinkle your nose like that. I paid good money to have those washed, and that coat is nearly new. There's a belt in here somewhere. We're about of a height, but I'm wider through the trunk than you are, so you'll need it." Dominick continued to dig through the bag, and with a noise of triumph pulled out a sturdy leather belt and laid it on top of the pile in Alfie's arms.

Alfie barely noticed as his mind had stuttered to a halt some moments before.

"These are… your clothes?"

Dominick fixed him with a look. "I've been flashing too much coin lately to buy a full set without the wrong sorts noticing. Wouldn't have even gotten you a coat, but it'll look peculiar if anyone sees you out at night without one, and the last thing you want when committing a crime is to be memorable."

"No, of course." Alfie said, more calmly than he felt. "I'll just go put these on then, shall I?"

He escaped from the kitchen as quickly as he could without drawing notice to how the idea of wearing Dominick's clothes was affecting him. He laid the garments out on his dresser and stripped down to his drawers. Each time he reached out to pick up an item, he remembered Dominick at Bonheur et Fils, standing naked behind a curtain with nothing to protect his modesty because he never wore anything underneath his clothes. These clothes.

Alfie's cock throbbed. He slipped a hand into his drawers and hissed with pleasure, Dominick's shirt clutched in his other hand. Dominick's clothes had covered him, caressed every part of his body kept secret from Alfie.

And Dominick had handed them over so easily, literally given Alfie the shirt off his back. Oh, but that would have been even better, Dominick stripping down in front of him, his clothes still warm from the heat of his body, slightly damp with sweat and smelling of him. Alfie slid his hand up and down his length while he raised the shirt slowly to his nose...

"What's taking so long?" Dominick called up the stairs.

Alfie bit back a gasp at the sound of Dominick's voice. His hand flew from his drawers guiltily. How pathetic he was, to be brought to such a state just from a worn set of clothing. To be completely infatuated with the man inside them was one thing, but this was just pitiful.

"Just a moment!" he rasped.

Right, no more of that. They had work to do. Dominick had only given him these because they were necessary, not for any other reason.

The thought did little to quell Alfie's arousal, but he determinedly ignored it, slipping the shirt over his head and reaching for the trousers. As he buckled the belt, he noticed himself turning his head into the collar and had to jerk his chin up.

Stop being ridiculous, he told himself sternly. The risk Dominick was taking tonight to help him was immense and Alfie could not be distracted by such base impulses. Besides, Dominick had said the clothes were freshly laundered, so there would be none of the scent of blood and gin—iron and juniper—that he associated with Dominick.

He felt his cock twitch feebly at the thought anyway. He leaned his head against the dresser and groaned.

CHAPTER 18

By the time Dominick heard Alfie's footsteps coming down the stairs to the kitchen, he had checked all his equipment and repacked the bag twice. It had been years since he had committed any major thefts, having known too many men who got themselves nabbed and hanged. He didn't want Alfie to know how nervous he really was.

"Well, how do I look?"

Dominick turned and was struck silent. He thought he'd grown used to how handsome Alfie was, but seeing him in normal clothes, *Dominick's* clothes, hit him hard in the gut. It was like Alfie had been stripped of all the gilding, all the fussy ornamentation and useless decoration, and what lay underneath was even more beautiful.

Without the distractions of fine materials and glittering threads, Alfie's eyes shone like the jewels they were. His hair was copper shot through with gold, and in Dominick's rough clothes he looked like a statue wrapped in muslin to protect it on some dangerous journey.

The collar of the shirt was too wide on him. It revealed just enough of his chest and the delicate arch of a collarbone to make Dominick want to just forget the entire plan and drag Alfie down onto the floor. The portion of skin revealed had to be smaller than Dominick could cover with a single hand—a theory he now desperately needed to test—yet if it affected him this much, how would he survive seeing Alfie's entire body bared to him?

It doesn't matter, because you'll never find out.

The thought was like a bucket of ice water, waking Dominick from his thoughts and dragging him back to reality. As he looked Alfie over to make sure there was nothing extraordinary about him—aside from the obvious —that would stand out, he realised that this was how Alfie would look if he'd remained in Spitalfields.

If someone else had been chosen instead, and by some miracle Alfie had survived the workhouse and the streets long enough to grow into a man, this is how he would look every day.

If he had survived. It was a miracle Alfie had lasted it as long as he had; he would have never made it to full adulthood. Not sweet, open, vulnerable little Alfie. The man before him was a lie, the ghost of someone who would have died years ago had Dominick and fate not intervened.

"Boots."

"Excuse me?"

"I didn't think to get you a pair of boots. Those are far too fine." Dominick sighed, shaking off his melancholy thoughts. "Still, better that you're in a well-fit pair. Just try to walk in a lot of mud along the way."

He slung the bag over his shoulder and walked out of the kitchen without another word.

✳ ✳ ✳

The street Alfie's cousin lived on was almost everything Alfie's was. Almost. The houses were almost as grand, the lanes almost as wide, the park almost as green. But even Dominick could tell that it wasn't *quite* there.

"Here we are, number 263," Alfie whispered under his breath.

He had done remarkably well so far, listening while Dominick laid out the plan as they walked, and answering all the questions Dominick had about the building as well as he could. He was smart enough to admit when he didn't know an answer rather than give Dominick a guess that could get them caught. Dominick nodded, but flicked only the tiniest glance over at the house before continuing on their way. They turned at the corner and kept walking, just two men on their way home from the pub, not planning on loitering anywhere that might disturb such fine people or be noticed by suspicious servants.

"Did you see there were no lights on?"

"I did," replied Dominick. "You're sure the household will be asleep?"

"They know not to expect him back, so by this time they should be. I don't know if he has a kitchen boy sleep by the front door to let him in, or if he just makes enough racket trying to get his own key to work that someone hears him anyway, but as long as we stay off the ground floor we should be fine."

Dominick nodded. They were fortunate then, that like Alfie, St. John had his study on the more secluded first floor rather than the fashionable ground level. As they walked over, they had decided the study was the most likely place any incriminating documents would be kept. Once upon a time, Dominick would have been able to search a room just down the hall from a sleeping servant, but he was out of practice and Alfie was completely untested in the fine art of housebreaking. But the first floor up presented its own set of challenges. Namely, how were they going to get in?

They walked around the block once more, enough that Dominick felt confident that no one was keeping a particularly watchful eye, but also not enough to draw notice from the casual observer, before going to the mews around the back. Here they caught their second bit of luck.

Alfie had been unable to tell Dominick the layout of his cousin's carriage house, it not being an area of the home he had ever visited, and Dominick had feared the only doors would have been the large ones that allowed St. John's coach to exit the building. Such doors would have been difficult to open without attracting attention and would have forced them to sneak through the entirety of that building before they even made it into the main home.

However, there was a narrow gate set just to the side of that door which opened directly into the townhouse's private garden.

"Keep an eye out," whispered Dominick before dropping to his knees. His skills with a set of lockpicks weren't as rusty as he had feared, and it was a matter of less than a minute before he was able to push the gate open carefully, wary of squeaky hinges. Pleased with himself, he smiled at Alfie as he rose back to his feet and brushed off his knees. But the worry in Alfie's eyes apparently left little room for awe at Dominick's skill; he just gave Dominick a quick bob of the head before ducking ahead of him into the garden.

From there, it was simply a matter of sticking to the shadows as they crossed the small area, watchful not to step on any of the raised beds and the first delicate shoots of green they contained. If they did this right, no one would know the house had been burgled until they confronted St. John with whatever proof they found. Leaving great big footprints all over the garden would be suspicious indeed.

When they reached the back wall of the home, Dominick instinctively pressed Alfie flat against it with one hand so he could not be seen from the windows above while Dominick concentrated on the next step in his plan.

Unlike Alfie's townhouse that had a flat back wall which rose in a sheer, impenetrable cliff face, the back of his cousin's house was terraced with each floor receding slightly from the one above it. As a result, they could easily climb onto the roof of the ground floor and have plenty of room to work while Dominick found a way to break into the first floor. This presented its own challenges, they would have to walk on cat's feet on the roof to keep from being heard within, but far better that than having to scramble up and cling to the window ledge while he worked.

He looked back across the yard to the carriage house, then up as best he could towards the windows above. Even if someone was still awake, he and Alfie would be hard to spot. The night was black as pitch, no moon in the sky. If there was just a little fog to muffle the sound of their footsteps, it would be the perfect night for housebreaking.

"Right then," Dominick whispered, leaning as close to Alfie as he dared. He realised his fingertips were still resting on Alfie's chest. "Give me a lift up, and when I've got the window open I'll pull you up after me."

Alfie nodded wordlessly, eyes wide in the dark, then dropped to one knee and interlaced his fingers. Dominick took just a moment to enjoy the sight before putting his foot on Alfie's hands. He counted off a quick three and they moved as one, Dominick stepping up as Alfie pushed. It was so easy that Dominick was almost surprised when he found himself at eye level with the roof of the ground floor, and nearly forgot to take hold. He finished clambering up, less gracefully than he would have liked, and froze. He counted quietly, waiting to see if anyone in the house had heard him and was coming to investigate. After several minutes without any sign of movement in the house, he leaned over the edge and nodded down at Alfie before turning back to the window.

He peered through the glass. The drapes were drawn tightly, so he had no way of knowing which room was which. The other windows along the back would likely be the same, so it was better to just stick with the one he had, rather than traipsing all over the place. He trusted Alfie when he said no one should be on the first floor at all this time of night.

The window itself was simple enough, two sashes, one above the other with several panes of glass in each and a latch where they met in the middle. Since only the bottom half of the window would open when he got it unlocked, it would be a bit of a squeeze for Dominick to get in and not the best for a quick exit, but Alfie would probably be able to dive through like a swan. He chuckled softly at the image as he pulled a long blade from the bag. Too flimsy to be any good in a fight, the thin metal was perfect for bending through tight spaces. He slid it up into the crack between the sashes and closed his eyes to better focus. It was only a second before he felt resistance as it caught the lock.

Easy now, slow and steady. He pushed, wincing when the lock gave a slight creak, then tried again even more slowly. After several agonizing moments, he felt the blade slide through the crack, having pushed the lock completely out of the way. He opened his eyes and smiled. He jiggled the window just a little to see if it would rise, and it did. He turned to go pull Alfie up onto the roof, and nearly screamed.

Alfie was sitting directly behind him, staring over his shoulder with an enormous grin on his face.

"What the hell are you doing?" Dominick hissed.

"Watching you work," whispered Alfie. "That was amazing, you got it open in no time!"

"Watching me have an apoplexy is more like. How did you even get up here?"

"Like you said, no one was better at climbing." He nudged Dominick's shoulder with his own. "Hurry up before someone sees us."

Dominick grumbled under his breath but went silent as he carefully slid the window up, listening for any more creaks that might give the game away, or any noises from within the house that said it already had. He held up his hand, and Alfie sat perfectly still, waiting while Dominick listened. Hearing nothing, he held the sash up and nodded for Alfie to go through. As he'd suspected, Alfie slid in with a lithe grace that suggested he spent every night breaking into the houses of his relatives. He held the window in turn while Dominick climbed through, then propped it open with the small beam laid on the sill for just such a purpose.

From what little Dominick could see, the room appeared to be a library, but from the staleness of the air, it was not one used all that often. He closed the curtains behind him to hide the fact the window was open, and on feel alone, pulled two dark lanterns from his bag and lit them. He handed one to Alfie.

"The study is the first door on the right. If there's any evidence to be found, it will be in there," Alfie whispered.

Dominick stopped him before he could open the library door. He was meant to be protecting Alfie after all, and that included protecting him from any crazed housekeepers wielding candlesticks who might be lying in wait. He peeked into the hall, which was thankfully empty, and let out a low exhale.

This was the other part of why he had stopped committing burglaries. The unending tension. The knowledge that at any moment everything might go crashing down and it would mean his death. It was better when he was working with Jimmy and at least knew there was someone watching his back. But after Jimmy had retired to run the pub, Dominick had run a few jobs with less savory crews, and those were enough to make him quit the entire enterprise for good. Give him a good clean fight any day, where he could look danger in the eye rather than waiting for it to stab him in the back.

They crept down the hall into the study, and Dominick risked opening the lantern a little wider to let out more light. Christ, the place was a mess. They would never find anything.

"There's a safe in that side cabinet," whispered Alfie. "I'll search his desk while you work on that."

Dominick tried everything he knew on the safe. It was an older model, which helped, but safe cracking had never really been his strength. Finally though, it yielded. He hissed at Alfie, who rushed over with bright eyes. Dominick preened under the warmth of his silent praise.

The feeling was short lived however, when the safe opened to reveal nothing more than a bottle of champagne. Dominick grunted in frustration.

"Who keeps their drink in a safe and all their important papers strewn about?" He hissed.

Alfie squeezed his shoulder. "If it helps, that's a very valuable vintage. Here, I found a locked drawer, come open that for me."

Dominick went over to the desk with his lockpicks. The wide center drawer in the middle of the desk was the one that locked. Compared to the safe, it was simple and only a matter of seconds before Dominick had it open. He had barely slid it out more than a few inches before he heard Alfie take a sharp breath.

Lying right on top were several sheets of the same paper the blackmail note had been written on.

Alfie reached out with a trembling hand and picked one up. Even by the faint light Dominick could see the same uneven edge of raw pulp of the blackmailer's letters. The page was blank, but there was already a stamp attached to the back, ready for St. John or his lackey to write his next demands and put it in the post.

Dominick pulled the drawer further out to see what else was inside. Suddenly, the entire bottom of the drawer crashed to the floor with an almighty racket. Dominick swore and jumped back. There had been a false bottom to the drawer and when he'd pulled too far the entire thing had come clattering down.

From deep within the house, he heard several voices raised in alarm.

"Hold this!" Dominick shouted, thrusting the open bag at Alfie. There was no longer any reason to keep quiet. The secret drawer seemed to have been filled with files and letters, as well as small tokens too indistinct to make out in the dark. He scooped as many as he could in the bag, as well as a few of the blank sheets of paper before pushing Alfie towards the door. The voices in the house grew louder as the pounding of footsteps descended from the servants' quarters in the attic.

"Go! Run!"

He pushed Alfie again, who followed Dominick's order immediately and bolted, bag of evidence clutched to his chest. Dominick took one last frantic glance around the room. The lanterns could stay, there was no way to link them to him. His eyes fell on an object near the leg of the desk. One of the trinkets that had fallen out of the drawer, no doubt. There was no reason to go back for it, they had enough evidence, but Dominick did, rushing the few steps and grabbing it up before tearing out the study door.

He heard a shout, and looked back just in time to see the nightcap-clad head of some butler or valet round the corner of the landing as Dominick dashed into the library. He grabbed a chair and braced it under the doorknob. It would buy them a little extra time to get away at least. He turned to the window just in time to see Alfie pull his feet through. He crouched on the roof and beckoned Dominick furiously.

Dominick lunged, and cleared most of the window in one motion, feeling Alfie tug his coat and jerk him through the rest of the way. They skittered over the roof and dropped into the garden, uncaring how much noise they made in their haste to get away. Alfie still had the bag held against his chest with one arm. They cleared the gate of the carriage house just as the commotion from the main building turned to full shouts of alarm.

"This way!" Dominick grabbed Alfie's free arm and yanked, sending them careening pell mell down the alley, boots sliding in the mud as they made their escape.

Behind them, the alarm was being picked up in the streets, but they ran on, Dominick leading Alfie down every side street and alley they came across, until there was no chance of their pursuers catching them. Still they ran, putting as much distance between themselves and St. John's house as possible. Eventually, the streets started to look familiar, and Dominick recognized them as those he walked every day to Alfie's house.

Alfie twisted in his grip.

"Trust me," he panted. And Dominick did, without question.

Alfie took the lead, weaving them down side lanes and courtyards Dominick hadn't even noticed, but Alfie must have known about for years. As they passed one house with a lit gas lamp burning over the door, Dominick risked opening his still clenched hand to see what the gewgaw was that he'd braved the hangman's noose to go back into the study for.

Glinting dully in the lamplight was his pewter ring.

CHAPTER 19

Alfie gasped as they crashed through the kitchen door. He had Dominick's bag tightly clasped to his chest with one hand and bodily dragged Dominick through the doorway behind him with the other, kicking it shut and throwing his back against it. He finally unpeeled his stiff fingers from Dominick coat and numbly reached down to turn the lock before sliding to the floor. Dominick was already there, lying on his back in front of the stove, gulping in deep panting breaths. Under other circumstances, Alfie might appreciate the view, but he was currently too busy trying to catch his breath to focus much on it.

"Are you… well?" he eventually wheezed.

Dominick made no verbal response, but raised a hand, before dropping it down next to his head. There was a distinct thunk as his wrist hit the flagstones.

"Ow." Dominick breathed.

Alfie started to giggle. He didn't know what it was, whether it was the giddiness of nearly being caught, or the lack of air, or just something about Dominick being too exhausted to even flinch when he hurt himself, but Alfie just couldn't stop. He laughed until he couldn't breathe again and that just made it worse.

Dominick rolled his head to look at him. "Shhh!" he hissed.

At that, Alfie fell over, clutching his aching sides. "You shhh!" He hiccupped. "No one… to hear us. Unless… unless someone's broken in!"

That set Dominick off as well, and they lay there side-by-side, laughing and hushing each other until they had tears in their eyes.

Perhaps it was whatever strange combination of emotions that had set off the laughter, or just the sheer joy of being up to mischief with his old friend again, but Alfie suddenly felt free. It was as if for the last thirteen years he had been a bird so blinded by the splendor of its surroundings that it did not realise it had landed in a gilded cage. And now had been there so long, it had forgotten it used to fly.

But with Dominick back, the door to the cage had been thrown open. Here, on the cold stones of the kitchen floor, in the strange dark hours before dawn, he didn't have to be the perfect son and consummate aristocrat. He didn't have to mind his manners or his dress. He didn't even have to be The Right Honorable Alfred Pennington the Earl of Crawford. He could just be Alfie.

As a weight he hadn't known he carried lifted off his chest, all the things Alfie had tried to keep hidden finally bubbled to the surface. He would be scared and hunted no longer. He was free now, and his freedom made him bold. He would never know if the risk was worth the reward if he never took the risk at all.

With this in mind, Alfie raised himself onto an elbow and before he could think better of it, leaned down and kissed Dominick.

The kiss was light, the barest press of heat, but

Alfie's intentions were unmistakable. He had the fleeting sensation of chapped lips beneath his own, before his new-found courage faltered. He pulled back, feeling a hiccup of breath against his skin that could have been laughter or shock or any number of things.

He flopped back down onto his side. Part of him, the part that had gotten used to the cage, wanted to curl up, turn away, deny the moment ever happened. But the part of him that had been freed was stronger, and he lay there with his hand half-stretched between them, watching Dominick and waiting for his response.

And this time, when Alfie looked at Dominick, Dominick finally looked back. Alfie couldn't breathe for an entirely new reason as he watched understanding dawn in Dominick's eyes. A slow, delighted smile spread across his face, and he reached out and took Alfie's hand his own. Alfie didn't hesitate, spreading his fingers so Dominick's interlocked with his.

"We need to celebrate." Dominick rubbed his thumb along the back of Alfie's knuckles. Alfie felt it like a caress along his spine.

"What exactly are we celebrating?"

"Many things." Dominick rocked their entwined hands slowly back and forth. "Your first successful burglary. Being alive. Being together."

Alfie's heart soared. Such sentiments seemed too precious to be spoken while lying on the floor of a darkened kitchen in the middle of the night. But he didn't care where they were said, a kitchen floor, Buckingham Palace, or the very tops of the Himalayas. As long as it was Dominick saying the words, Alfie would follow wherever he must to hear them.

But he could think of somewhere much closer and far more cozy than the ends of the Earth for their celebration. He tugged Dominick to his feet without unlinking their hands, and kicked the bag to the corner of the room. Tonight they would celebrate; they could deal with unpleasant realities tomorrow. He noticed Dominick drop something small into his pocket, but since he didn't comment on it, Alfie decided he had far more important concerns.

He pulled Dominick up the stairs. At the first floor landing, Dominick tried to keep going—the bedrooms were on the second floor—but Alfie laughed and dragged him into his study instead. One thing at a time.

"I think," he said, crossing over to the sideboard. "It is only appropriate that we celebrate the robbing my cousin's house with a very fine bottle of port he gave me."

"And how shall we celebrate the rest of it?" He heard Dominick say from somewhere behind him.

"I'm sure we can think of something. We are criminal masterminds after all."

He heard Dominick laugh, but focused all his attention on trying to open the bottle. The cork finally came free with a pop, and Alfie poured them each a glass of the deep ruby liquid. Leaving Dominick's glass on the sideboard, he took a sip to test the flavor as he turned back to face the room. Another jest sat on his tongue, but instead he nearly choked when he saw Dominick.

While Alfie had been struggling with the port, Dominick had stripped off his coarse workman's shirt and now stood waiting by the empty fireplace with Alfie's green silk banyan draped over his shoulders, the golden embroidery sparkling in the lamplight. The garment hung open and loose, hiding nothing of the exquisite chest underneath, those firm muscles half-wrapped in the most decadent packaging. Alfie stood helpless as Dominick stalked towards him with unmistakable hunger in his eyes. He threw back the rest of the glass in one, and licked his lips.

"You're meant to wear a shirt under that," he teased.

"And you're meant to wait for the other person to drink a toast," Dominick reached out and cradled the side of Alfie's head in his palm. The gesture was as sweet as it was possessive. Alfie found himself leaning into it, all but nuzzling into Dominick's hand. His eyelashes fluttered as Dominick rubbed his thumb gently over Alfie's lips.

It was too much. He grabbed Dominick by the silk collar and pulled him in.

Dominick's mouth was hot on his, feverish with desire. He used his grip on Alfie's head to angle him slightly, and yes. This was perfect. He felt lost, like everything he'd ever known had been flung away, leaving him with nothing but Dominick's mouth on his and Dominick's body against his own.

Alfie pressed closer, hoping to feel those miles of warm skin against him, the softness of the golden hair on Dominick's chest, but felt nothing except the rub of the coarse shirt he was still wearing. He whined and bit at Dominick's mouth in punishment.

"What's that for?" asked Dominick, pulling away just far enough to speak, his lips brushing Alfie's in a maddening tease.

"For looking like that while I'm still in these scratchy things."

Dominick chuckled, and leaned in to deepen the kiss. An acceptable distraction.

Alfie shivered as Dominick ran his tongue against his in a long, sinful slide. Whether it was mere moments or hours later when they finally broke apart, he couldn't say. The room was spinning around him. He arched into Dominick and felt his hard cock rub against Alfie's own.

"You're amazing, Alfie." Dominick murmured. He put his hands on Alfie's waist and skated up, his fingers tickling against Alfie's sides as he slowly pulled the shirt, *his* shirt off him. He threw it into some forgotten corner and wrapped his arms around Alfie's back, drawing them together. Alfie sighed and draped his arms over Dominick's shoulders, trying to get as much of their bodies into contact as possible. The room spun around him and he was finally warm for the first time in years.

Warm. Too warm. The room began to spin even faster. And faster. Alfie gasped as his stomach lurched. Something wasn't right.

A sharp tingling began to climb up his arms and legs, like stinging nettles slowly being drawn toward the center of his body. He clutched at Dominick, his lips numb, unable to speak. Dominick said something but Alfie couldn't hear him, the blood rushing in his ears as darkness closed around the edges of his vision.

The last thing he saw before everything went black was the look of terror on Dominick's face.

CHAPTER 20

"Alfie? Alfie!" Dominick shook the motionless body in his arms, his heart galloping.

Alfie's head lolled bonelessly with the motion before coming to rest against Dominick's neck. Dominick froze, body rigid with terror, until he felt the faintest puff of breath against his skin.

He let out a sigh of relief. Reaching up, he cradled Alfie's head as he carefully lowered them both to the floor. His fingers shook as he brushed an errant lock of hair from Alfie's face.

Alfie didn't stir even when his arm flopped off Dominick's shoulder and hit the rug with a resounding thud. With a whispered apology, Dominick tried desperately not to think of the phrase "dead weight". He laid Alfie down gently, grabbing a pillow from the settee and placing it under his head.

A soft moan escaped Alfie at the movement. Dominick let out a breath that caught in his throat with a rattle.

"Shh, I'm here," he said, taking Alfie's hand. "Lie still, love, I need to get help."

He ducked down and placed a quick kiss on Alfie's forehead, then forced himself to let go. He didn't look back, he couldn't. If he did, he wouldn't be able to bring himself to leave Alfie's side.

Get help, get help, get help.

Sprinting from the room, his knees almost buckled underneath him as he took the stairs as fast as he could. He grabbed onto the banister and forced himself to breathe. Every second he wasted was a second his Alfie was on the floor alone, but if Dominick tumbled down the stairs and broke his neck, there would be no one to summon help at all. Mrs. Hirkins would find his body crumpled at the foot of the stairs in the morning, and who knew what would have happened to Alfie by then.

He tried to focus. Alfie needed him, he could not give in to panic.

Think of it as a fight. Your man in the ring is down and not getting back up. What do you do?

When he'd been down, Alfie had bought his salvation. But what good would money be against this strange sickness that had so suddenly come over the man he loved?

Stop thinking like a gutter rat. If a rich man is down, he doesn't bind his wounds with rags, he uses his money to—

"Summon the doctor."

The echo of his words in the silent house gave Dominick the focus he needed to continue. He descended the last few steps with greater caution, but as soon as his feet hit the polished marble of the ground floor he was off like a shot, pausing only long enough to rifle through the small desk by the front door for the bag of coin he'd seen Alfie use to tip the odd delivery boy. He only prayed it held enough. He didn't know what a proper physician like Doctor Barlowe charged, but damned if he would trust Alfie's health to any of the leeches Dominick knew.

Out on the front steps, he peered into the darkness and

swore. At this late hour, the square was quiet in a way that the streets of Spitalfields never were. There was not a single soul about, even the link boys having gone home to their beds. He hesitated a moment before turning south and taking off in the direction of Great Russell Street.

If I can't find a cab there, I'll head west. By God, I'll run all the way to Harley Street and carry that doctor back if I have to! Dominick panted as the echo of his boots hitting the cobblestones bounced off the rows of darkened houses.

As he rounded the corner of Russell Street, he glimpsed a hack making an unhurried turn onto Tottenham Court. He called out and with a burst of speed caught up to it before it disappeared around the corner, startling the horses and driver both.

"Oy! What in the hell do you think you're doing?" swore the driver as one of the horses reared up in its traces and the other threw its head back in alarm.

"Harley Street..." Dominick panted, lungs burning. "Fetch Doctor Barlowe of Harley Street... It's an emergency."

The driver sneered. "And why should I be doing any such thing for the likes of you?"

It was only then that Dominick felt the bite of the night air across his bare chest. He shivered as the damp breeze raised gooseflesh on his skin. What a sight he must look, a half naked man running out of the darkness, draped in silk. Little wonder the driver had made assumptions. Assumptions that were not entirely false, either. He tried to pull the banyan tighter around himself, but the belt was missing, lost somewhere in his flight.

The driver sneered again, and snapped the reins, urging

the horses onward. Dominick lunged forward, grabbing the harness of the nearest horse.

"Now listen 'ere!" The driver rose in his seat, brandishing his whip.

"Silence!" Dominick shouted, pulling himself up to his full height. This man might not listen to a destitute boxer and whore like Nick Tripner, but Mr. Dominick Trent would be heard—and obeyed.

"There's an emergency at Lord Crawford's house on Bedford Square. You will fetch Doctor Barlowe of Harley Street *immediately* and bring him there. Am I understood?"

The driver nodded reluctantly. Dominick threw the money purse to him without bothering to check the contents.

"There's twice that again when you return, now go!" He slapped the horse on the flank for good measure and it started forward, the other quickly matching its gait. Dominick heard the driver swear as he nearly toppled, then shout at the horses for even greater speed. He watched the hack disappear into the darkness.

His shoulders slumped and he allowed himself the luxury of one long exhale. Then he turned on his heel and took off again, back to Alfie.

CHAPTER 21

Alfie was still lying on the floor where he had left him, but he groaned feebly when Dominick collapsed to his knees by his side.

"Hush, Alfie. You're safe."

"Nick?"

"I'm here, and the doctor's on his way." Dominick placed a comforting hand on Alfie's shoulder, frowning when the skin that had been so warm under his touch only minutes before was now worryingly cool and clammy. His heart clenched as Alfie shivered under his touch. "We should get you in bed. Can you stand? I don't know if I can get you up those stairs on my own. Nearly took a header down them once tonight, and there's some things even your Doctor Barlowe can't fix."

"I think so."

Dominick arraigned himself behind Alfie and wrapped his arms carefully but firmly around him. In any other circumstances, the position would thrill him, but his fear overrode any such thoughts.

"On three. One... two..."

As they lifted him into a sitting position, Alfie groaned and doubled over, clutching at his stomach. Dominick held him and rubbed soothing circles on his back. He glanced desperately at the clock on the mantle. How long had it been since Alfie had collapsed? More importantly, how much longer until that blasted doctor arrived?

"I think... standing may be beyond... my capabilities at present," Alfie hissed between gritted teeth. "The settee?"

It took them nearly five minutes to move Alfie the few feet to the settee and another ten to get him up on it. By the end, he was panting, eyes screwed tight with pain as he clutched his stomach, crying out as spasm after spasm wracked his body. Dominick found himself on the verge of tears, ready to tear apart whoever or whatever was responsible for Alfie's sudden illness.

In between kneeling by Alfie's side during the attacks, he busied himself around the room, if for no other reason than to keep himself from darting back and forth between the window, the clock, and trying to wrap Alfie up and spirit him away to some magical place where nothing could ever hurt him like this again. He removed Alfie's boots and draped a blanket he had found stashed away over him, tucking the edges in tight.

"Like a... broody hen," Alfie mumbled. Dominick tucked the blanket even tighter in response and had to stop himself from checking the temperature of Alfie's brow for the fifth time in as many minutes. Instead he forced himself to step back and give Alfie room to breathe. He looked for something else—anything else—to do with his hands to keep them occupied. He spotted the glasses Alfie had poured sitting on the sideboard, one empty, one full.

A wash of cold fear ran down his spine.

He slowly approached the glasses, bending down to eye them carefully. There seemed to be nothing wrong with the glasses themselves, no strange films or residues he could see. He lifted the full glass and sniffed it.

The glass clicked against the wood as he set it back down roughly in irritation. It wasn't like he knew what untainted expensive port smelt like, never mind one that had been laced with poison. Besides, hadn't he seen Alfie open the bottle himself? How could poison have gotten into a clean glass from a sealed bottle when they were the only two in the room?

But that was what this had to be, poison. He clenched his fists. As soon as the doctor arrived and Alfie was safely under his care, Dominick was going to go back to that townhouse and beat St. John to death with his bare hands. That cold reptile had given Alfie a bottle of poison and waited, all the while taunting him with nasty letters. Maybe he had hoped the stress would drive Alfie to drink, or perhaps he got a thrill from knowing that death was there, waiting for Alfie, and it was only a matter of time.

A rough sob escaped him, and he slammed his hands down on the sideboard, rattling its contents. If Alfie died, Dominick would do more than beat St. John to death. He would find a way to make it slow, agonizing. There were plenty of places in the city where a person could be taken and the neighbours would ignore the sound of screams, others where screams wouldn't be heard at all. And Dominick knew where to find each and every one of them.

He slammed his hands again, images of vengeance filling his eyes, and barely noticed when something light tapped against his knuckles. The cork had rolled from beside the bottle and come to rest against his hand. He picked it up and brought it closer to the light. There, impossible to see from the top but clearly visible on the bottom of the cork, was a tiny pinprick.

Dominick's white hot anger settled into a cold fury. That was how. That was how St. John had tampered with the bottle, he'd injected something terrible into it and left it for Alfie. He clutched the cork tightly in his fist. This was all the proof he needed. He was going to find that bloated, thrice-damned, pox-ridden—

"Lord Crawford?" A voice called from down below. "The door was open. Is anyone home? I was told there was an emergency."

"Doctor Barlowe!" Dominick called out in relief, slipping the cork into the pocket of his banyan. Revenge could wait, Alfie needed him now. "Upstairs! Quickly! It's Al-Lord Crawford!"

He rushed to Alfie, running a hand through his sweat dampened hair as the doctor's footfalls pounded up the stairs. "Hear that, Alfie? The doctor's here now. He'll get you all fixed up in no time."

"What's happened here then?"

Dominick turned, the story of St. John's treachery already on his lips, when he took in the queer look on the doctor's face. He realised abruptly how it must look, him in just the banyan with hands all over Alfie, who was shirtless under the blanket. For the second time that night, he drew upon his new self, the self Alfie had made for him, had given him along with all his laughter and warmth and kisses. The devil take what Doctor Barlowe thought of Dominick, it was only Alfie that mattered.

"Lord Crawford came down ill very suddenly. I have reason to believe he may have been poisoned."

"Poison!" The doctor exclaimed. "Bah! I'll be the judge

of that. I'm sure it's just a case of too much rich food on an empty stomach."

Dominick stepped back and let Doctor Barlowe take his place by Alfie's side. He tried not to hover as the doctor examined Alfie's eyes and took his pulse, but couldn't help the instinctive step forward when the doctor's prodding of Alfie's stomach caused him to cry out in pain.

The cry cut off abruptly however, as Alfie promptly rolled over and violently cast up his accounts over the side of the settee. Dominick was far enough away to avoid being hit by the mess, but Doctor Barlowe's shoes and trouser cuffs were not nearly as fortunate.

"For Christ's sake!" swore the doctor as Alfie groaned and retched again. This time the rug took the brunt of it as Doctor Barlowe retreated to a safe distance, cursing and muttering in a manner hardly befitting a man of his training. Dominick picked up one of their discarded shirts and went over to Alfie, wiping gently at his face as Alfie spasmed and vomited again.

"There now, get it all out. You'll feel better after."

When the worst of it seemed to be over—Alfie having eventually exhausted the contents of his stomach and spitting the last traces of bile onto the carpet with a grimace—Dominick handed the shirt over for him to wipe his mouth again and rose to face the doctor.

Fat lot of good he was.

Doctor Barlowe was seated as far from his patient as he could be in the room, one handkerchief pressed over his face while he used another to wipe vomit from his shoes with obvious disgust. Dominick was distinctly unimpressed. The man acted all high and mighty while taking out a few stitches, but Dominick had seen worse than this in any pub in Spitalfields on any given night. Even the most gin soaked East End surgeon wouldn't blink to be covered up to his elbows in shit and blood, yet this fancy Harley Street man quailed at a bit of sick?

"It would appear my services are no longer required," said Doctor Barlowe.

"Apologies, Doctor," Alfie mumbled, rolling onto his back and closing his eyes. "Please send a bill for the cleaning of your garments."

Dominick stared in disbelief as Doctor Barlowe merely nodded and went to collect his bag.

"That's it then? He could have been murdered and you're just worried about your shoes?"

Doctor Barlowe raised an eyebrow. "Murdered? Come now, Mister... Trent, was it? We met before? Leave the hysterics to the fishwives and leave the medical assessments to me. Lord Crawford simply had a disagreement with his supper and lost. Nothing a good night's rest won't cure."

Dominick opened his mouth to tell the good doctor exactly where his assessments could go.

"Nick," Alfie shook his head, then made a face as if the movement triggered another wave of nausea. "There's no need to involve-"

"Are you mad? He's a doctor, for Christ's sake. If he testifies in court that your cousin tried to poison you, then we don't need to worry about... the other thing."

Dominick winced. He'd let his fool mouth run and nearly said something he shouldn't in front of the doctor. He was making a right bollocks of this whole mess. How could he protect Alfie when he couldn't even think straight for fear of something happening to him?

"Other thing?" Doctor Barlowe asked.

Dominick clicked his teeth shut.

"I assure you gentlemen, anything said in my presence is held in the strictest of confidence."

Dominick glanced at Alfie. It was his decision to make, but even though they now had proof that St. John had been blackmailing him, Dominick knew they still couldn't take him to trial for it. Never mind the fact they had gotten their proof by breaking into St. John's house and *stealing* it, a jury would still want to know what Alfie was being blackmailed for, and that being made public would ruin him.

But if they could convince the doctor to testify it was poison, they could go after the bastard for murder instead. No jury would have any questions about why the next in line for a title would attempt murder, and any allegations St. John made from the stand would be considered nothing more than a desperate attempt to save his own skin.

But none of that would happen if the doctor didn't believe Alfie had been poisoned.

Alfie said nothing, but looked torn. An understanding air came over Doctor Barlowe, and he spoke with incredible sympathy.

"Lord Crawford, I have known your family for many years. It burdens my heart that I was not able to extend your parents' lives further when their times came, but I hope I was at least able to ease their suffering. Your mother, I know, was particularly distraught at leaving you alone in this world. Althea feared that you might develop the same morose temperament as your father. If there is anything I

can do that would lessen her son's strain or suffering, you
need only ask."

At the mention of his mother, Alfie let out a deep sigh.
"I'm being blackmailed."

The kindly expression on Doctor Barlowe's face froze as
the warmth in his voice changed to shock.

"Blackmail!"

"It's true," said Dominick, when it was clear Alfie was
too weak to continue. He chose his words carefully. "Mr. St.
John has obtained information about Lord Crawford that,
if brought to light, would badly damage his reputation and
has been attempting to blackmail him with it. We have
proof, but bringing it to trial might do more harm than
good."

"I see. No, that won't do. That won't do at all." Doctor
Barlowe shook his head and drummed his fingers softly
on his medical bag, deep in thought. "And in addition to
blackmail, you have reason to suspect he poisoned Lord
Crawford?"

Dominick fetched the bottle of port and the cork. "St.
John gave him this. It was sealed, but there's a hole in the
cork, where he must have injected the poison somehow."

Doctor Barlowe pulled out a clean handkerchief and
took the objects, inspecting them both before stopping the
bottle back up with its cork and wrapping them in the
cloth, careful not to touch either with his bare skin.

"These are very serious allegations. If you'll allow me,
I'll take these back to my office and see if there is indeed
any trace of poison on them, at which point we can discuss
what to do further.

"In the meantime, it appears Mr. St. John's plan has

failed. You will live, Lord Crawford, although I insist on bed rest for the next few days at least. I will send word with my findings when I have them. However, it may take some time. As you can imagine, poisons are hardly my area of expertise. Best to avoid your cousin in the interim, I should think."

"Let him believe his plan's still in motion, and I just haven't gotten around to drinking it yet?" Alfie croaked.

"Precisely. Besides, if word gets out that a lord has been poisoned, all the most fashionable members of society will claim to have been, and I'll be run off my feet!"

* * *

"Mr. Trent, a word?"

Dominick took another moment to ensure Alfie's pillows were properly fluffed before joining the doctor in the hall. Doctor Barlowe had helped him carry Alfie upstairs and into bed with a minimum of fuss from the patient. Dominick had been impressed by the strength still evident in the man. Of course, being a doctor wasn't just prescribing smelling salts to swooning ladies; he had to have strength enough to hold a thrashing patient still and operate at the same time.

"I thought it best to discuss this where Lord Crawford could not hear. It would not do to distress him further in his current state," the doctor said as they reached the front hall, pulling on his gloves. "As I said before, anything said to me is in the strictest confidence, whether it is of a medical nature or... otherwise."

Dominick nodded.

"As such, I will contact you as soon as I have any conclusive evidence one way or the other as to whether the bottle contains traces of poison."

He gave his medical bag holding the bottle in question a jaunty pat. "But until such time, I will not be making any accusations against his lordship's cousin. To do so would only be ruinous in society and bring scandal upon the family name, which must obviously be avoided at all costs. And the unnecessary stress to the patient as well of course."

"Of course," Dominick added dryly, already eager for this conversation to be over so he could return to Alfie.

"As a gentleman, I assume I can rely upon your discretion in this matter as well?"

Dominick couldn't help the huff of laughter that escaped him, "Don't worry, Doctor. I don't mix much with society."

"Good, good." Doctor Barlowe said with a crisp nod before rummaging in his bag. "I almost forgot again. I meant to give these to Lord Crawford when I removed his stitches, but they completely slipped my mind. His medication."

"Medication?" Alfie had mentioned no such thing to Dominick.

Doctor Barlowe nodded. "You seem to be good friends with his lordship, I ask then, have you noticed any... strangeness in his behavior?"

Dominick's brow furrowed in confusion.

The doctor sighed and looked up at something on the wall. Dominick followed his gaze to the painting hanging there. It was the portrait of Alfie's parents, the one of them dressed in the exotic garb of their travels.

"I knew his lordship's mother when she was a girl. Kind, gentle, all fine traits that she passed along to her son. She was the model of respectability, a paragon of what a well-bred lady should be. In a just world, she would be among us still, an example and inspiration to all decent folk.

The doctor's kindly face twisted into a scowl. "But her husband somehow coerced her into haring off with him to parts unknown, and when they returned... I only met the man after he had already fallen ill, so I do not know if his neurasthenia was a result of his travels or the cause of it, but the late earl's madness was becoming more pronounced by the day. That he passed before his eccentricities could shame his wife and son further was almost a blessing."

The doctor sighed heavily, and touched the painting's gilt frame with reverence.

"But his death sent poor Althea into such mourning. I had hoped that free of his influence, she would recover and become her old self again, once more respected and celebrated for her virtue. But those hopes were in vain. And now I fear for the current earl. To have a morbid heredity from one parent is trouble enough, and his cousin acting in such an atrocious manner is most worrisome as well. I fear the risk of shame being brought upon the family did not die with the father."

He handed Dominick a small bottle of unlabelled brown glass. "These drops are merely a precaution. Be sure not to give him these until the poison has passed completely from his system; it would be best to wait until his lordship is up and out of bed. I would also appreciate a note being sent so I can update my records when he begins treatment. Three drops in water, after supper. Any more could prove dangerous."

Dominick took the bottle grimly.

"I appreciate your concern for your friend," Doctor Barlowe called over his shoulder as he walked out the front door and climbed into the waiting hack, the same one Dominick had chased after before. Dominick handed the driver the promised coin—liberated from a stash in Alfie's desk—and closed the coach door behind the doctor.

Doctor Barlowe leaned out the open window and whispered, "I warn you to be careful. This sort of thing often looks better before it gets worse. Feel free to call me again if he should take a turn."

Dominick started. He hadn't considered that. If the poison—and it *was* poison—still remained in Alfie's body, he could be in danger even now. He hardly waited for the hack to pull away before he was slamming the front door behind him and rushing back upstairs.

❊ ❊ ❊

Dominick sat heavily on the bed and breathed a sigh of relief. Beside him, Alfie's chest rose and fell evenly in his sleep.

It could have been minutes or hours that he sat there, matching his breaths to Alfie's own. If Alfie stopped breathing, Dominick realised vaguely, he would too. Maybe not right away, but to have gotten Alfie back after all these years, to have felt the soft touch of his lips and the silken warmth of his body beneath Dominick's hands only to then lose him? That would kill Dominick as surely as any poison.

The thought did not particularly shock him. After all, he couldn't remember a time when he didn't love Alfie in one way or another.

He pulled the covers of the bed up, tucking them in more firmly around Alfie's bare shoulders. Alfie mumbled something in his sleep, fighting briefly against his cocoon of blankets before giving up with the smallest huff. Dominick's heart swelled with fondness. Like this, swallowed in his giant bed, the lines and cares of the day erased by slumber, Dominick saw nothing of the lord Alfie had become, just the street urchin he had once known; sweet, brave, and far too good for the ugliness around him.

It was a precious thing, to be so in love with such a man. He only hoped that Alfie did not love him back.

Dominick sighed, turning away from Alfie to look down at his own hands. Even now, in the quiet and beauty of a lord's mansion, they were clenched into fists, ready to fight. His palms were coarse and rough from honest work when he could get it, and his knuckles pitted and scarred from when he couldn't. As for Dominick's body... He knew there was a rough appeal there, he'd made enough pennies on his knees or braced against the bricks of dark alleys to know that, but that was only on the surface. Inside he was all the ugliness he had ever tried to protect Alfie from. A cheap fighter and a cheaper whore, a thief and a ruffian. A man who could be counted on to do almost anything, if it bought him bread enough to live another day.

If he had done any good in his life since protecting Alfie all those years ago, Dominick could not think of it, and he knew that when his time came, that one act would not be enough to balance the scales of all that had come after it.

For now though, he could watch over the man he loved and be there for him when he awoke. Maybe that would count for something.

CHAPTER 22

Alfie tugged at the collar of his cleanest—and itchiest—shirt. Dominick had told him to keep watch while he eavesdropped on the fancy folks having tea with the governor. The rumor was they were here to hire a new maid or kitchen boy and if Dominick could find out who they'd picked before anyone else did, he and Alfie could get a head start on claiming their things.

The fine carriage parked in the workhouse yard was an unusual sight. Alfie was so distracted by its liveried footmen pointedly ignoring the taunts of some of the braver children that he didn't notice the boy sneaking up behind him until it was too late.

"Off with very fairies, were you?" Baz said with a vicious flick to Alfie's ear. "That'd be about right. Get a good look in while you can, that's the last time you'll see anything so nice."

Alfie rubbed his stinging ear and looked up at the taller boy. Dominick said he'd start growing any day now, and end up taller than Baz and him both, and who'd be flicking whose ears then! He straightened up as much as he could.

"You never know, they could pick me, and in a few years I'll be wearing a fine uniform just like that and riding on the back of an even fancier coach."

Baz laughed viciously, "Well, mind you don't get any mud on the doors opening them or I'll order you whipped. Didn't you hear? They're not here for a servant, you ninny. They're looking for a child on the sly like to say is their own. Raise to be a proper lord with beautiful ladies and bags of money and whatnot."

He sneered down at Alfie. "Not going to pick a scrawny weakling like you, are they? Rich folk don't like a little mouse, always hiding in the shadows. They want a real man like me."

"I think they'd want an heir who wasn't so stupid he'd confuse his soup bowl for his chamber pot."

Alfie immediately regretted his words as a brutal punch to the stomach brought him to the ground. He raised his arms to protect his face from the kick he knew was coming. He braced himself for the pain, but it never came.

Instead there was a shout as Dominick burst out of the building and threw himself directly onto Baz. He fought like a demon possessed, landing blow after blow until Baz kneed him in the bollocks. Alfie winced in sympathy and tried to go to his friend's aid. Baz rolled them over, but Dominick still had strength enough to grab a hold of him and keep him from going for the knife in his boot. The two wrestled furiously in the dirt, teeth bared like dogs and spitting curses in between savage jabs.

Still gasping, Alfie pulled himself to his feet, and staggered a few steps before he was stopped by a voice behind him.

"Such a pity! And he seemed most promising too!"

The nasal crack of the lord's voice was enough to silence the whole yard. Even the two fighters came to a halt at the sound. Alfie turned. The fine man and lady stood on the stairs to the main building. She had a hand pressed over her mouth in shock, but the look on him was outraged disappointment. Beside them the workhouse governor groveled and sniveled.

"Many, many apologies, Your Lordship. We have unfortunately had quite a few problems with that one. Would your second choice still suffice? As you see, here he stands, quite wisely staying uninvolved in the squabbles of his lessers."

"I suppose," the lord sighed, and flicked a hand at the waiting footmen.

"No!" Baz screamed, struggling to break Dominick's grip, "It's meant to be me! I'll kill you! I'll kill you both!"

Alfie squinted in confusion, then two sets of heavy hands landed on his shoulders and began to drag him away.

"Nick? Nick!" he cried.

Dominick smiling at him from the dirt, teeth bloody and eyes sad, was the last sight Alfie had of the only person who had ever loved him.

❋ ❋ ❋

"Nick? Nick!"

Alfie thrashed and struggled against the footmen holding him back. Then with a gasp he awoke and immediately wished he had not. His entire body felt as if he'd been dragged through Whitechapel behind a cart, and his mouth tasted as if he'd been licking the gutter the entire way. There was also a hazy recollection of Dominick tucking him into bed, but he must be getting the past confused with the present.

"I'm here, I'm here," said a deep voice. "Christ, you still scrap like an alley cat, don't you?"

Alfie lay still, blinking as his nightmare dissolved back into the memory it was. Slowly this time, he tried to sit up, only to be stopped by a heavy weight across his chest. He looked down and his breath caught in his throat. Dominick sat on the very edge of a chair by the side of his bed with one thick arm splayed across Alfie's chest, pinning him down. His head rested on top of the coverlet by Alfie's hip, face turned away and hair mussed as if he'd slept in that uncomfortable position all night.

The blankets had slid down just far enough in Alfie's struggles that the side of Dominick's thumb rested against his bare skin. The single point of contact felt like a brand, burning Alfie and filling him with memories of the night before. Of Dominick bathed in the glow of lamplight, those strong arms pulling Alfie against him, stripping him of his shirt...

Of what might have happened next, if his thrice cursed cousin was not a murderous fiend.

Alfie sighed, loathed to let such dark thoughts intrude on the present. He squirmed until he was able to free an arm from his blanket prison, and hesitated only a moment before laying it down on top of Dominick's. His pulse sped as his fingers traced along the raised veins and defined muscle, entranced by the potent *maleness* of his form. Dominick's arm hair tickled against his wrist as Alfie gently stroked a fingertip over the backs of still tender-looking knuckles, humming absently to fill the sudden silence of the room.

The hand beneath his twisted, coming palm to palm with Alfie's and interlocking their fingers. He smiled as Dominick lifted his head from the covers just enough to turn to face him.

"Good morning?" Alfie whispered.

"Evening," replied Dominick with a tired grin. "You

slept the whole day away. I was just starting to drift off myself when you decided to wake so dramatically."

Alfie shivered as Dominick pulled their entwined hands down to press a kiss against the back of his hand.

"How are you feeling?"

"Better. A bit like the time I spent 10 hours in a pub after completing my finals at university and woke up in a mail coach bound for Aberdeen, but it's fading."

Dominick chuckled. "I'd like to hear that story sometime."

"It's not much of a story. Before we even crossed into Lincolnshire, I had been sick all over myself multiple times and was kicked off at the first inn to make my way home in disgrace."

"Sounds like some nights I've had."

Dominick gave Alfie's hand another kiss, then pulled away. The sad whine Alfie let out surprised and embarrassed him, but Dominick only laughed.

"I'm not going far. You'll be hungry once you brush the sleep off. Mrs. Hirkins left enough stew to feed an army on to warm for you in the kitchen. A proper fussock she was, I had to convince her I'd sit awake by your side all night, Bible open in my lap and hands clasped in prayer, before I finally convinced her to go home."

Alfie whined again. He'd never be able to look her in the eye after this.

Dominick winked. "Now you stay right where you are. If I'm going to be awake all night with you in bed, I can think of much better ways to spend it than reading the Bible."

The fire that rushed through Alfie's body with those

words was hot enough to burn away the last wisps of lethargy from his mind. Hardly had the door clicked shut behind Dominick, before he was up. He shivered in the cold of the room and grabbed the robe draped absently across the back of a chair to cover his naked body. Flushing at the realisation *someone* had stripped him before putting him to bed, he tried to put the thought from his mind, but could not fully drive away the hope that Dominick had liked what he'd seen.

He looked around for his slippers, but not seeing them immediately, padded barefoot over to the washbasin. A quick scrub with tooth powder removed the foul taste, but a glance in the mirror was enough to confirm that he still bore the aftereffects of his poison. His skin was even paler than usual, a poor contrast to Dominick's healthy glow, and dark circles weighed down his eyes. He ran the backs of his fingers over his cheeks, debating the merits of a quick shave, but decided not to deprive himself of what little colour the copper stubble lent him. The idea of leaving it was shockingly improper, but then again, so was what he and Dominick were about to do.

He pulled his mind from such thoughts with difficulty, nerves and excitement jumbling the images in his mind. He could already feel his body responding, and it would not do to have the race half run before Dominick even returned.

He huffed out a laugh. His hands were shaking too much to safely hold a razor anyway and doubtless Dominick was far more used to the feel of stubble on a lover than he was.

He scowled. He didn't blame Dominick for what he had

done to survive and would not begrudge any that he had taken to his bed willingly, but the idea that other men had paid so cheaply to have such a treasure as his Dominick, to have used him and discarded him for the price of a few coins, was enraging. His heart broke for the boy Dominick had been, and the man he was now, still so strong and caring, still rising to his feet with the same breathtaking smile Alfie remembered from boyhood, no matter how many times the world knocked him down.

No more, Alfie decided. When this business with his cousin was sorted, he would ensure Dominick was taken care of and would never have to worry about where his next meal was coming from, never mind resorting to selling his body to pay the rent.

He cursed aloud and looked away from the mirror, unable to bear his own reflection any longer. All this time he had been so selfish, focused only on himself and his immediate concerns while Dominick had been watching out for him as always, and Alfie had taken it for granted.

"No more."

Aloud, the words seemed even more of a vow. Tomorrow, he would start taking steps to ensure Dominick was the one protected in future, but for tonight, Alfie could show him, with his words and body, that he was safe, cherished, *loved*.

Resolved, Alfie nodded to himself and crossed to the fireplace, needing some task to occupy his hands. He had gotten the fire built up with enough logs to last the night and sat back on his heels to admire his handiwork, when he heard a deep voice from behind him.

"I thought I told you to stay in bed?"

Dominick stood framed in the doorway. He set the tray in his hands down on the dresser and leaned against it with his arms crossed. Amusement was clear in the quirk of his smile and the glitter in his eyes. Alfie's breath caught, the image before him so much like his fantasies that he hardly dared move lest he disrupt the moment.

"Well?" Dominick raised an eyebrow. "Are you going to do what you're told?"

Alfie licked his lips. "Make me."

There was a moment of stillness like the terrible calm before the storm, then Dominick was upon him.

Alfie barely had time to rise to his feet before Dominick was there, cupping his face with both hands and pulling him in for a kiss. Alfie gasped into it in shock, before quickly coming to his senses and returning the kiss in full force. He licked against the seam of Dominick's lips, and was delighted when they parted for him, Dominick welcoming him in.

He dissolved into the moment, feeling drunk and lightheaded. The room spun, but there was no poison in his system this time, just want and *need*. He pulled Dominick into him with one arm around his back, while he twisted his fingers of his other hand into Dominick's hair and *pulled*.

Dominick snarled and broke the kiss before diving in to capture Alfie's bottom lip between his teeth, biting down hard. He laved the sting away with long, soothing laps of his tongue. Alfie whimpered, and his eyes fluttered shut. No fantasy could compare to the feeling of Dominick in his arms, savage and caring in turns; filled with such passion that Alfie could not think, or plan. All he could do was tip his head back to allow Dominick greater access as he moved his biting kisses from Alfie's abused lips to pepper them along his jaw and throat.

"We shouldn't," Dominick murmured, punctuating his words with a kiss just below Alfie's ear. But before Alfie's confusion could turn to worry, he continued, "You were poisoned yesterday."

"I'm fine, I swear."

"You should be in bed."

"I agree," said Alfie, shivering all over as Dominick found a particularly sensitive spot and began to nibble. "What are you going to do about it?"

Dominick growled and absently Alfie felt himself being moved backwards, but it was still a shock when the backs of his knees hit the bed. He lost his balance, falling backwards with a startled cry to land with a huff amongst the disordered bed linens. At the sound of Dominick's laughter, he scowled.

"Was that really—" the words died in his throat.

Dominick stood at the side of the bed, the fire behind him casting his features into shadow. With his outline thrown into such a clear silhouette, Alfie realised for the first time exactly how immense his friend really was. For a moment, he felt the same frisson of fear that Dominick's opponents must feel stepping into the boxing ring and seeing him waiting for them.

The light gleamed off his eyes and teeth, like he was not a man but a demon here to devour Alfie and drag him down into the pits of sin. Dominick put a hand on each of Alfie's knees where they hung off the edge of the bed. Slowly he drew them apart, stepping in between them before leaning down and running his hands up Alfie's bare thighs.

Any fear Alfie felt immediately turned to excitement. In one movement, he wrapped his legs around Dominick's waist and knocked his elbows out, twisting their bodies as Dominick fell so that he came out on top. He smiled down smugly from his perch atop his defeated opponent.

"I see you didn't forget everything I taught you," Dominick said cheerfully. "Or do you get in many scrapes with other lords? Fighting over the best seats at the opera perhaps? Or who gets to bring Lady such-and-so a glass of ratafia?"

He placed his hands back on Alfie's thighs. Alfie blushed to realise that the robe he had thrown on so quickly had come loose, barely concealing anything at all. He forced himself to remain still as Dominick's hands moved back and forth along the tops of his legs, not pushing, but simply caressing. As if there was nowhere else in the world Dominick would rather be than lying under Alfie, and he was in no hurry to do anything else. Alfie relaxed and sat down more heavily, only to realise that Dominick might be slightly less composed than he seemed, if the hardness poking into Alfie's backside was any indication.

He bit his lip and risked a slight roll of his hips. The effect on Dominick was immediate. His fingers clenched into the meat of Alfie's thighs and his eyes darkened.

"You're a wicked one, aren't you?" he murmured, voice as deep and powerful as the sea. Alfie had the distinct impression he was about to be wrecked upon it. He found he didn't much care.

Slowly, Dominick slid his hands up, and at Alfie's nod, tugged gently on the end of the belt. The already loose knot unwound immediately and the robe fell open. Dominick kept his eyes locked on Alfie's as he pulled the two sides apart, giving him a full view. Alfie tried not to squirm under the scrutiny, his nails digging into his palms to fight the impulse to cover himself as the moment dragged on and on.

He felt Dominick's gaze on him as hot and heavy as any touch, moving down his chest, following the blush Alfie felt spreading down from his face, his cheeks blazing from the combined sensations of embarrassment and lust. He felt it sweep past his nipples, pebbled in the chill of the room the fire had yet to warm, and continue steadily downwards, past the flat planes of his stomach until it finally rested on his cock, fully hard and throbbing for attention. Alfie choked as a drop of clear fluid slid from the tip, and Dominick's eyes flared.

"Perfect," he said, almost too softly for Alfie to hear.

Then suddenly Alfie was once more on his back, robe pooling as Dominick leaned over him.

"Perfect," Dominick said again.

That was all the warning Alfie had before Dominick's mouth was on him, taking him in to the root and sucking hard. He cried out, back bowing off the bed in pleasure. He was distantly glad Dominick had sent Mrs. Hirkins home, because there was no way he was going to be able to keep quiet under such exquisite torment.

Dominick sucked again, before pulling back to lick and kiss the head of Alfie's cock as if it was some rare treat. Alfie shuddered. None of his experiences had ever been a fraction as erotic as this. He felt as if he was going to fly apart at any moment from the unbearable sensations. He was unable to take one more moment of Dominick's mouth upon him, but would die if he stopped.

"Please, please, please…" he begged. He dug his fingers into Dominick's hair, the silky strands all that anchored him to the very earth.

Dominick released him with an obscene pop, moving back just far enough that his breath panted over wet skin, electrifying Alfie's nerves and sending sparks of lust shooting throughout his body. A thin line of saliva still connected his bottom lip to Alfie's prick, and Alfie groaned as he licked it off.

"Please, what?" asked Dominick innocently, cursed devil that he was.

Alfie was too far gone to articulate his desires any further.

"*Please.*"

Dominick pressed his cheek against the inside of Alfie's thigh, dropping a kiss there so light and sweet Alfie felt his heart rip in two. His stomach caught in his throat, and he croaked, trying to say something, anything of the feelings Dominick awoke in him, but before he could, Dominick dived back down, licking and sucking. Alfie's eyes closed in bliss as Dominick wrapped his lips around him, taking him in impossibly deep.

Alfie tried to gasp out a warning, fingers tightening to the point he worried he might be hurting Dominick, but then Dominick hummed and it was too late. Alfie felt the crest of pleasure rising from within his very soul, and with a shout, he came. He felt Dominick swallow around him, drinking down pulse after pulse. The filthiness of it all wrung another jolt of climax from him.

His shout turned into a sob as he pried his eyes open, unsure of when he had closed them, to take in the sight of Dominick lying fully dressed before him, arms wrapped around Alfie's hips to hold him down as he licked the last traces of spend from Alfie's cock. His eyes were heavy lidded and self-satisfied, but still burned with need for his own release. He was wicked. He was debased.

He was beautiful.

Too far past words to say any of this aloud, Alfie tugged on Dominick's hair again, this time trying to pull him upwards. With a chuckle Dominick obeyed, laying his clothed body over Alfie's bare one. He was in a fine shirt and pair of trousers that Alfie had bought for him, but even the expensive fabrics felt rough against Alfie's over-sensitised skin. He wrinkled his nose at the sensation, earning him another chuckle, before Dominick's mouth descended on his.

This kiss was not the wild, desperate act of before, but was filled with no less passion. Alfie drifted in the blissful haze of his release and let Dominick explore his mouth, charting with lips and tongue like a conqueror discovering as he claimed.

As he came back to his senses, Alfie responded more thoroughly with licks and even nips of his own, until they reluctantly parted for breath. Dominick rested his forehead against Alfie's chest, the rise and fall of his body brushing in interesting ways against Alfie's. Alfie felt himself begin to stir once more and nearly whimpered when Dominick glanced up at him wickedly.

"How much have you done with other men?" he asked, moving his way down Alfie's chest to one of his nipples.

Never breaking eye contact, he took it lightly in his teeth, giving it the same treatment of sharp bites and soft tongue that he had given Alfie's lips and neck. It felt like there was a direct line between Alfie's nipple and his prick, the sensation flooding down his body. He went lightheaded as his cock filled again.

"I... what?"

"How much have you done with other men?" Dominick asked again, mercifully pulling back enough that Alfie could think. "There's more I want to do with you, *much* more, but I'm not sure how much you've done. Though, I'm not sure I should ask. I'm going to be embarrassingly jealous no matter what you say. I just want to be so good for you, Alfie."

He looked away as he spoke, and Alfie's heart broke all over again. Once more, he'd been selfish, taking his pleasure without giving Dominick his own. Because it wouldn't have always been good for Dominick would it? It might have even been terrible sometimes. But here he was with Alfie, his heart still so gentle that Alfie couldn't help but love him.

The wave of love should have been drowning, but instead Alfie felt buoyed by it, letting it raise him above his embarrassment enough to admit the truth.

"That was it, really. Or rather, I've had that once before. A mouth, I mean. A man's mouth that is, or well, a boy's really. But not—it was when we were at university you see. And then several times I've..." He carefully unwound his fingers from Dominick's hair to gesture crudely, his courage beginning to fail him. "But with the risk of being caught I've never... well."

"Go on," Dominick said, crossing his arms on Alfie's chest and looking at him with poorly-concealed amusement. "I'm sure I have no idea what you mean. Perhaps if you mime it more fully? Or we could play charades?"

Alfie cuffed him lightly upside the head. "You're a beast."

Dominick hummed noncommittally.

"Look in the side table then," Alfie said. "I'm sure you'll figure it out."

With another more interested hum, Dominick rolled off him and sat up to investigate.

"Oh," he said softly. He pulled the contents from the drawer.

"Yes, 'Oh'." Alfie said. The bottle of oil he had hidden away looked small in Dominick's broad palm. He sat up and placed a hand on Dominick's arm to get his attention.

"I haven't before, but I want to with you." He whispered. "I want you in me, Nick. *Fuck* me."

He kissed Dominick fiercely and felt him shudder against him.

"Right," said Dominick eventually, "Christ, stop that, I need to think. Right. How shall we do this?"

Alfie lounged back against the pillows, feeling every inch the wanton as Dominick's eyes raked over his bare skin. It was powerful, this feeling. Intoxicating.

"I may not be the expert," he drawled, his confidence returning. "But I believe that for best results it helps if both parties are unclothed?"

Dominick looked down as if he had never seen a shirt and trousers before in his life and had no idea how they had appeared on his body.

"Right," he said again with a long pause before trying to shed all of his clothes at once, tangling himself in his shirtsleeves almost immediately.

Alfie laughed and kneeled up to help, nearly tearing the buttons off Dominick's shirt in his haste while Dominick unfastened his trousers. Alfie's eyes lit up and he reached out for his prize, only to have Dominick gently push him back onto the bed.

"Money may be no object to you now, but I know what these togs are worth, and I won't have you ruining them just because you can't wait two minutes."

Alfie huffed and rolled his eyes. He understood, but who would have believed that the boy who had thought that washing clothes meant wearing them out in the rain would now be so careful about removing his shoes and laying out his stockings on a chair so they wouldn't wrinkle. Although... This was a show Alfie could still enjoy.

He wrapped his hand around his cock, now fully hard once more. He slid his fingers slowly up and down the length, the touch barely more than a tease as he watched Dominick shrug his shirt from his shoulders and meticulously inspect it for any tears or creases. His back was a thing of beauty, the colossal planes of it rippling with muscle as he bent to lay his shirt upon the chair. His loosened trousers hung low, revealing two dimples just above the swell of his arse. Alfie's heartbeat thudded loudly in his ears and he tightened his grip.

"Turn around," he croaked, licking his suddenly dry lips.

Dominick glanced over his shoulder at him and went perfectly still, before straightening and turning around, standing tall and proud. It was Alfie's turn to look his fill, and he took his time. He'd seen Dominick without his shirt before, it was almost becoming a habit now, but he'd never really gotten a chance to *look* at him.

He licked his lips in a vain attempt to draw moisture to his suddenly dry mouth. From the front, Dominick's physique was even more impressive, dark golden hair thick across the heavy muscles of his chest, the rich curls narrowing down his chiseled stomach before tantalizingly thickening again above the waistline of his trousers. It gave an illusion of softness that Alfie knew he wouldn't find. He had thought before that Dominick was like a bronze statue, but in the firelight, it was clear he was not cold, unfeeling metal, but more like a statue straight from the forge, the bronze still glowing with heat. To touch him would be to invite catastrophe.

"Come here."

Dominick walked over to him without hesitation. Giving himself one last squeeze, Alfie scrambled to his knees on the edge of the bed, putting him almost at a height with Dominick. He draped his arms languidly over his friend's shoulders and pulled him in for a kiss. He led this time, Dominick responding to his every touch as if Alfie had given him orders aloud. Alfie pulled back to trace his fingers down a length of string knotted around Dominick's neck like a necklace to the ring that hung in the center of it.

"What's this?"

"Something of mine I found recently." Dominick

hummed, running his nose along the edge of Alfie's jaw, once again finding that sweet spot that made him shiver.

"That sounds mysterious."

"It is." He traced the shell of Alfie's ear with his tongue. "But I want to think on it a bit first."

"Very well," said Alfie graciously despite the breathiness of his voice. "I suppose I shall have to find my distractions elsewhere."

He felt Dominick's grin against his cheek as he released the ring and pushed his hands down further still, taking Dominick's trousers with him as he went. They dropped loose to the floor, and finally, *finally* he had all of Dominick revealed to his eager eyes.

His cock was as impressive as the rest of him, long and thick, standing proudly from a dense thatch of hair. There was already slickness gathered around the head, and Alfie didn't even realise he was reaching out to touch until Dominick hissed. He pulled back.

"No, no, keep going. Please, Alfie."

Carefully he took the member in his hand, sliding from root to tip. At Dominick's groan, hot and wet in his ear, he grew bolder. Firming his grip and giving just a bit of a twist at the end, the way he himself liked, while his other hand cradled Dominick's sac.

Dominick dropped his head to Alfie's shoulder and sighed. "Bloody *perfect*."

Alfie gave him a few more long strokes, but could take it no longer. Seeing Dominick like this, touching him, holding him, only made Alfie need him more. His body clenched with desire. He leaned back slowly, guiding Dominick down with him onto the bed.

"I think," he said, feeling the blush rising again on his cheeks. "That it would be better if I followed your lead for a bit. I'm not entirely sure how best to proceed from here."

Dominick nodded, dropping another of his sweet, world-ending kisses lightly against Alfie's lips. "Happily."

He then began arranging Alfie to his satisfaction, pulling the blankets off the bed entirely and propping a pillow under Alfie's hips before digging through the sheets with a curse, looking for the abandoned bottle of oil. He came up with a triumphant cry, bottle in hand, before spreading Alfie's bent legs a little further and situating himself between them.

Alfie turned away, feeling horribly exposed. He could feel the burn of his embarrassment from the tips of his ears to the center of his chest. A light but insistent touch pressed against his chin, turning him back to face Dominick.

"Hey now, none of that," Dominick said. His eyes were dark with passion, the clear blue a narrow ring around the wide black of his pupils. But there was still concern there, and something else that made Alfie's heart beat even louder. "It's just us. Just me."

Alfie exhaled, not realising how tense he had become until he felt his body relax. It was Dominick. His Nick. The one person he had trusted and loved before he even knew the meaning of those words. The one he wanted so badly he ached at night, and all he had to do was trust him just a little bit more. He nodded, but instead of the pressure against his entrance he had been expecting, Dominick swept him up in another kiss, and then another and another, until Alfie felt dazed.

When the touch he'd been expecting finally came, it wasn't the immediate push he'd feared, but a light brush, Dominick tracing well-oiled fingers gently around his entrance, resting in the center just long enough to steal what little air remained in Alfie's lungs before slowly circling the edge again until Alfie feared he would go mad.

"Look at you," Dominick whispered, his voice carrying a note of reverence. "You're so beautiful like this, Alfie. So gorgeous."

Alfie panted, and looked pleadingly up at Dominick, begging without words.

"So beautiful." Dominick whispered again as his finger finally breached Alfie and pressed inside.

"Oh," was all he could say, the word drawn out as Dominick withdrew his finger and pressed in again and again. "Ohhhhhhhhhhhh."

The feeling was like nothing he had known before. The difference between doing this to himself and having Dominick do it to him was indescribable. Discomfort tingled along the edges, but mostly all he knew was such a sense of fullness and completion that it was as if until this very minute, he'd been walking around his entire life half-whole and never realised it until now.

"Nick…"

"Hush, my love. I know, I know. One more now."

The discomfort rose momentarily as on the next pass, Dominick slid a second finger in alongside the first. The stretch was more, a slight sting of pain accompanying it as Dominick stretched and prepared his passage, fingers curling and pressing.

On the next stroke, Dominick's fingers tapped the spot

inside him that had Alfie arching off the bed with a howl.

"Ah, there it is," Dominick said smugly.

He pulled back and pressed his fingers in again, this time with force. When he hit the spot, Alfie dug his nails into Dominick's shoulders. He snapped, pulling Dominick down into a kiss that was more teeth than lips, biting and crying out as Dominick thrust repeatedly, each time hitting the spot that had choking pleasure ricocheting throughout his body.

He barely noticed when two fingers became three so lost he was, a creature mad with pleasure, trying to pull his lover into him and tear him apart at the same time. Dominick's thrusts were relentless. Alfie thought he would die there in the bed, his heart beating faster and faster until it beat right out of his chest. It was even worse when Dominick leaned back, gently pulling his fingers from him. The loss was unbearable, and Alfie yanked at him, trying to get him back where he belonged.

Dominick laughed and something thicker, blunter, rested against Alfie's entrance. "So greedy. Is this what you want then?"

His words should have felt crude, debasing, but there was no malice in them, and no shame in Alfie when he moaned, eyelids fluttering in anticipation. "Yes. Please, Nick. I need you."

No sooner had the words left his lips than Dominick was pushing in with a loud groan.

Alfie clung to him, locking his arms around Dominick's neck and his legs around his waist. He held on for dear life as Dominick filled him, pressing his slick cock deeper and deeper until Alfie thought he would never end. Finally, he reached as far as he could go and stayed there. Through the swirl of pain and pleasure that wracked Alfie's body, he could feel Dominick trembling, fine quivers running through him as he fought to stay still. Alfie breathed deeply and tried to adjust. The moment he felt the pain begin to recede and the pleasure take over, he kicked Dominick in the side.

The effect was as immediate as if he had spurred a racehorse. Dominick flew into action, snapping his hips and driving into Alfie wildly, thrust after powerful thrust. Alfie bucked his hips, his body taking over from his mind and reacting on instinct, trying to meet the assault head on and draw the greatest pleasure from it. Dominick growled. Alfie had no time to realise how tightly his lover had been holding on to his control until it was gone.

He grabbed Alfie's waist in a bruising grip and pulled him onto his cock. Alfie cried out, the new angle causing Dominick to hit that spot inside of him with every thrust. He writhed and panted, overwhelmed but still needing more. He could almost taste his climax; he was so close, but it was just out of reach. He sobbed and grabbed Dominick's arse with both hands, feeling the strong muscles flex as he drove into him.

He blinked away his tears of pleasure and looked up at his lover. Dominick was fierce, magnificent and all his. Alfie clenched down and Dominick gasped, teeth white and sharp as he grinned ferally.

Alfie grinned in return and did it again.

Dominick leaned back, pulling Alfie half into his lap and took Alfie's prick in hand. The touch was the missing piece he needed. Dominick had barely wrapped his fingers around him before Alfie was coming. His vision darkened around the edges as he flew out of his body. He was distantly aware of the hot splash of his own spend against his stomach and chest but was too lost in pleasure. Blindly, he reached out and felt Dominick take his hand, sucking two of Alfie's fingers into his mouth, drawing a moan from Alfie's lips and another surge of spend from his cock.

Alfie floated softly back to earth, becoming aware of himself in tingling degrees. Dominick tilted him gently back onto the sheets and slowed his thrusts but didn't stop, each one indolent and deep, setting off aftershocks throughout his body. He released Alfie's cock when the touch became just a shade too much, but kept Alfie's fingers in his mouth, nipping and sucking as he thrust.

"Nick," Alfie groaned. He tried to move, to bring Dominick to climax, but found he could do little more than lie there and take it.

He could speak at least, he realised foggily, and tried again. "Nick, so good. So good for me. Please. Faster, you're almost there."

Dominick pulled Alfie's fingers from his mouth with a groan and bent down, nearly bending Alfie in half as he buried his face in his neck. The ring on his necklace pressed a hard circle between their chests, warmed by both their bodies. Alfie reached up weakly, and twined spit slick fingers through his hair once more, pulling him impossibly closer.

"That's it, Nick. I want to feel you come in me. Please. There's been no one else, just you. Feels so good in me. I'm all yours."

With one last brutal thrust, Dominick came, biting

down on Alfie's shoulder with a muffled shout. Alfie felt the hot rush deep inside him as Dominick climaxed. Alfie held him as tightly as he could, wanting to keep him there forever. He made the moment last as long as possible, whispering filthy encouragements in Dominick's ear, but eventually Dominick sagged against him, completely spent.

Just when his weight was becoming too much to bear, he kissed Alfie's shoulder and gently pulled out.

"Sorry, sorry," he repeated as Alfie hissed.

The discomfort was forgotten as Alfie watched him stumble from the bed on satisfyingly shaky legs, and wet the cloth by the pitcher before returning to Alfie and cleaning him all over. That task done, he collapsed back onto the bed beside him and let Alfie draw the covers over them both.

They smiled at each other giddily, the fire having burned down a little, but still bright enough to catch each other's grins.

"Well?" Dominick finally asked.

"Well, what?"

"Well, what did you think?" His face grew serious. "I didn't hurt you, did I?"

Alfie stretched. He felt sore and well-used, with a deep throb that promised deeper aches on the morrow, but mostly he felt overwhelmingly *good*. He found Dominick's hand under the blankets and placed it on his hip where Dominick had grabbed him so tightly before. He watched Dominick's eyes darken as he remembered and felt his fingers twitch against Alfie's skin as if he couldn't help himself.

"Not too much," Alfie smiled.

"And the rest of it? It's not... not everyone likes it, but you seemed to?"

Alfie had to bite his lip to keep from laughing. He considered his words carefully. "Well, I don't know."

"You don't? I'm sorry, I thought—"

"I suppose I don't have anything to compare it to." Alfie interrupted. "I can hardly say how that rated if I've only had one experience. That would not be scientifically sound at all. No, I think further testing is required. Extensive, *rigorous* testing. In every manner we can think of and as frequently as possible, I should expect."

Dominick stared at him, incredulous.

Alfie nodded to himself. "Yes, I firmly believe—"

His yelp turned into a laugh as Dominick used the hand on his hip to pull him firmly against his side. "You're going to be the death of me."

Alfie snorted.

"I suppose science can wait until morning," he said magnanimously, arranging himself with his head pillowed on Dominick's chest, his arm draped across his middle and Dominick's hand still resting low on his hip.

"Mmm," hummed Dominick, already half asleep.

Alfie waited until he felt Dominick's breathing change, the chest beneath him rising and falling in the deep breaths of slumber, before he leaned up and pressed the lightest of kisses against his cheek.

"I love you," he whispered, before letting feelings of security and *home* sink him into a deep sleep.

CHAPTER 23

Dominick blinked awake with the morning sun and a bone-deep feeling of contentment. Outside the window, he could hear birds chirping in the square, the clop of hooves as horses pulled carriages down the cobblestoned streets, and a thousand other sounds blurring together to form the chorus of a city waking up to the promise of a sunny day. Although it could be hailing brimstone and locusts for all he cared, the source of his serenity was not the weather, but rather the lump of stolen blankets that was currently drooling on his shoulder.

He gave a halfhearted tug at the nearest corner of blanket, but was rewarded only with an indistinct muttering and Alfie cocooning himself more tightly. Apparently some things never changed. Dominick laughed softly and rather than wait around with only the lightest of sheets to preserve his modesty until Alfie awoke —although that was a fine idea for another time—he extricated himself, and with a last kiss to the top of an ear peeking out of the nest, went to his bedroom to change and prepare for the day.

The spare bedroom. Not *his*.

It was too fine a morning for thoughts like that however, and he was nearly whistling by the time he made it down to the kitchen.

"I take it the patient has recovered then?" Mrs. Hirkins asked, swatting his hand away from a bowl of fresh berries and cream.

"Completely. Although I'm sure one more day in bed wouldn't do him any harm." Not that he intended to let Alfie sleep for any of those hours, but she didn't need to know that.

"I'm sure," she agreed briskly. "Just as well. Better than most he is, and finding a new employer at my age would be a trial."

Dominick glanced down at the breakfast tray laden down with not only bangers and eggs, but also the aforementioned berries and cream. And toast. And kippers. And bacon. And the fresh sticky buns she was just now pulling from the oven. A wiser man than he knew when to keep his bone box shut however, so he bit back any reply and waited for her to squeeze the teapot into the last bit of space on the tray, before he carefully lifted it and headed towards the door.

Pausing just long enough to tuck the newspaper and early mail Mrs. Hirkins had left on the hall table under his arm, Dominick continued up the stairs past the dining room. It took some maneuvering to get up the extra two flights, and even more to open the door to Alfie's bedroom, but he managed without spilling a single drop of tea. He must have made enough noise to rouse his sleeping lover though, as he entered the room just in time to see Alfie emerge from his bundle of blankets, blinking and soft with sleep. His auburn curls, normally so violently bullied into order, now crowned his head in a wild riot of colour and confusion.

He looked completely dishevelled. Dominick's cock throbbed and he wondered how quickly he could change that look to *debauched*.

He hesitated in the middle of the room. On the one hand, Alfie must be starving after so long without a proper meal, and it would be a shame to let this one grow cold. On the other hand…

"You brought me breakfast in bed?" Alfie smiled at him, sitting up fully. One of the blankets that had been wrapped so tightly around him slipped down, revealing a pale shoulder rubbed red by Dominick's stubble, and shadowed here and there with the bruises from his teeth.

Right.

Dominick set the tray down on the nearest table with a clank and advanced on the bed. Breakfast could wait until later. Much later.

* * *

Much later, he dropped back against the pillows, sweaty and sated. Alfie hummed contentedly as he burrowed against Dominick's chest, composing them both for his greatest comfort. How lucky Dominick was, to have found him again. To be able to hold him like this in the quiet of the morning as the world came to waking around them and a new day, unseasonably bright and filled with promise, began.

Alfie's humming transformed into a tune while they lay together, something from a music hall, light but forgettable. He ran his fingers through Dominick's chest hair as if he was petting some great beast. Dominick snorted. If he was a beast, then he was one that had been thoroughly tamed.

Alfie's hand passed over the ring on its cord without comment. Maybe he didn't care, or maybe it was enough for him that Dominick had promised to tell him about it at some point. Either way, it was something Dominick would have to deal with sooner rather than later. He'd had time to think during the long day he'd sat beside Alfie's bed as he slept, watching his chest for every breath and praying the doctor had been correct when he said that Alfie had gotten enough of the poison out of his system before it could do any real harm. Dominick knew he was not the smartest man, but he liked to think that his mind ground slow but fine, and he had come up with several possibilities as to how his ring could have ended up in St. John's study. All of them would involve going back to Spitalfields to do some investigating and probably some headbreaking.

He sighed. Dragging himself from a warm bed and naked Alfie to face the mud and stink of the rookery sounded like a torment sent from hell, and a stupid idea to boot. Still, the sooner he confirmed his suspicions and handled any unpleasantness, the sooner he could return to Alfie's side. A tamed and loyal beast indeed.

Alfie groaned in protest as he tried to gently disentangle himself.

"You're making this more difficult than it already is," Dominick chuckled. Alfie only clutched at him tighter.

"If you don't let me up, then I can't fetch you those sweet rolls Mrs. Hirkins baked."

He could almost see the wheels turning in Alfie's mind as he pondered this predicament.

"You're a cruel man to make me choose," Alfie sighed, loosening his hold.

"That I am. Cruel. Coarse. Savage. Depraved…"

"Mmm."

"And you, love, are insatiable." Dominick laughed and dropped a quick kiss on Alfie's lips, his face upturned for just such a purpose. He then removed himself from further temptation and fetched the tray, grabbing some bacon and toast and wrapping them in a napkin to take along before hunting down his clothing. Alfie tore into his breakfast the moment the tray hit his lap, heading straight for the sticky buns as Dominick knew he would.

"I have some things need doing today, but I'll be back by supper. Can you keep yourself out of trouble for a few hours?"

Alfie rolled his eyes and didn't deign to respond, his mouth probably too stuffed with pastry to do so anyway. He began to flick through the mail on his tray pointedly.

"The doctor left you some medicine," Dominick continued, holding one shoe in his hand but unable to find its partner. "Said to let him know when you were up and about and to wait to take it until after supper. So stay out of that too. Oy, you don't see my—"

Alfie cried out and Dominick spun around to see his eyes wide with horror. In his trembling hands he held the newspaper up for Dominick to see. From across the room, most of it was too small to read, but the headline sent ice running through his veins.

BURGLARY AND MURDER!!!

CHAPTER 24

...The body, found early yesterday morning in an alley off of Drury Lane, has been identified as that of a Mr. Reginald St. John, late of Red Lion Square and cousin to The Rt Hon Alfred Pennington the Earl of Crawford.

Servants at Mr. St. John's home report that he had not been seen for the last two days, never returning home the evening before the body was found. Most shocking however, the same night Mr. St. John was last seen, his home was the subject of a most brazen and outrageous burglary. The impudent thieves were chased from the house in the dead of night, but despite the courageous actions of Mr. St. John's valet and several footmen, none of the reported team of four to six criminals has yet been apprehended. It can only be assumed that this audacious crime and the heinous murder of Mr. St. John are connected.

The deceased was found still in possession of his pocket watch; however, he had no money on his person. It is assumed that this upstanding member of society was brutally attacked but his murderer or murderers perhaps being interrupted, had time only to grab his pocketbook. Finding the poor soul's address therein, they then continued their night of terror, ransacking the dead man's house. Albeit as yet, no connection has been confirmed...

Alfie put the paper down. His hands were shaking too

hard to read any further. His cousin dead? And murdered the same night he and Dominick had broken into his home? Good lord, *they* were the team of criminals! Had he been recognized? Were officers of the law even now climbing the front steps to arrest them both for burglary *and* murder?

Everything started to go a bit grey around the edges.

"Easy, there, easy. Deep breaths." Alfie found himself tipped forward, a warm hand rubbing soothing circles on his back. The new position brought his nose just inches from the paper in his lap. The accusing words began to swim before his eyes. He snapped them shut and tried to focus on his breathing.

"There now, in and out. Christ, what a shock."

Alfie felt the paper being taken from his lap. There was a long period of silence broken only by his still too rapid breaths.

"What's 'impodent'?"

He looked up to see Dominick squinting at the paper closely, mouthing the words as he read.

"What?"

"'Impodent'. It says 'the impodent thieves that robbed your cousin's house.' I want to know what they're saying about us."

"It's pronounced 'impudent'," Alfie groaned, dropping his head again in misery. "It means bold, shameless, cheeky."

"Well, that's fair enough then."

"*Dominick.*"

"No, I see. Your cousin's been killed and they think it might have been the same ones who robbed his house that did it. Although we know it wasn't because that was us. I'd say I'm sorry for your loss, but I'm not. If I hadn't been spending every moment of that night by your bed, praying you'd live to see morning, it might have been me that got him. After what he did to you, I'm inclined to put the word out that I'll stand a round at The Barge for the ones that did."

Alfie could barely focus on what Dominick was saying. His cousin was dead. He knew he should probably feel some sense of remorse, but all he felt was *relief*. Reginald had been an awful man. A crude, self-absorbed bully. He'd made everyone who'd met him miserable. And that was even before he'd tried to blackmail and kill Alfie.

No, he would spare no tears for his cousin.

It was not his grief that had sparked such a reaction when he saw the article. It was partially the shock, of course, but mostly fear. If someone realised he and Dominick had been the ones to ransack his cousin's home that evening, would they believe that the two of them were murderers as well?

Most likely he would suffer little consequence, perhaps have to go live on the continent, though that was no great loss. But Dominick? Dominick would hang. No matter how much Alfie spent on his defense or how many bribes he paid, the murder of the heir to an earldom by a commoner? And once word got out that Dominick had been a male prostitute there would be nothing Alfie could do.

His vision began to swim, the edges going grey. Then there was an almighty whack between his shoulder blades.

"I said to breathe, Alfie. Not to work yourself into a fit. Here."

Dominick climbed onto the bed and leaned back against the headboard, manhandling Alfie to sit between his legs. In this position, Alfie could feel Dominick's strong chest pressed against his back. He tried to relax against it, matching the rise and fall of Dominick's breaths with his own. It was as if Dominick was breathing through him, a part of Alfie's own body. Steady and sure and as vital to life as his own heart and lungs.

"I see you managed to get me back into bed," Dominick said several minutes later.

"I did," Alfie chuckled weakly. "Sorry. I just started to worry—"

"That Bow Street might somehow connect us to the burglary and think we were the murderers too?"

Alfie nodded.

"I thought as much. Listen, when they get here, just stay calm."

"What do you mean, '*When* they get here'?" Alfie cried.

He tried to turn around, but Dominick's arms kept him locked in place. He struggled, but only weakly. In all honesty, he very much needed to be held right now. His world was spinning apart and Dominick's embrace was the only solid thing left.

"You're a lord and your cousin's just been murdered. For certain, there will be a constable or two showing up to break the news gently. Not often do they get the chance to gander at a lord's house. Reporters will show up too, I'll wager, but you won't want to talk to them. Remember, no one at your cousin's house got a good look at us, and no one would ever expect an earl to be a cracksman. You'll do fine. Just try not to say anything to the constables about how if anyone deserved to be shot in a dark alley, it was him."

"Stabbed," said Alfie. "I suppose he deserved to be shot too, but the article said he was stabbed. Well, had his throat slit, to be precise, but I'd rather not envision it."

Dominick suddenly stilled, arms locked around him.

"Dominick? What is it?"

"Nothing," said Dominick eventually. Alfie turned his head. He could make out little more than Dominick's profile at this angle, but his features were rigid.

Dominick spoke slowly, "I was just thinking it might be best if I clear out for a bit. I shouldn't be here when the constables come by anyway, and it'll give me a chance to look into a few things."

There was something wrong with the way he said it, but Alfie couldn't quite pin down what.

"Very well," he said, aiming for a nonchalance he didn't feel. "Will you be back early enough for supper or shall I have Mrs. Hirkins prepare something that can be eaten cold?"

Dominick gave him a tight squeeze and then slowly let go. "If I'm going to lie low and avoid arousing suspicions, I can't just be sneaking back here for meals like an alley cat. It'll be best if you don't see me for a while, maybe a few weeks. That'll give the fuss plenty of time to die out and me time to figure out what I need to."

A few weeks? Alfie was speechless. Surely all Dominick had to do was go to the pub for a few hours until the constables had come and gone. His cousin was dead and with him, the blackmail, death threats, all of it was over. Alfie wanted to take Dominick out for dinner or to Vauxhall, something to celebrate the occasion, but instead

Dominick wanted to leave him on his own for weeks?

If he ever comes back. A niggling doubt began to creep into the back of his mind. Alfie tried to ignore it but couldn't help the sharpness of his words. "What aren't you telling me?"

"Nothing!" Dominick fired back. "Listen, you hired me to protect you, didn't you? So the less you know, the less you'll have to lie about if asked. Now go get dressed. I'm sure the constables won't appreciate the sight of you in your altogethers as much as I do."

Alfie jerked out of bed and stalked across the room, suddenly furious. He flushed with both anger and embarrassment as he struggled to put on the first thing he could find. His banyan. Of course it was that fucking banyan. He tried to tie it but couldn't find the belt so he just wrapped his arms around himself to keep it closed. That he must look like a blushing maid only rankled him further.

"Get out," he snarled. He barely restrained from stamping his foot. Dominick was already keeping him in the dark and ordering him about like he was a child, it would hardly do to act like one.

"What's got your knickers tied up in knots all of a sudden? All I'm saying is that it isn't always getting dressed in fancy clothes and eating costly dinners, sometimes looking out for you means keeping things from you. Things that won't do you any good and would only hurt you to know."

Dominick looked oddly solemn as he spoke. Then he shook himself and laughed, "Keeping you from getting hurt is what you're paying me for, after all."

Alfie felt like he'd been slapped. He had honestly

forgotten all about the money. It had just seemed so natural when they were spending time together. He had money, Dominick didn't, so of course he would pay. And of course he'd offered Dominick a salary when he'd first hired him, but it wasn't as if Dominick was his servant...

Hired him. He had, hadn't he. He'd hired Dominick to be his bodyguard. Not his friend or-or whatever they had become. His heart sank to his stomach. What he had *thought* they had become.

His mind went back over the weeks. It wasn't as if there had been much for Dominick to actually do as a bodyguard, had there? No wonder then that he took Alfie up on any distraction, whether it was a lunch at his club or sharing his bed. After all, it wouldn't be the first time Dominick had slept with a man for money.

Alfie began to feel sick. Is that what this had been to Dominick? A distraction? A way to kill time? Or worse, had Alfie somehow led Dominick to think that pleasing him was a part of his duties? Alfie was sure he hadn't been particularly subtle in his desires, and after the way they had met, Dominick could have easily assumed that sleeping with Alfie was an unspoken part of the arrangement. Alfie had been the one to instigate that kiss in the kitchen and everything that had happened after. Had Dominick really been responding to his advances, or just reacting?

Alfie felt a fine tremor begin in his hands as his anger turned into guilt and shame. At best, Dominick might have considered their time together a bonus of his employment. At worst, he just saw Alfie as another in a lifetime of men who had paid to use him.

Either way, it was a good thing he was asleep when Alfie told him he loved him. He would have looked like such a fool.

"Take whatever money you need and go," he snapped, ashamed of himself. He turned away to face the fireplace so Dominick wouldn't see him blink the tears from his eyes.

"Alfie? What—"

"And take whatever else you're owed as well. If my cousin is dead then the danger is over. I won't need a bodyguard anymore and this has all just been a colossal waste of everyone's time. You know where the money is in my desk. There's a hundred pounds in there. That should more than compensate you for your services."

Alfie stared down into the cold grate of the fireplace. He'd have to let Mrs. Hirkins know to expect visitors today. Which room would be best for receiving a constable? The drawing room was the obvious choice, but considering the occasion perhaps the library would be a more somber option?

He kept his eyes locked on the grate and pretended he wasn't straining to hear every one of Dominick's fading footsteps echoing through the house. He managed to hold himself together until he heard the awful finality of the front door click shut. Then he sat down on the floor and wept.

CHAPTER 25

Dominick set the empty tankard down with a thud and slid it across the bar. He'd hoped the first pint would drown the self-pity and disgust, but it hadn't. Neither had the second. Or third.

He felt like a whore. Strange that he could bend over in any number of back rooms and never feel so dirty as he had when Alfie had turned his back on him and told him to take his money. He'd thought... He didn't know what he'd thought. Alfie had hired Dominick for a job, knowing what he was. And now that he no longer had need of Dominick's services, he had dismissed him like all his other unneeded servants. He should have known it was coming. Alfie didn't even keep live-in staff, of course he wouldn't want Dominick hanging around when he was no longer required. And as for the rest...

Dominick fingered the fine material of his shirt cuff idly. He had gotten more perks out of the job than he'd expected: fine meals, well-made clothes, even just the chance to spend weeks out of the mud and stink of Spitalfields. So he supposed it was fair enough that Alfie got to take some perks out of it as well.

The memory came to him of Alfie smiling up at him from the bed sheets, eyes bright and hair in hopeless disarray.

He pressed the heels of his palms against his eyes. He was moping. And what was worse was that he was moping about moping. He should have just enjoyed his time with Alfie, taken his money with a smile and a "Thank you, milord" and gone on his merry way. But instead he'd become *attached*. He was like the lowly farm-girl in one of the stories he used to tell, who fell in love with the handsome prince in the castle. But instead of ruling side-by-side and living happily ever after, he was back in the dirt where he belonged.

And thanks to his damned pride, he didn't even have anything to show for it but the clothes on his back. He hadn't been able to bring himself to take Alfie's money from the desk or even his new clothes from the closet. As if not getting paid made it more meaningful somehow. It did, to him anyway. Christ, he was a wreck.

"Another pint!"

"Don't you be taking that tone with me," Maeve McVitie came out of the kitchen with her arms crossed. "You may have the look of a kicked dog but that doesn't mean I won't give you another kick if required."

He sighed. "Please?"

"That's better." She waited, drumming her fingertips on her elbow. "Coin?"

He searched through his pockets. There was nothing in them but a handkerchief wrapped around a few crumbled bits of bacon and crushed toast, and a button he'd picked up off the floor this morning. He'd meant to return it to Alfie, to tease him about whether it would be worse to try to fix it himself or try to explain to Mrs. Hirkins exactly how it had come loose.

He shook the handkerchief out over the bar and held it out to her. "Will this do? It's real silk."

Maeve pursed her lips and gave him an unreadable look. She then snatched the handkerchief from his hand. But rather than pouring him another round, she marched into the kitchen. A minute later she was back, the handkerchief tied up neatly in a small package that smelled of mince pie.

"Go on, get out of here," she said brusquely, but not without a touch of warmth. "You've had enough already and it hurts my heart just to look at you. Won't get a single *paying* customer in here with you sighing and drooping all over the place."

He nodded and took the handkerchief back. The warmth of the food inside had already begun to seep through the material. She held her hand on it a moment before letting go, her mouth open as if to say something else, then shook her head.

"And not a word about that to anyone," she sniffed. "I have a reputation to maintain."

※ ※ ※

Back on the street, Dominick noticed that the morning had gotten well into the afternoon while he'd been in The Barge. His stomach, now used to regular meals at set hours, rumbled. He picked apart the knot on the handkerchief. The pie inside looked just as good as it smelled. He smiled faintly. He'd never be able to introduce Maeve to Mrs. Hirkins. They'd probably be able to overthrow the Empire if they combined their efforts, but at least it would be a well-fed revolution. He bit into the pie while he considered his next move.

He still had a few coins saved up in his rooms, he wouldn't starve just yet. And he'd get a good price trading in these clothes to a barker for a more useful set. It would be hard to go back to coarse and ill-fitting duds after all this, but he'd have to get used to it. And after that? He tried to plan his next steps, but the nagging thought that he had unfinished business would not let him focus.

There was still St. John's killer to deal with.

He cursed under his breath. An idea had been growing for a while now, but he hadn't wanted to worry Alfie, not until he knew for sure. He rubbed at the heavy ring hidden under his shirt.

If St. John had been killed by a random footpad just for being unlucky enough to choose the wrong dark alley for a tryst or a piss, then there wasn't anything to worry about —the blackmail was truly over and Alfie was safe. But if he had been killed by someone else, someone who was quick with a knife and knew how to blend into the shadows of the city and disappear just as quickly? Someone who knew where to find St. John, had perhaps even planned to meet him? Someone who had been his accomplice in Alfie's blackmail and attempted murder? Then that person was still out there, and still just as much a danger to Alfie.

Dominick shook his head. He'd loved Alfie his entire life, had once watched him go and been glad, knowing that he would spend the rest of his life safe and happy because of Dominick's actions. It was the same now. He still loved Alfie, and even if Alfie didn't love him back, it didn't matter. Dominick would still act, would still protect him. He would likely never see his love again, but he could do this one last thing to make sure he was safe.

And then?

He groaned, wiping the last traces of pie from his hands and tucking the handkerchief back neatly into his coat pocket. He would deal with "And then" when it arrived. For now, he had a murderer to catch.

❊ ❊ ❊

Hours later, he stumbled up the steps to his rooms, exhausted and footsore. He'd trod half the city, turning over every rock and rookery for the vermin he sought, but the man had apparently gone to ground. Dominick was tired and miserable, and wanted nothing more than to collapse into a large, soft bed with clean sheets and freshly laundered pillows that smelled faintly of lavender.

His shoulders relaxed at the memory of such luxuries, enjoyed only hours ago and not truly appreciated while he had them. He tried to steer his mind away from the direction those thoughts led, but eventually gave up. He was too tired to fight anymore. He let the fantasy unspool in his mind as he reached the unlit landing, counting the steps to his door by memory.

He would collapse face-first onto the imagined bed, sinking deep into it and stretching out. It was so big his fingers wouldn't even reach the sides.

"You poor thing," would say a voice from behind him. That same person would start to gently remove his shoes and rub his aching feet through the silk of his stockings. "Let's get you out of all this and see if I can't find a way to make you feel better."

Dominick couldn't help the sad smile as he pushed open the door to his rooms and stepped through. There would be a light kiss to his shoulder and then… He froze.

Why had his door been unlocked?

He jumped back just as the light from his solitary window caught on a blade slicing towards him. A line of pain slashed across his stomach. He bellowed, striking out on instinct. His fist connected with flesh with a crunch. There was a howl of pain as his attacker fell back and Dominick advanced, shouldering his way into the room.

He risked a brief glance down. There was a long tear across the width of his waistcoat just between the fourth and fifth buttons. As he watched, the edges of the gash began to darken. He reached down and his hand came away red.

It couldn't be too bad, he told himself, if his insides were still insides. He aimed to keep them that way. He squared he shoulders and brought his fists up. His opponent might be armed, but he was Nick "The Terror" Tripner.

His rooms were in shambles. The thin mattress was torn open, straw ticking everywhere, his few pieces of furniture smashed and overturned. He flicked a look to the loose floorboard. As he feared, it had been pulled up and his precious tin box upended, the last few coins scattered across the floor and Alfie's cravat, stained with Dominick's blood, crumpled and kicked aside. His eyes leapt to the shadow standing in the corner of the room, one hand clutched to its nose, the other holding out a knife.

"I don't know why you had to make such a mess," Dominick said more calmly than he felt. "You already knew where that box was from the last time you broke in, Baz."

Baz Watts stepped into the light with a dark chuckle. The hand prodding his nose dropped. Dominick's impulsive blow must have been more glancing than he'd thought. The hand holding the knife stayed up, unwavering and pointing directly at Dominick's heart. His eyes glinted with hatred.

"I thought you might have wised up and hidden your valuables somewhere better after last time. But you haven't got any have you? You're either more of a cork-brained fool or a cheaper whore than I'd figured." He squinted at Dominick, then laughed. "Or are you taking your payment in socks and sleeves now? 'Another go for only a shirt, sir! You'll be shocked at what a boot will buy you!'"

Dominick tried to ignore how closely Baz's comments came to the truth. "I'm smart enough to know you were St. John's accomplice."

Baz scoffed. "Want a prize for that, eh? I tell you, it's not nearly as fun as you'd think. I'm minding my own business in a hell when some rich toff comes up and asks if I'd like to make a real wage taking care of his cousin. I'd never tried blackmail before, had I, so I was certainly interested. Turns out it's mostly just sneaking around and sending a few threatening letters. I offered to just slit the molly's throat and be done with it, but no, this St. John wants his fancy lord cousin to suffer, don't he? Get him all scared so he'd be willing to hand over as much money as we asked."

Dominick had been slowly edging his way towards a broken table leg, not wanting to go up against a knife with fists alone, but something Baz said didn't add up. This whole time, they thought St. John was trying to kill Alfie because he knew he wasn't the rightful earl, but from what Baz had said it didn't sound like St. John knew at all. "Wait, you said St. John was threatening him because he's—"

"A molly?" Baz sneered. "A madge cull? A backgammon player? "A cata—"

"Enough!"

Baz laughed. "A tradesman such as yourself? I will say you getting involved fouled up our plans right proper. It was all thought out neat-like. St. John would bring his cousin down to the stews to take in a boxing match and oh, what do you know? They get separated in the crush. Then this nice little boy tart I'd found happens to lead Crawford to some quiet room where lo and behold! St. John comes stumbling in at just the wrong moment! Of course he'll keep his cousin's vile secret, for a price."

Baz scowled and lunged forward with the knife. Dominick ducked and sidestepped just in time, but there was little space to maneuver in his cramped rooms and he wasn't sure he'd be as lucky next time. The table leg was now firmly out of reach, so he furtively scanned the room for another weapon.

That Baz knew about Alfie's preference for men was bad. That he correctly assumed that Dominick had been with him intimately was worse, but fortunately, he seemed oblivious to the idea that any feelings might have developed, at least on Dominick's part. Perhaps he couldn't even consider such things were possible between two men, or maybe it was just that there was nothing but bitterness and hatred in Baz's own heart, so the concept itself was foreign. Whichever it was, it meant that if Dominick died here, gutted in squalor, Baz was that much less likely to go after Alfie as well.

Especially since, he now realised, Baz had called him "Crawford", not Alfie. Could that mean in all his time working for St. John he never realised that the man he was being paid to destroy was the same little boy he had tormented ceaselessly for years?

Dominick sent up a muttered prayer of thanks. It was hard to see *Alfie* sometimes under all the layers and trappings of The Right Honorable Alfred Pennington the Earl of Crawford. At least until you felt the warmth of his smile under your hand, or watched his eyes fill with fear or joy. No matter what happened to Dominick himself, he swore Baz would never get close enough to Alfie to see either.

Baz was still talking.

"But instead he had to go panting into the night after you, didn't he?" Baz spit. "That made my job a lot harder. If you'd have just taken up my offer in the pub to go in on it, it would have been a quick fix. But you've always been too stubborn for your own good. So I got creative. It was one thing to watch the two of you swanning all over London and see you spend the blunt everyone knew you earned on your back, but I had to prove it."

Dominick nodded, "Which is why you stole my ring and gave it to St. John. He could say he found it in his cousin's home and you wouldn't even have to pay off any witnesses to say it was mine."

He may have gotten the motives wrong, but everything else Baz was saying fit into the theory that had begun to form even before they'd broken into St. John's house and he'd found his ring. He hadn't forgotten Baz's cryptic offer of a job, or the threats that had followed. Baz had all but told him he was being hired to do a rich man's dirty work. St. John being found with his throat slit only confirmed his suspicions. He hadn't said anything to Alfie because he didn't want to worry him. Better for him to be safe and think it was all over while Dominick handled Baz.

As he'd crisscrossed London looking for Baz that afternoon, Dominick had hoped he could convince him the blackmail wouldn't work now that they had the ring back, not to mention the proof of the fine paper found in St. John's study, and the letters on that same paper in Baz's own hand. If Baz walked away, then all the better. But if he didn't…

Dominick let out a long breath to steady his racing heart. If he didn't, then it was better Alfie wasn't involved in what Dominick would have to do.

There was only one question that still bothered him.

"Why bother trying to kill Crawford before you got the money out of him? St. John gave him that bottle of poisoned port *before* they went to the match."

Baz halted his steady advance.

"Poison? I wouldn't know anything about that." He cocked his head to the side and shrugged. "Not my style, is it? St. John must have been trying to scare him, I suppose. Or it was a case of putting the cart before the horse. Impatient old sod's been nagging me worse than a fishwife to get this handled."

"Is that why you killed him?"

Dominick expected Baz to laugh and start bragging about all the criminal cunning it took to knife a man in the dark, but instead Baz stood up straight, the knife lowering just a fraction.

Dominick tried to take advantage of his momentary distraction, but Baz danced back, bringing the knife up again. His free hand dropped back behind him, and Dominick watched it carefully. There would be a smaller blade in that hand now, dropped from a sleeve and ready to throw. If he wanted to stop Baz, he'd have to get in close.

"St. John's dead? Well, I can't say I'm surprised. A man like that must have all sorts of enemies. Not me of course, I'm as saintly as a nun."

And there was the laugh Dominick had been expecting, followed by a slow grin full of low cunning.

Baz wagged the blade in front of him back and forth. "I'd been thinking of playing the cousins off against each other to see who'd offer the most for my silence. But if the old gudgeon is dead... Well, I'll just have to take my cut from the molly himself. Too bad for you if he's not interested in paying. His fancy friends in society might not listen to me like they would have listened to St. John, but I'm sure the constables will. I know where he hid all the proof and once I've dealt with you, it will be the easiest thing in the world to retrieve it."

Dominick didn't react to the obvious gibe. Baz had had it in for him ever since they were children. Especially after watching Alfie being carried off to join the same fancy society he now sneered while Dominick ground his face into the workhouse yard. Keeping his eyes on Baz, he lifted his chin and reached under his shirt, slowly pulling out the cord. The ring swung in the air between them.

"Give it up Baz. I know where the blackmail material

was hidden too, because I broke in and stole it. You have no patron and no proof. Best to just cut your losses now and walk away. You put your word up against a lord's alone and I don't think you'll like how you fare."

Baz looked as if he'd walked into a brick wall. Dominick wanted to crow in triumph, but the feeling was short-lived as the look of shock quickly changed to one of disgust. Baz spat on the floor.

"I guess I'll just slit the bugger's throat and be done with it then!"

He ran at Dominick, his hand flicking out from behind his back as he did so. Dominick leapt to the side, but there was nowhere to go. He hit the wall and felt the sickening sensation of metal against bone as something lodged against his ribs.

Instinctively he yanked on it and pulled it out. The throwing dagger was small, and had mostly got caught in the fabric of his coat, but had still sunk deep enough that this second injury was bleeding worse than the first. He swung out. His fist caught Baz's forearm, blocking the strike aimed at Dominick's heart. Dominick swung again, knocking his opponent back.

He roared in pain and fear, "I'll beat you to death with my bare hands before I let you lay one finger on Alfie!"

"What did you call him?"

Too late, Dominick realised his mistake.

"What did you call him!" Baz screamed the question this time, spittle flying from his mouth. "It can't... oh, I see it now. That simpering little git made a fine little lordling, did he? I knew there was something familiar about him but oh, oh this is too good."

He began to laugh again, but there was something wrong about the tone, too shrill, too fast. There was no sanity in the sound. A chill raced down Dominick's spine as he pulled himself once more into a fighting stance. He shuffled into position the best he could, his stomach and ribs burning, and made sure he was between Baz and the door. If Baz wanted to get to Alfie, he would have to go through Dominick to do it.

"Still the loyal dog, Tripner?" Baz snickered. He pulled yet another knife from somewhere hidden. "Were you sniffing his arse then too? This really is prime. I'm going to gut you for ruining my chance all those years ago, and then I'm going to carve the life he stole from me out of him, piece by piece. I'm going to make it last for hours. He'll be begging for the end long before I've even started to take my share. I'm going to enjoy this."

He stalked forward, no mad rush this time, but a determined attack. His madness seemed to have sharpened his mind to a solitary, destructive focus.

Dominick waited until he was within range, then bobbed down under the swing of the first knife and came up for an uppercut under the ribs. The hit connected, but so did the knife in Baz's left hand, tearing into Dominick's arm as he struck and weakening the blow. He ignored the pain and hit Baz with his other fist, hook after hook in quick succession. Baz fell back, out of range, but Dominick followed, forcing him to retreat further with each step.

Baz threw another knife. Dominick sidestepped out of the way, but it was only a distraction. The moment he broke eye contact, Baz charged.

They hit the floor with an almighty crash that shook

the thin walls of the building. Dominick shouted in agony as his head slammed back against the floorboards. His vision swam, and he fought to stay conscious while blindly fending off Baz's attack. He grappled, trying to break free, but Baz was on top of him, both hands wrapped around a dagger as he drove it down towards Dominick's throat. Dominick threw his hands up just in time. He gripped Baz's wrists tightly, and stopped the blade a hairsbreadth from his skin.

Baz laughed that feral laugh again, his eyes rolling like a mad horse's. He leaned his full bodyweight onto the dagger. Dominick tried again to push him off, but he could feel his wounded arm weakening as blood trickled down inside his sleeve. His other injuries had already slowed him down and sapped his strength.

The point of the knife pressed against his throat, drawing up a single bead of blood. He was nose to nose with Baz now, the man's stinking breath from behind rotten teeth filling Dominick's lungs on each shallow inhale.

Dominick turned his head away and closed his eyes, not wanting to have to look at that as he died. He tried to think of Alfie, the way he'd looked that morning when Dominick brought in the sweet rolls. Or wrapped enticingly in that silk banyan he loved so much. Or lying on the kitchen floor laughing after they'd robbed St. John's house. Or that first night they'd met, the very first night all those years ago, rubbing tears from his eyes with tiny fists and looking up at Dominick with so much courage for such a tiny boy.

Dominick smiled.

"There's one thing you need to know, Baz," Dominick

swallowed and the blade sunk deeper. "Alfie didn't take your place. You were never the Crawford's first choice. I was."

CHAPTER 26

"Oh Freddie, you will let me know if you hear anything? Dreadful business."

"Yes, of course," Alfie said, for what felt like the hundredth time today. He rose, hoping Mr. and Mrs. Stockton would take the hint that their visit was over, and nearly wept with joy when they did.

It took a moment for Charles Stockton to stand, the trend of overly tight waistbands not allowing for rapid movement. Alfie offered his arm to Mrs. Stockton and ushered her to the front door perhaps more rapidly than was chivalrous, having to lean slightly to the side to make way for her bonnet of truly commodious proportions. The door finally closed behind their condolences and less than subtle enquiries into whether he had been told any more about his cousin's murder than was in the papers. He sagged against it.

He had barely been dressed and shaved when the constables knocked on his door to officially inform him of his cousin's death and ask if he knew of anyone who might wish his cousin harm.

The whole ordeal had felt like it was happening to someone else. It was as if he was observing himself from a distance playing the innocent and lying about having no idea as to who might have done such a thing. And to hear that his cousin's home had been robbed as well? What a shock. He'd offered to help in any way he could, of course. But really he hadn't been to his cousin's home in months and was sure he would have no idea what, if anything, had been taken.

By the time they'd left, he had just long enough to dash off a quick note of thanks to Doctor Barlowe for the medicine and his care, and to let him know that Alfie was up and would begin his new medical regimen that evening. He got halfway through a letter to his solicitors letting them know to expect to hear from St. John's firm about his will, when the doorbell rang again, and the first of an endless stream of well-wishers arrived.

Vultures, the lot of them. Not a single one would he have counted as a friend, and now they were all offering a shoulder to cry on, in exchange for a bit of gossip about the crime. They seemed to fall into two groups and he wasn't sure which was worse. The first were Reginald's drinking cronies who kept saying what a dreadful business it was, but did Alfie happen to know if any markers had been found in the ransacked house? Alfie made a note to amend the letter to his solicitors to expect to hear from several creditors as well.

The second group was the society mamas who clucked about how difficult it must be for him to lose his last blood relation and only months after his mother had died. Their sympathy was rather undermined by the presence of the eligible daughters they had brought with them and heavily weighted comments about what a shame it would be if the Crawford bloodline ended without an heir. As the visits went on, he was tempted to tell them it had, that the real earl had had his throat cut two nights ago on his way home from a Covent Garden brothel, and that they were throwing their precious daughters at an orphan from the stews and a sodomite to boot.

The looks on their faces might almost have been worth it.

The hall clock struck five, and he wiped his hands across his face. The only good part was that he hadn't had time to think about Dominick all day. He felt guilty over the way they had left things, which made no sense. Dominick had been upfront from the beginning that he was just there to do a job. Now that the job was over, of course there was no reason for him to stick around.

That said, Alfie could have handled it better, perhaps offering to help Dominick find new lodgings or arrange the delivery of his wardrobe. That would have let him know Dominick's new address as well, so that if he ever happened to be in the neighbourhood...

But no, it was better to have a clean break. Still, he shouldn't have snapped at Dominick like that. He'd been kind enough to Alfie to call him "friend" while their working relationship had lasted, it wasn't Dominick's fault Alfie had gone too far and fallen in love with him.

He was broken from his maudlin thoughts by the rumbling of his stomach. While Mrs. Hirkins had brought up a fresh tray with every set of visitors, a man could not survive on tea and cakes alone. He had let his foul mood out on her as well, snapping at her once or twice as the day wore on and she announced yet another group come to call. He should go find her and make his apologies, and maybe even grovel a little cheese and pickle out of her before supper. He reached for the bell, but reconsidered. If he was going to grovel properly, it would be best to do it in her realm, not his. He practiced his most remorseful looks as he took the stairs down to the kitchen.

※ ※ ※

"No need to pretend around me that you're sad the jack-weight is dead," Mrs. Hirkins said without looking up from a ball of dough she was kneading. "He was a bully and a lech and we both know the world is better without him in it."

She threw the dough on the floured counter with emphasis. "God rest his soul."

Alfie couldn't help but smile. Mrs. Hirkins had always been the one person in this house he didn't have to walk on eggshells around. She'd patched more than one skinned knee and pretended not to notice how many petit fours went missing before tea. But more than anyone, she had also been the one to show him how life among the nobility worked. Even if that did occasionally take the form of chasing him out of the scullery with a broom as it was no place for young gentlemen.

And now it was just the two of them.

"I actually came to apologise for anything I might have done to offend you today, Mrs. Hirkins. It's been... rather trying and I'm afraid I haven't been at my best."

"You were no worse than you usually are, I suppose," she said with a twinkle in her eye. She crossed over to the sideboard and returned with a plate of cutlets and fruits that had already been prepared. "Here now, this should tide you over until supper, although I'll be as busy as the devil in a high wind trying to get that ready by a decent hour after you've had me running back and forth with trays all day."

"I'm sorry," Alfie replied, tucking in. "I should have hired more staff after my mother passed."

He hadn't realised how hungry he was until she had set the plate down before him, and focusing on the food gave him an excuse not to look at her as he spoke again. "No need to go to any great lengths for supper. I'll be dining alone."

"Oh?" she said, and Alfie wished he could read more from her tone without seeing her expression. "Is Mr. Tripner otherwise engaged this evening?"

"No. I mean, yes. That is, I don't know what he's doing. He won't be dining here this evening though. Or any other evening. He's moved on."

"Has he indeed? Well, that is a shame."

Alfie swallowed around the lump in his throat. "Quite."

Mrs. Hirkins went back to kneading the dough, discussion apparently over. Alfie picked at his food, his appetite having suddenly diminished.

"When I was a girl," she said after several minutes had passed, the only sounds between them being the crackling of the kitchen fire and the rhythmic thump of dough on board.

"When I was a girl, I lived in a little village near York. But there weren't room enough for all of us, so I was sent to live with an aunt here in London. Every night I cried. Missing my mam, frightened of all the noise and people. It seemed like I had been tossed ashore on a strange land all alone. You had the same look about you when your parents first showed up with you on the doorstep, calling you their son but forgetting you were there at all from one minute to the next. Such a sweet thing you were too, until you opened your mouth. Then such filth I had never heard!"

Alfie blushed. He knew that Mrs. Hirkins knew, or at the very least suspected, that his origins were much lower than his parents claimed, but he hadn't fully appreciated her loyalty in never saying anything. She gestured, and he sprinkled a handful of flour on the table as she held the dough aloft.

She nodded and continued kneading. "So. Frightened and miserable I was. But one day, I met a neighbour lass who lived on the floor above. Jenny."

She stopped, and stared at the dough, before giving her head a quick shake and continuing.

"Oh, what a delight she was. We went everywhere together. She knew all the best jokes and hiding places. Beautiful too, with hair black as night and the sweetest brown eyes. She had a box full of ribbons from men trying to court her, but she would have none of them, though she could charm the birds from the trees if she felt like it and could make you laugh with just a look. I was never so happy as when I was with her."

Mrs. Hirkins had stopped kneading again, her knuckles clenched white in the dough but her eyes empty, staring through it to a time long past. Alfie's mouth was dry. It certainly sounded like... But he didn't even know if there was a word for two women who were like he and Dominick were. He gently laid his hand on the back of hers. She startled.

"Were you…" Alfie wasn't entirely sure what he was asking. *Were you in love? Were you the only one who felt that way? Were you heartbroken when you discovered things between you weren't what you thought they were and you were left alone?*

"I don't know." She spoke softly, and that said more to Alfie than anything else. Loud, strong, fearless Mrs. Hirkins, who was never afraid to say exactly what she thought, quieted by the memory of a girl she'd known a lifetime ago.

"What happened to her?" he whispered.

"She died. A fever that winter. One day we were laughing and stealing sips of mulled wine, and the next she was gone."

She put her other hand on top of Alfie's and just stood there, her rough and flour caked hands clinging to his. "That spring I met Mr. Hirkins, and the rest you know. He's as good a man as any other, and I wouldn't trade my babies and grandbabies for the world. I have no regrets there."

She looked up at Alfie then, her eyes filled with her old determination once more. She spoke slowly, as if each word was a point he was not allowed to miss.

"Since you came to this house, Master Alfred, I have never heard you laugh so much as you have these last few weeks. It's a precious gift, that. And it warmed my old heart to hear it as I walked the halls. I think-I think my Jenny knew how I felt. I think she had to. But I was always too scared to say the words aloud. And then she was gone. I would have given all the years of wondering for just one chance to let her know."

Alfie thought about it—all the years stretching out

before him, empty and alone. Maybe he would find someone else someday, someone who was "as good as any other" but that person could never replace Dominick. Dominick had been in his heart almost since the day he was born, and Alfie knew he would be there until the day he died. He'd been thankful before, that he'd never told Dominick he loved him, but now he couldn't bear the thought.

But unlike Mrs. Hirkins and her poor Jenny, Dominick wasn't dead. Alfie still had a chance. And maybe he had been right this morning, and Dominick didn't feel the same, but if he did... If he did!

He jumped up, knocking back the stool he'd been sitting on.

"Thank you Mrs. Hirkins. Thank you." He gave her hands another squeeze and kissed her on the cheek. "I'm sorry, I have to go—"

"Off with you then," she coughed, trying to cover a sniff. She tossed him a kitchen rag. "Making an old woman cry. And look at the state of you! Best wipe that flour off if you're going to be presentable. And don't you worry about supper, I'll be here to make sure you have something warm when you get back. And I'll make enough for two."

Alfie gave her another quick kiss and dashed out of the kitchen, barely remembering to grab his coat and cane as he clattered out the front door. He had gone thirteen years without Dominick, and didn't plan on spending a minute more alone.

CHAPTER 27

The cab took him close to Spitalfields, but no amount of money could convince the driver to roam the streets while Alfie searched for a landmark. He had only the vaguest remembrance of where Dominick lived, having only visited it the once and at night to boot, but Alfie was not going to let that deter him.

He paid the driver and set out on foot, stride as fast and confident as a man who knew his business. His hand gripped his sword cane in such a way as to suggest to any potential thieves or muggers that there were easier pickings to be had elsewhere. Despite appearances though, he really did have no idea where he was heading.

The sun began to set, and he feared he'd have to call off his search for the night. His steps slowed. Who was to say Dominick was even at the same rooms Alfie had seen all those weeks ago? Surely with the hundred pounds Alfie had told him to take, he could have already found himself a place in a much nicer area. Or he could have even left London entirely.

Alfie's steps slowed. As far as he knew, Dominick hadn't any real reason to stay. He had no family of course, Alfie knew that, and he hadn't seemed to have any close friends either. He'd spoken warmly once or twice of the man Jimmy, who'd been the one to throw in the towel for him that night in the ring, but that was all. He might already be beyond Alfie's reach forever.

Just as the thought was beginning to fill him with despair, Alfie looked down the narrow street and saw a sign for a pub with a cur carved roughly into the wooden panel, its once bright paint now flaking but still recognizable in colour. The Red Dog. The same pub where he had first seen Dominick boxing and followed him out into the night. His heart beat faster. They hadn't gone too far from the pub to get to Dominick's rooms. If he was still around, Alfie could be with him in just a matter of minutes. *If* he could remember the way.

He cocked his head for a moment, trying to remember, then turned left. This time, his determined gait as he strode into the gathering night was not just an act.

✳ ✳ ✳

Alfie was pleased when only two wrong turns later he was standing in front of Dominick's lodging house. He stepped inside and hesitated. Would it be better to plan out what he was going to say or to go up immediately and beard the lion in his den, so to speak? On the one hand, he knew he had to get his words exactly right, as he would likely never have another chance. On the other, the suspense was already driving him to distraction, and he doubted dragging it out would improve matters.

The sound of an almighty crash followed by a howl of pain in a familiar voice ended his deliberations. He ran up the stairs, tripping over his own feet as he took them two at a time in the darkness.

He reached the third floor, vaguely noting that none of the other occupants of the house had been drawn out by the fight. He didn't blame them. On the streets, minding your own business was the best way to keep out of trouble, but another cry from Dominick had him longing for reinforcements. He rushed down the hall without considering his own safety. He didn't need to know what he was rushing into. If Dominick needed help, Alfie would be there.

The door to Dominick's set of rooms was open, and Alfie stood a moment in the doorway, letting his eyes adjust enough to the low light to make sense of the scene before him. Two men were struggling on the floor. Based on size and bulk alone, the one on his back was clearly Dominick, but Alfie at first did not recognize the man on top. Then the man leaned forward into the shaft of moonlight coming through the window and Alfie remembered his face. It was the same man he had seen watching the carriage when Dominick had bought them pies from that pub. This close, Alfie was struck again by the thought that there was something familiar about him, but that was immediately rendered unimportant when the light caught the edge of a blade in his hand. The man had a knife to Dominick's throat.

Alfie inhaled sharply. Neither of the fighters had noticed his presence, too consumed in their combat. He raised his cane, meaning to strike Dominick's attacker, when Dominick turned his head towards Alfie as if he knew, even though his eyes were closed, that Alfie was there. Then he spoke.

"There's one thing you need to know, Baz. Alfie didn't

take your place. You were never the Crawford's first choice. I was."

Alfie let out a cry of shock. If that was true, Dominick was the one who should have been an earl. He was the one who should have lived the last thirteen years in comfort rather than fighting to earn a few coins or having to choose between whoring himself out and starving. Dominick should have been whisked away to a life of privilege. Alfie was the one who should have been left behind. But if he had, he would not have survived. He had never been as strong as Dominick, and the things Dominick had endured would have killed him.

And even as a child Dominick knew it, and made the choice. He *had* intentionally started the fight that day, not to stop Baz, but to save Alfie.

Dominick opened his eyes at Alfie's cry. There was such a look of wonder there, of shock and joy and fear, thirteen years—a *lifetime*—of meaning in just one look. Alfie only hoped Dominick could read a fraction of the same feelings on his own face.

"*You*," hissed Baz. He reared back. Alfie reached forward, trying to stop him. Dominick turned and looked up at his attacker, just as Baz brought the knife down and sunk it into his chest.

Alfie screamed as Dominick crumpled, curling in on himself and rolling on his side away from Alfie. *No! Please, God, no!*

Baz rose to his feet and stalked towards him. The knife in his hand was red and dripping. Behind him, Dominick groaned weakly. Baz glanced back at him and spat.

"Ignore him, he'll bleed out in a minute or two. This is

between you and me."

Alfie was still as a rabbit caught in a predator's sights. It wasn't possible, it wasn't allowed. Dominick couldn't be dying. Not ever, and not now, not when Alfie hadn't had a chance to tell him he loved him, had always loved him. He was so close, just feet away, but Alfie couldn't get to him.

Baz's whine of a voice barely broke through the anguished keening of his thoughts.

"Well, if it isn't little Alfie. You do clean up fine. I guess it don't matter now which of us it was supposed to be. I'm going to take every penny of it out of your hide. Why don't you put that stick down and I'll go easier on you, eh? Maybe I'll even be kind enough to slit your throat *before* I cut out your tongue?"

Alfie realised he was still holding his cane aloft and brought it down hard. Baz caught it and sneered, his ugly face twisting until he looked like every nightmare Alfie had ever had. He had spent his entire childhood believing that one day Baz would kill him if Dominick wasn't there to protect him. It looked like he was right.

"Not so brave without your cocksucker to protect you, are you? I was going to be nice and let you kiss your whore goodbye, but now I think I'm going to start by slicing up that pretty little face of yours instead."

"Don't talk about him that way!"

"The whore? He's trash. A flea-bitten dog that should have been put down years ago. You know I offered to let him in on your cousin's scheme and he was too stupid to take me up on it? And now it turns out he could have been the one to have everything you got, but look where he is instead. Bleeding out in a filthy room, where he'll either rot until the neighbours complain of his stink, or be taken by resurrectionists. Fitting, eh? That the whore's body gets sold even after he's dead?"

Alfie's fear turned to rage, blinding hot in its intensity. Everything inside him fell quiet.

"If he doesn't leave this room alive, then neither do you."

Baz still clutched the end of the cane, so Alfie pulled back. He flicked his thumb over the hidden catch and drew the sword within from its sheath.

Before Baz could realise what had happened, Alfie lunged. His body, honed by years of pouring out his fears and frustrations through fencing, moved instinctively with a perfect attaque au fer, knocking the knife from Baz's hand.

Baz looked shocked and stumbled back. He recovered quickly, stepping away from Dominick's prone form. In a flash he had another knife in his hand. He spat and cursed under his breath, but Alfie didn't react. He advanced slowly, step by careful step, until he could strike again, this time a cut across Baz's arm that had him shrink back, but not drop the knife. Alfie attacked again and again, a remise of small moves keeping Baz on the defensive.

"Dominick is a good man, the best man I have ever known," Alfie said, never halting his flurry of strikes. Baz was bleeding freely now from several smaller wounds, but Alfie wasn't done with him yet. "He is kind, and brave, and generous. He makes me happy."

Here Alfie's voice broke. His hand wavered just a fraction. Baz parried the sword aside with the cane sheath he still held and leapt, the knife in his other hand slicing through the air over his head.

Alfie dropped to a knee and drove up with all his might.

There was a gasp followed by a gurgle. Baz was suspended over him, pinned in place with Alfie's sword stuck straight through his chest, a direct strike to the heart. Alfie watched the knife slip from Baz's slack fingers and rose, pushing the blade through his body to the hilt. He leaned in close as Baz's eyes dimmed.

"He makes me happy," Alfie whispered. "And I love him more than a vermin like you could ever comprehend."

He let go of the sword and let it fall, taking Baz's lifeless body with it, the man already forgotten as Alfie walked over to Dominick and dropped to his knees beside him.

"Please," he said, hand hovering over Dominick's back, too afraid to touch him in case he was already still, unable to roll him over just to find him slack in Alfie's arms.

"Please, don't go. We haven't had a chance to go on our adventures yet. Remember? You promised. Please don't go, Dominick. I can't be without you again. I love you."

He closed his eyes and set his hand down on Dominick's shoulder. There was no movement.

Then a warm, broad palm wrapped around his own.

CHAPTER 28

Dominick panted shallowly. Each breath sent another tongue of fire lapping across his chest. He wanted to just curl up and wait for the pain to end, but he couldn't. He'd heard everything Alfie said. By some miracle of miracles, Alfie loved him back, and that alone was reason enough to go on. He grit his teeth as he let Alfie carefully roll him onto his back.

"That's it, Nick. I've got you. I'm sorry, I'm sorry." Alfie's hands fluttered over his chest, making quick work of Dominick's vest and shirt to get to the wound. Dominick left him to it. His Alfie. So brave. He'd come for Dominick, had said he loved him. The thought gave Dominick the strength to reach up and cup Alfie's face in his hand.

"I love you too," he said.

Alfie looked stricken, and Dominick tried to soothe the look from his face. He rubbed Alfie's cheekbone with his thumb, leaving behind a smear of blood.

"Nick, no. Don't leave me, please."

Dominick huffed, the movement sparking another flash of pain. "Not going anywhere. The bastard missed all the vital bits because you distracted him. You saved me, Alfie."

"Not as much as you saved me."

Dominick rubbed Alfie's cheek again, coaxing the

smallest of smiles out of him. Content, he let his hand drop and watched as Alfie finally got his shirt out of the way. He risked a glance down. His instinct was right, Baz's knife had gone in a little south of his shoulder, through the meat halfway between his collarbone and his armpit. It hurt like the devil, but he'd had worse.

"I'll live," he said with a pleased hum.

"You'd better," Alfie croaked, face suspiciously wet as he unwound his cravat and pressed it to Dominick's chest to slow the bleeding. "This is the second cravat I've ruined because of you."

"The first one's over there, if you want it back. I'll hang on to this one for now though."

He put his hand over Alfie's, and was rewarded with Alfie leaning down over him for a quick kiss, and then another. He finally broke away but didn't go far, resting his forehead against Dominick's, their noses brushing. Dominick might have to get himself stabbed more often if it got him rewards such as this. First love declarations and now kisses. He opened his mouth to say as much, but thought better of it.

Alfie must have caught the movement however because he sighed and pulled away. "We need to get you to a doctor. Can you walk?"

"I think so," Dominick replied. "I'll need help getting up though, and the stairs might prove tricky."

Alfie helped him to his feet, a process that involved more bitten off curses than usual, but finally he was standing. He leaned heavily against the wall to catch his breath and surveyed the wreckage of his room. There would be no way to hide what had happened here. Blood was spattered across every wall and soaked into the floor, every piece of furniture he owned had been destroyed. And then there was the matter of Baz's corpse lying right in the middle of it all with Alfie's sword sticking out of him.

"Well, we can't leave that there."

Alfie turned, horrified. "Of course we can't! He's dead! We have to alert the proper authorities!"

"What? No, not Baz. Your sword. Get the rest of the cane too. The outer bit. We can't have anything that traces back to you."

Alfie's brow furrowed in confusion.

"How exactly do you think you could explain this?" Dominick asked gently. "There's a dead body, in the lodgings of a known male prostitute, with an earl's cane sticking out of him. It's better if we just disappear and let Spitalfields handle its own."

Alfie opened and closed his mouth a few times like a fish. Dominick could tell he wanted to object, but eventually he would realise Dominick was right. Alfie let out a sigh when acceptance finally rolled over him, his shoulders drooping. He walked over and surveyed the body a moment, before pulling the sword out with a sickening squelch. He wiped it on Dominick's already ruined bed linens, then picked up the outer part as well, sliding the sword back into its sheath. It appeared to be a harmless gentleman's stick once again. Dominick reached out and Alfie passed it over without a word.

Leaning heavily on the cane, Dominick took a last look around his rooms. There was nothing of his own he needed to take with him.

"Your cravat from before," Dominick pointed. "Get that

too, just to be safe."

Fortunately, Alfie didn't ask why Dominick had kept it. It was just as well, he couldn't think of an answer that wouldn't be hopelessly sentimental. Alfie picked it up, and when he did, he took an extra moment to pick up the little tin box, and the few coins that were scattered close by. He handed them all to Dominick, who shoved them roughly in the pocket of his coat, blushing at how much the small gesture meant to him. They may have been a pittance to Alfie, but Dominick had earned every one of them and the fact that Alfie understood that warmed his heart.

"Is that everything?"

At Dominick's nod, Alfie came around to his injured side and wrapped an arm around his waist.

"Then let's get you to Doctor Barlowe."

Dominick shook his head. "Just take me home."

＊ ＊ ＊

Dominick groaned as the poorly sprung hack hurdled over the rough streets, each bounce a fresh agony. Alfie had his arm around him still and was making soft shushing noises, like one would a startled horse, and brushing Dominick's hair back from his brow.

Night had fallen and the scarce streetlamps cast little light into the compartment, hiding Alfie's face, but Dominick didn't need to see him. Alfie's care radiated more brightly than any lamp. Although that may have been the blood loss talking.

"I wish you'd let me take you straight to Doctor Barlowe's."

Dominick winced as the hack hit a particularly deep rut. "Too far. Your house is closer. Better to let him come to us. One of the perks of nobility, eh?"

Alfie didn't seem to have anything to say in response to that. They had barely gone another half block though before he asked, "Who was that you were talking to when I came back?"

Dominick smiled. The trip down the stairs had exhausted him, so he had rested there while Alfie went in search of a coach, probably willing to drag the horses into Spitalfields by himself if need be.

"One of Maeve and Jimmy's kiddies. The squeakers are worse than you for getting themselves into trouble. I gave her a tuppence and told her to tell her ma there's work for her brothers at the boxer's place."

"Her ma's brothers?"

"Resurrectionists," Dominick said darkly. Baz didn't deserve any better after threatening Alfie. "It was his idea after all."

"Ah."

Dominick had a moment to worry Alfie might be disgusted with him for even suggesting such a thing, but Alfie just pulled him closer as they rounded the corner to Bedford square. "At least he'll finally do some good for someone other than himself."

Between the two of them, they eventually got Dominick out of the hack. He leaned heavily on the cane, but was able to shamble up the front stairs on his own while Alfie paid the driver and sent him off to retrieve Doctor Barlowe.

The house was dark when Alfie opened the door and

called out for Mrs. Hirkins.

"She said she'd stay even if dinner was going to be late. She likes you, you know."

"Of course she does," Dominick said. "I'm very charming. But if she sees me bleeding all over the front hall, it'll undo all my hard work."

"You think there's somewhere else she'd rather you bleed all over?" Alfie snapped. Dominick might almost be offended if he couldn't tell Alfie was clearly worried about him.

"I handled the front steps just fine, I can handle a few more. If we get me to bed by the time the doctor arrives, we can contain the blood to one room at least. I'm sure she'll approve of that."

"I'm sure she won't approve of it at all," Alfie muttered, but went to Dominick's side. Dominick dropped the cane on the floor to grip the banister, and with that on one side and Alfie on the other, they slowly began their ascent.

They made it up to the first landing before Dominick had to stop, and Alfie carefully maneuvered him into a chair in the hall. He lit the oil lamp on the table next to it before kneeling at Dominick's side, looking up at him with such concern and love that Dominick was rendered speechless. Alfie's hands were sure as he lifted the makeshift bandage from under Dominick's hand and checked his shoulder. He let out a pleased little harrumph.

"It's stopped bleeding. That's good. We've gotten through the worst of this mess, and the rest will be over soon. Just wait until Doctor Barlowe gets here, and he'll take care of everything."

"Yes," said a voice from the darkness. "I will."

Doctor Barlowe stepped out of the shadowed depths of the study. In one hand he held the little brown bottle he had left for Alfie to take. He sighed.

"My dear boy, this would have been so much more pleasant if you had just taken your medicine."

In his other hand, he held a pistol.

CHAPTER 29

"Do forgive my dropping by unannounced, but I rather expected the patient would be in bed. Imagine my surprise."

The pistol was steady in Doctor Barlowe's grip. Alfie stood, instinctively putting himself between Dominick and any potential shot.

"Where is Mrs. Hirkins?" Alfie asked, his voice calmer than he felt.

"Who? Oh, the quarrelsome old woman. Stashed in the drawing room. I'm afraid I rather lost my temper when she told me you were out. Bit of a bump on the head, but she should be fine in the morning."

Alfie was at a loss. None of this made any sense.

"You poisoned the port." Dominick's voice rumbled with sad certainty.

Doctor Barlowe leaned to get a better look at Dominick, but Alfie stepped in his way.

"Well, aren't you a clever one," Doctor Barlowe tutted. "You'd best have those injuries seen to. In my experience, more men die from infection than the wounds themselves."

"Why?" Asked Alfie. He felt stuck in a dream. A nightmare, where everything was rushing around him and he was too slow to keep up. He understood the words that were being said, but they still made no sense.

Doctor Barlowe shrugged. "Why did I poison the port? Simple opportunity. The day I treated your gunshot wound, on my way out I saw the bottle your oaf of a cousin had left for you. A good doctor has an ample supply of syringes on him at all times, so it was only the work of a minute. Besides, you can understand my frustration, I had been trying for quite a while to make it look like an accident. But you just wouldn't die, would you?

He laughed, sounding as jovial as ever, and that chilled Alfie more than anything else.

"Do you know," he continued, "I hadn't even taken off my coat on when that driver you sent knocked on my door? Oh, my heart did race then, I assure you. It wasn't until after I stitched you up I realised I still had the gun in my pocket!"

He laughed again as heartily as if he was sharing a joke amongst fellows at the pub.

"No!" Alfie protested. "You weren't the one behind those attacks. Reginald was. He had Baz try to scare me so I'd be more easy to blackmail, and Baz killed him when he didn't think he'd get a big enough cut!"

Doctor Barlowe's genial grin turned to a scowl. Alfie sensed Dominick behind him, struggling to stand. He pushed him back down without taking his eyes off the doctor.

"Baz didn't kill St. John, did he?" Dominick asked from around Alfie's side. "You did."

"That man was a cheating, drunken, vulgar disgrace to the family name," Doctor Barlowe sneered. "I had planned to ignore him. He was only related on your father's side after all, but when you told me he was blackmailing you, that couldn't stand. There could be no dark marks or rumors against you after you died or it would ruin everything I had worked for. What a repugnant fellow. You know, it took me less than an hour's search before I saw him stumbling out of that—that den of iniquity!"

Alfie's gorge rose in horror and revulsion. He swallowed back bile. "You slit his throat?"

"Of course," Doctor Barlowe blinked behind his spectacles. "A full set of scalpels is a crucial component of every doctor's bag."

Alfie clenched his teeth to keep from being sick. Dominick's hand pressed against his back and he leaned into it, needing both the warmth and support. His knees were weak. When he took a step to steady himself, Doctor Barlowe's pistol followed him, still pointing straight at his heart, but now a fraction further from Dominick.

When he finally felt like he could talk without being ill all over the carpet, his voice came out as small as a scared child's.

"But why did you want to kill me?"

Doctor Barlowe sighed and shook his head. "It was never about you, dear boy. I saw your mother again for the first time in decades when I was called to your father's sickbed. What an angel she was, so caring and proper. I realised immediately that all the scandals that clung to her name were your father's fault for forcing across the globe and not giving the least care for propriety! I swore then that I would do whatever was in my power to restore her good name. It broke my heart to see the fine girl I once knew tarnished by the life your father foisted upon her."

Alfie took another step to the side, greater this time and Doctor Barlowe turned to follow him unconsciously, lost in his own thoughts. Alfie didn't dare risk a glance at Dominick. If he could just get the doctor to forget he was there, Dominick might have a chance to… Well, in the state he was in, at best he might have a chance to escape, if Doctor Barlowe was too focused on killing Alfie. Although how far Dominick would get with his injuries before the doctor caught up to him, Alfie didn't want to think about.

Doctor Barlowe was still speaking. "I thought after your father died, she would be happy. She'd be free to marry someone *respectable*, and live the sort of life a good woman of refinement should, regain the honor she was due. But instead she sunk into the most dreadful state."

Alfie remembered how his mother had changed after his father died and Alfie became the earl. The sparkle in her eyes had dimmed and she'd shrunk away from the world, wearing her widow's weeds as if they were her own shroud.

A part of her had been buried with her husband; it just took three years for the rest of her to join him. Alfie missed her. They'd never been as close as he'd craved, but she was still the only mother he knew, and the months since her passing had only started to dull the edges of his loss.

Doctor Barlowe looked at him with understanding. "That's when I knew. You see that what happened wasn't her fault? Your father had corrupted her with his sickness. Whatever madness it was that made him shirk his duties and go larking off, dragging you poor mother with him. I thought I stopped him in time by speeding his passing, but it was too late. She had it as well. Instead of being happy at his death as I had hoped, I watched her low spirits turn to melancholy."

"'Speeding his passing'?" whispered Dominick.

Doctor Barlowe ignored him. "That's when I knew that while I had failed her in life, I could not fail her in death. I watched you carefully, hoping you had not inherited your father's madness. In you there might be some redemption, some way to return the memory of her to the high standing she deserved. You had always seemed such a serious and well-heeled young man. I had high hopes that the curse of the father had not passed to the son.

"But after her death, I began to see the same signs of malignant despondency in you, and I despaired. I could hardly restore her good name if her only son turned out to have the same disgraceful character as his father. You do see that I never meant it personally. But I had to stop you before you married and continued the family line, with your heirs inheriting the same unhealthy and contrary disposition until the Crawford name became so steeped in scandal that your mother's fine nature was forgotten forever."

He smiled sadly, as if he was disappointed in Alfie for corrupting his future children before they were even born. He lifted the hand that held the bottle and gave it a quick shake.

"But listen to me prattle on. I never meant to trouble you with any of this. I was just here to check in on my patient. If you had taken your medicine tonight as you said in your letter, you would have passed quickly and quietly in your sleep. A tragedy certainly, but a respectable way for a lord to die. But you are a willful and troublesome child, so now I suppose we will have to think of something else "

Alfie couldn't help his bark of a laugh. In the corner of his eye Dominick tensed, but it was just too much.

All this time, he'd thought someone was trying to blackmail and kill him because he did *not* have noble blood. But instead it had been one man trying to kill him to stop him from passing that same blood onto his children, while two other men tried to blackmail him for having no interest in doing any such thing!

"My apologies," Alfie said, letting out another hysterical titter. "It has been a very long night."

He gestured towards the study behind Doctor Barlowe. "You're right, if this is going to happen I should face it as a gentleman. Perhaps we can discuss my options? There must be a more elegant solution than just shooting me in the hall. Not very civilized. Think of how tongues will wag."

He stepped away before Dominick could stop him, knowing he would try. They were unarmed, injured, and exhausted. As long as Doctor Barlowe had the gun, at least one of them would not be walking away from the evening.

There was no good in trying to reason with the doctor. A man so obsessed he would see "malignant despondency" in an orphaned son mourning his mother would never see that he had been wrong. Alfie's father hadn't been a madman for taking his chance to leave the stifling society of London behind to see the world, he'd been an adventurer. And his mother hadn't been corrupted by his father, she'd been liberated. If anything was melancholy, it was not the tarnishing of their reputations, but the constraints they faced upon their return to London, wearing them down until there was nothing left.

Alfie had been lost and alone since their passing. But he understood now what they had felt. If he fell to a gunshot tonight, at least he would die with the memory of the last few weeks with Dominick, which had been the grandest adventure of his life.

But if Doctor Barlowe was going to kill him, Alfie was going to do everything he could to drag the bastard down with him.

He walked past Doctor Barlowe without waiting for his response. If he could only get him away from Dominick. Maybe Alfie could find something in the study to disarm him, a heavy figurine or a poker. He cursed the sword cane lying useless in the front hall below.

"I suppose we could try the poison again. I assume that's what you used on my father. Although that might prove suspicious. Perhaps I could be crushed by a bookcase while reaching for a tome of improving works? Or would that be too farcical?"

He looked back through the open doorway. The doctor hesitated for just a second and then followed, turning his affable smile on Alfie.

That second was all Dominick needed. With a roar he leapt at Doctor Barlowe, wrapping his arms around him and pulling him back. There was the sound of an explosion, and Alfie's legs went out from under him.

A moment later, the blinding pain struck. He howled and clutched his left leg, the fine material of his trousers was already turning red. There was a perfect hole in the fabric. He stared at it—uncomprehending—while the noise of a scuffle registered dimly in the background. Finally understanding made it through the fog of his pain-addled mind. He'd felt this pain before.

I've been shot.

He heaved as a fresh wave of agony hit him, the wound throbbing with every beat of his heart. He reached blindly for his cravat to stem the flow of blood, but there was nothing there. He'd already used it to tend to Dominick and no mere handkerchief would stop this. If he did not get help from a *real* doctor, and soon, Doctor Barlowe would have his wish. Alfie would die before having the chance to besmirch his mother's name any more than he already had by being a gutter rat and a sodomite.

He twisted onto his stomach and began dragging himself towards the doorway. In the hall, he could see Dominick and the doctor struggling. The lamp had been knocked to the floor and the rug was beginning to smoke and smolder. Alfie inched his way closer as quickly as he could bear. The two men were grappling at the top of the landing, the railing creaking under their combined weight.

"Dominick!" Alfie yelled.

His warning came too late. Doctor Barlowe heaved, and he and Dominick crashed backwards through the banister and fell from sight.

Alfie screamed Dominick's name again and crawled towards the landing, afraid of what he would see broken upon the marble floor below. Then he saw it. A hand, big and bloody, clinging to the bottom of the broken banister.

Alfie sobbed in relief. He wrapped his hands around Dominick's wrist. "I've got you! I've got you!"

Dominick let out a choked noise. Alfie dared peer over edge. Dominick clung by his injured arm, his shoulder bleeding freely and the strength visibly draining from him with every moment. His other hand clutched his throat where Doctor Barlowe clung to him, his arms locked tight around Dominick's neck and eyes mad with fear.

There was no time to think. Alfie grabbed the closest thing he could reach and threw.

Dominick ducked his head just in time. The lamp struck Doctor Barlowe directly in the face, shattering immediately. There was a rush of sound as the oil inside caught, engulfing his head in a ball of flame. He shrieked and let go of Dominick, beating furiously at his face as he fell. The noise was more animal than man, a high quavering wail that stopped abruptly with a sickening thud. If Alfie survived, he would hear that sound in his nightmares for the rest of his life. But there was no time to think about that now.

Dominick grabbed the landing with his other hand.

Alfie gripped his wrists again. Dominick looked up, terror writ large across his face.

"I've got you," Alfie said, looking deeply into those eyes he so loved. "On three. One. Two. *Three!*"

For just a moment, he felt himself being dragged forward by Dominick's weight and he thought they were both going to go over. But he kept pulling, and just when it seemed he was about to lose his balance and they would both fall to their deaths, Dominick got one elbow on the landing, then the other. Alfie grabbed the back of his coat and slowly, painfully, they pulled him up. Dominick collapsed on top of him, panting heavily, but alive. Alfie wrapped his arms around him, and buried his face in Dominick's neck. He stank of sweat and blood, but Alfie had never smelled anything sweeter than his love still breathing in his arms.

"I've changed my mind," croaked Dominick. "I'm not taking you on any adventures. I've had my fill already."

Alfie laughed, and kissed him. Dominick ran his fingers through Alfie's hair and gripped tightly, his fingers trembling against Alfie's scalp.

Too soon, they broke apart. Alfie noticed another smell in the air. Smoke.

"We have to go."

"Wait," Dominick said. He ducked down and kissed Alfie once more. "I love you."

"I love you too." Alfie knew why Dominick wanted to say it again now. Just in case. "I'm not sure I can make it down the stairs on my own, please don't leave me."

Dominick gave him one more kiss. "Never."

* * *

Together they made it down the stairs, clinging to each other all the while and coughing as thick black smoke rose around them. The front hall rug was completely ablaze. At the center of the inferno was a large lump consumed by fire that Alfie refused to look at too closely. The painting of his parents was the next to catch as flames rushed up the walls. For a moment, the fire imbued their eyes with a living light, and then they were gone. Alfie's eyes stung as the air filled with ash and hot embers.

They crawled on hands and knees. Through the smoke, Alfie saw the outline of the front door just ahead of him, but Dominick tugged his sleeve.

"Drawing room," he coughed. "Mrs. Hirkins."

Alfie nodded and together, they turned into the drawing room. The fire hadn't reached it yet, thank God, but the air was almost too hot to breathe. Mercifully, Doctor Barlowe hadn't tried to hide Mrs. Hirkins' unconscious body, just left her where she had fallen. Alfie took a quick moment to strip off his coat and drape it over her face to protect her from the heat and debris. Without a word, he and Dominick each grabbed an arm and pulled, dragging her with them towards the outline of a front door now completely obscured by smoke.

Somehow, between them they got the door open and emerged into the cool spring night. Alfie swooned as his lungs filled with fresh air.

They survived.

❊ ❊ ❊

The next thing he knew, he felt cool grass tickling the backs of his ears. Alfie leaned up on his elbows.

He was lying on the grass in the park square while liveried footmen and nightgown-clad neighbours dashed about raising the alarm and throwing buckets of water where they could. There was a length of cloth—perhaps a sheet or kitchen towel—wound tightly around his injured leg and to his left, a gaggle of maids wrapped in robes were fussing over Mrs. Hirkins. Her chest was rising and falling steadily and the maids seemed to have things well in hand, so he didn't let himself worry.

And to his right? To his right, Dominick was sitting upright and so close that Alfie's shoulder brushed against his thigh. He looked down at Alfie with clear worry. The parts of his face that weren't covered in blood were black with soot, and his clothes weren't even fit for the rag pile. His shirt gaped open, and against the drying blood, the ring on its cord dully reflected the light of the flames.

"You look a mess," Alfie croaked.

"You're one to talk," Dominick replied in a voice just as raspy. A furrow creased his brow. "Alfie, I'm so sorry. Your home... I don't think they're going to be able to save it."

Alfie looked. Flames were pouring out of the first floor windows already, and as he watched, there was the sound of glass cracking as tongues of fire licked out of the second floor ones as well. He had lived in that house for the last thirteen years. Had grown to manhood there. Had learned all the rules of this strange new world he had been thrust into. Had lived with a mother and father and servants. And one day, a wonderful man came to stay, who made him laugh, and who loved Alfie just as much as Alfie loved him.

And *that* was home.

He slowly sat up and looked Dominick in the eyes, trying to express all he felt and more. Dominick smiled and carefully bumped his bandaged shoulder against him.

As the smoke and wails of the fire wagons filled the air, they leaned against each other and watched the past burn.

EPILOGUE

June 1818

Dominick bit back a curse as the carriage hit another rut in the road and jostled his remaining injuries. The doctor—the *new* doctor—who'd looked them over after the fire had done a fine job patching him up, but it would take more than a few weeks for him to heal completely. Another bounce made him inhale sharply and set off a fit of coughing which hurt even more.

"Here."

A hand ran soothingly up and down his thigh as he continued to cough, and when he finally opened his watering eyes, he could just about make out Alfie leaning across the carriage and offering him his handkerchief. His throat would heal from breathing in too much smoke in time, as would the rest of him. Aside from some interesting new scars, the doctor claimed in a few months Dominick would barely remember what happened.

He doubted that. If his own nightmares weren't enough, more than once he had been woken in the night by Alfie's, his love crying out at the remembered horrors of that day and haunted by the faces of the men he'd been forced to kill.

Dominick would wake him then, secure in the privacy of the set of rooms they rented while everything was sorted out. He'd hold Alfie until he went back to sleep, then watch over him as long as he could to ensure the dreams would not trouble him again. If Alfie allowed it, Dominick planned to watch over him for many years to come.

"Feeling better?" Alfie asked, giving his knee a squeeze.

"Aye." Dominick handed back the handkerchief, leaning over so Alfie wouldn't have to move as much. His injured leg was propped up on the seat next to Dominick.

The doctor had not wanted Alfie to make such a journey while he was still recovering and Dominick agreed, but Alfie claimed to be sick of London and that the fresh air would do him good. Dominick bemoaned his plight at loving such an obstinate man, but Alfie remained unmoved. He could still put very little weight on his leg and required a cane for more than just protection now, but Dominick made sure that the one he picked to replace the cane destroyed in the fire along with everything else also had a blade concealed within. Just in case.

He watched as Alfie folded the handkerchief neatly and tucked it into the jacket that lay next to him on the seat. There was no need for formality. They were the only two in the carriage after all, and Alfie had told him they'd want to be as comfortable as possible for the long ride ahead.

Dominick readily accepted his judgment in this, especially if it meant he'd get to spend the day looking at Alfie in little more than his shirtsleeves. Perhaps if the day grew too warm Dominick could convince him that there was really no need for waistcoats either, and cravats were such a nuisance, and did a shirt really need to be buttoned that high...

"Stop that." Alfie began to dig around in a bag beside the

jacket without even looking at Dominick.

"Stop what? I'm not doing anything."

"You're thinking very loudly. And they are not thoughts that belong in public."

"It's a private carriage," Dominick argued.

"A private carriage on a public road with a public driver sitting only a very thin partition away."

"I can be quiet."

The look that Alfie shot him doubted that very much, and already disapproved of whatever clever quip Dominick thought he was going to make next. Dominick just smiled and leaned back in his seat.

Alfie had said the trip to Scotland would take a week at least, more likely two. He had time. Maybe time to talk too. They hadn't done much of that since the fire. Alfie had been too busy dealing with the insurance and paperwork and everything else that went with one's home going up in smoke.

The body found in the charred foyer had proven to be less of a problem than Dominick expected. With the law, at least. The papers were having a field day with the story of a heroic doctor who had accosted burglars in the midst of robbing his patient, only to be struck down by the villains before they set the house ablaze and escaped into the night. That said patient was a member of the nobility whose cousin had just been murdered and his house ransacked by perhaps the same band of ruffians had all London in a frenzy.

Mrs. Hirkins' wailing to any reporter or constable who would hold still about being struck by an unknown assailant—and a woman of her age after all, and just what was this world coming to?—had provided a wonderful distraction from who Dominick was, and what exactly he had been doing there.

While Alfie was busy, Dominick had spent his time getting Mrs. Hirkins moved into the new home that the generous pension Alfie bestowed upon her had purchased, and commiserating as Mr. Hirkins complained that with room for all the grandchildren, he would never again know a moment's peace. It was much easier to sit by a fireplace with the dog, scratching behind its ears while the old man feigned annoyance, than it was to think about what was going to happen next.

When Alfie had shyly asked Dominick to accompany him to finally visit his family seat in Scotland, he'd leapt at the chance. The only good thing London held was sitting across from him right now. Let the city keep his secrets and memories both.

"I'm sorry," Alfie said, interrupting his thoughts. He'd pulled a sheaf of papers from his bag and was fidgeting with the edges. "If I had known you were still in such pain I would have postponed our trip. I should have thought. I was just so ready to leave—"

"You're the one with the hole in his leg. If that wasn't going to keep you in one spot, I certainly wasn't going to try. I do wonder though, how exactly you're planning on explaining my presence when we get there."

Dominick cleared his throat. "I don't suppose you'll have much call for a bodyguard. I'll warn you in advance that I'm going to make a terrible valet. I could be your secretary I suppose, if you'd like all your correspondence to go out in block capitals with half the letters backwards."

Alfie's hands stilled on the papers. "Nick, you didn't come with me because you thought you were my servant did you?"

"Of course not! I came because I love you."

The startled look on Alfie's face reflected his own. It was true of course, but he hadn't meant to be so blunt about it. Still...

"You could look less shocked," he teased. "I did tell you that before."

"You did." Alfie smiled, a small, sweet thing. "I suppose I'm just not used to hearing it. I love you too, you know. I have mentioned it a few times, but you weren't, strictly speaking, awake for all of them."

"Well." Dominick squirmed, no more used to hearing the sentiment than Alfie was. "Good, then. I'm glad that's settled."

A quiet slipped over the carriage with the drowsy sounds of the wheels bumping along the road and the steady cadence of the horses' hoofbeats.

"I was thinking you could be my cousin," Alfie finally blurted.

"Your cousin?"

"When we get to Scotland. I thought we could tell people you were my cousin. Not Reginald, of course, that would be revolting. But some other cousin no one has ever heard of. I'd hardly be the first Crawford to show up with an unexpected relation. At this point it's practically a family tradition."

"Your *cousin*?"

"From Cornwall."

Dominick, speechless, raised an eyebrow.

"A distant cousin. Very, very distant."

Dominick couldn't help but grin as the beginning of a blush crept over Alfie's cheeks. "All right then. How do you toffs say it? Mr. Dominick Trent, late of Cornwall, very, very distant cousin of Earl Alfie Crawford, at your service, sir."

Dominick bowed as much as his seated position and aching chest would allow.

Alfie laughed, then sniffed theatrically, "It's 'The Right Honorable Alfred Pennington the Earl of Crawford' actually."

"A bit of a mouthful to call out in bed, but I'll give it a try."

"See that you do."

Dominick was able to hold in his laughter for a few moments, but as soon as he saw Alfie's lips twitch it was over. The pair descended into hilarity, and it was at least a mile before they regained some semblance of composure. Dominick's last chuckles triggered a coughing fit that had Alfie's handkerchief back in his hands. The man himself levered his way over into the seat next to Dominick, his injured leg across Dominick's lap and a hand rubbing Dominick's chest in soothing circles. Even after the coughs died out, Alfie kept up his ministrations. Dominick closed his eyes and leaned back, content and warm in Alfie's love.

"Do you have a sixpence?" Alfie whispered.

Dominick frowned slightly at the odd question. Alfie had plenty of his own, clearly. And besides, it wasn't as if there was anything he needed to buy right at the moment. It wasn't worth opening his eyes or moving out of Alfie's hold to investigate however, so he fumbled blindly for his discarded jacket and pulled a coin of the right size out by feel.

He passed it over. "Try not to spend it all in one place, Your Lordship."

The hand on his chest stilled before moving to take the coin from his hand.

"That's that then," Alfie whispered, but it sounded more like he was saying it to himself than to Dominick. Dominick opened his eyes and turned in his seat enough to look at Alfie, but he wasn't looking back at him. Instead he was staring at the coin in his hand before giving a decisive nod and putting it away, reaching for the papers he had been fussing with before. The action pulled him away from Dominick, who put a hand on Alfie's hip to keep him from falling off his lap and damaging his injured leg any further.

"I visited my solicitor quite a bit before we left London," Alfie said, sitting back up with a sheaf of papers in his hand. Dominick kept his hand where it was. "In part because of well, everything. But also because I wanted to make a gift. To you."

"Alfie, you've given me—"

"Nick, please, I need to say this all while I can." He took a deep breath.

"You've saved my life more times than I can count, both in the last few months and in all our years together growing up. Not only that, but you started the fight with Baz intentionally so they would choose me instead of you. I would have died in that workhouse without you, and when I think of all the terrible things you had to endure while I lived the life you should have had..."

His hands were shaking now.

"Alfie..."

"Shush. I want to give you a gift not because of all that though, or out of some sense of thanks or obligation, but because I love you, Dominick. I always have, and if I have any say in the matter, I always will."

He laughed wetly, and Dominick could feel tears pricking in the corners of his eyes. "The solicitor wouldn't let me make a *gift* of what I had been planning, but he agreed to let me make a sale for a fair price. I decided to set that price at a sixpence."

With that, he handed the papers to Dominick. He squinted, trying to read them, but between the jostling of the carriage and the fine, spidery lettering, he couldn't make it out.

"What does it say?"

"It starts with a long section about the parties named herein, a Mr. Dominick Trent—"

"Of Cornwall." Dominick mumbled.

"Of Cornwall," agreed Alfie with a nod. "And a Right Honorable Lord So-And-So, etc. etc. but in short? Almost half of everything I own is now yours."

"*What?*"

"I know, it would've been more fair to make it an even half, but quite a bit of it is entailed and sorting that out was more than I wanted to put my solicitor through. The poor man seemed distressed enough even after I had explained that following the untimely death of my cousin Reginald, it was only right that I wanted to ensure my only other— very, very distant—relation was well cared for."

Almost half of everything Alfie owned. Dominick had no concept of how much that could be, but he guessed it was more than he would have made in a hundred lifetimes.

A hundred-hundred maybe. He opened his mouth, but no sound came out.

Alfie jumped back in quickly, as if afraid of whatever Dominick would say. "The paperwork is binding. As soon as you handed over the asking price, it was yours."

At this he turned to look at Dominick for the first time since he'd begun speaking. Dominick fell in love all over again at the fierce expression on his face, as if Alfie had conquered him in battle and Dominick had no choice but to accept the terms of surrender. Which in this case meant being forced to accept thousands upon thousands of pounds. Dominick had no idea what expression he was wearing, but whatever it was caused Alfie's look to soften.

"There are no conditions or anything of that sort," Alfie said. "It's all yours outright, the money, the properties, everything. If you want, you can take it all now and go. I'd have no claim on it or you. But I was hoping... I was hoping you would come to Scotland with me anyway. To stay. For good. Or for as long as we want to stay. I never forgot the stories you used to tell me of faraway lands and extraordinary journeys. Someday I'd like to travel like my parents did. I'd like to see some of those places with you, and have our own adventures."

What could Dominick even say to that? To this wild, beautiful, brave, caring, ridiculous creature who he loved and who, by some miraculous turn of fortune, loved him back?

He finally settled on, "I'd like that too."

The smile Alfie gave him in return was worth more than any sixpence, or thousands of pounds, or manor houses, or the whole lot of them rolled in together.

Alfie took the papers back from Dominick and began shuffling through them.

"In that case, if you look at the bottom of page eight... No, Dominick, stop looking at me, look at the contract. At the bottom of page eight you'll see that you now own several properties throughout the country.

"On the way to Scotland we will happen to be passing rather close to several of them. Mostly smaller things. Hunting lodges and the like. They've only been in use occasionally, loaned out to my parent's friends, so there would be no staff. Only us. But as it will take some time for the household in Scotland to prepare for our arrival, I thought a good way to begin our adventures might be by visiting each and examining them all in thorough detail."

"Only us, you say?"

Alfie looked up at him through his eyelashes. The coy minx. "Why yes. Most of them are close to inns where say, a coachman could stay with the horses and from which meals could be delivered, but we'd be very much on our own."

"And we should do our inspections in thorough detail?"

Alfie hummed thoughtfully and tilted his head, bringing his butter-wouldn't-melt mouth that much closer to Dominick's. "It might take a few days. Each. Accounting for travel and any unexpected delays, the process will take at least the whole summer, perhaps longer, depending on how much exertion your injuries can handle."

"Not to mention your leg. That sort of inspection can be quite strenuous," Dominick agreed, scratching his chin in mock contemplation. He leaned in, stopping with his lips just a breath apart from Alfie's. "I don't suppose we'll be passing anywhere near one of these properties by say, tonight?"

Alfie gasped, "You *did* read the contract!"

Dominick rolled his eyes. They were so close that Alfie's self-satisfied smile filled the entirety of his vision. He'd spent the happiest years of his life chasing that smile and it looked like he was destined to spend the rest of them the same way. There was no choice but to accept his fate.

So with a long-suffering sigh, he did. He tossed the contract aside and pulled Alfie in for a kiss filled with promise for all the years and adventures ahead.

The End

HIS LORDSHIP'S MASTER

Book Two Of His Lordship's Mysteries

Scotland 1818

Still reeling from the horrific events in London, Alfie thinks Balcarres House, the seat of his earldom, will be just the place to recover. But unexplained noises in the night, figures that vanish into thin air, and ghostly tales of the infamous Wicked Master all make for a less-than-restful stay. When one of the household turns up dead, matters only get worse.

While Alfie tries to solve this mystery, his lover Dominick struggles to fit into his new station in life. It feels like the mud from the slums still sticks to his fine new clothes. He begins to worry that he'll never be able to stand by Alfie's side, and about what will happen when Alfie realises the same.

But Balcarres House holds secrets that cry out for blood. If Alfie and Dominick aren't careful, they may become the next ghosts trapped within its walls.

Available Now

AUTHOR'S NOTE

This novel has been an absolute labor of love and I am so happy to finally be able to share it with the world. I began with little more than an idea, the desire to finally sit down and write, and the confidence that I knew a lot more about Regency England than turned out to be the case.

A month into writing the first draft, I had the opportunity to visit London to further my research. All of the places mentioned in the book exist or existed at the time, from Alfie's townhome to the Glasshouse Yard workhouse in Spitalfields. I even kept a list of good pub names I saw as I wandered for use in this and future books. Much of the information on Alfie and Dominick's early lives came from the incredible Foundling Museum, which is well worth a visit if you have the chance. The token system I describe in the book, such as Dominick's ring, was a real process used by the original Foundling Hospital and many others. There is a collection of unclaimed tokens on display in the museum and it is just as heartbreaking as you'd think.

Even once I'd wrangled all the research, I couldn't have written this book without the help of many people, first and foremost Margot, who has been with this project from the first multiparagraph rant over text to the final proofreading. Thank you also to Emily for being my beta reader and looking this all over with a keen romance lover's eye.

The writing community has been incredibly gracious and welcoming. I've received tips from authors I've read for years and had absolute strangers help me figure out everything from appropriately villainous character names to figuring out a release schedule.

Finally, I want to thank my family for all their love and support. Without their encouragement, I might not have ever had the determination to finish this book, and to start on even more adventures of Alfie and Dominick to come. At time of writing I have the rough draft for book two already sitting on my computer, and ideas enough for several more.

Thank you, dear reader, for coming with me so far and I hope you stay for the adventures ahead!

ABOUT THE AUTHOR

Samantha SoRelle

Samantha SoRelle grew up all over the world and finally settled in Georgia, USA where the humidity does all sorts of things to her hair.

When she's not writing, she's doing everything possible to keep from writing. This has led to some unusual pastimes including perfecting fake blood recipes, designing her own cross-stitch patterns, and wrapping presents for tigers.

She also enjoys collecting paintings of tall ships and has one pest of a cat who would love to sharpen his claws on them.

She can be found online at **www.samanthasorelle.com**, which has the latest information on upcoming projects, free reads, the mailing list, and all her social media accounts. She can also be contacted by email at samanthasorelle@gmail.com, which she is much better about checking than social media!

BY SAMANTHA SORELLE

His Lordship's Mysteries:

His Lordship's Secret
His Lordship's Master
His Lordship's Return
His Lordship's Blood
Lord Alfie of the Mud (Short Story)
His Lordship's Gift (Short Story)

Other Works:

Cairo Malachi and the Adventure of the Silver Whistle
Suspiciously Sweet
The Pantomime Prince (Short Story)

Made in the USA
Columbia, SC
31 October 2023

24780132R00198